Praise for Into The Arms

'Mesmerising in its familiar
moments of Rei's life that to

'An exquisitely sensitive, rich and raw tapestry that weaves its way through the life of a young girl into womanhood in full transparency, exposing lies dressed up as love.'

'This is a book of true courage and strength in the face of persistent forces, showing how integrity and quiet resolve can undo the greatest of evils.'

'A true masterpiece. Raw, real and relatable, that very cleverly reminds you to listen deeply to yourself and the truth within.'

'Fascinating and enthralling to read. A truly empowering tale of a young woman's journey to being in her power, showing the reader how to stand up to abuse with integrity and love.'

'A thoroughly enjoyable and totally gorgeous book with incredible insights into life. I smiled, I laughed out loud, I felt humbled and at times saddened, but most of all I felt honoured to be reading it.'

'Unlike any book I have read before in style and flow. Utterly unique, Into The Arms, is a disarmingly real account of abuse and the prevailing light of a young woman.'

'A deeply touching read that exorcises what is un-dealt with within and brings to expression the purity of what we are all made of through the eyes of pure Love and Wisdom.'

'Compelling and illuminating. This humorous, poetic and playful story showcases the raw horror and pain of abuse, suicide, and lovelessness.'

'An intimate telling of a life. Clever, wise, beautiful and brutal all at once. I have winced, teared up, laughed, been shocked, frustrated and saddened reading it.'

'A heartbreaking novel and eternal classic that serves as a huge warning to us all…about what happens when we don't listen to our inner compass…tender and deeply touching.'

'Richly abundant, beautiful and moving… moments and experiences intertwined that unfold you into the arms of your own inner knowing.'

'A novel with a moral vision that's both powerful, sensitive, and hard hitting whilst observant and unengaged by the horror within it. It's alive and deeply responsive to the tenderness and beauty that exists from such vulnerability.'

'Like a series of Japanese screen prints the structure of the book gives way to a series of seemingly random awarenesses, each hugely healing in their unearthing. A beautiful and masterful narrative.'

'Have you ever blamed yourself for anything? Felt wrong for even breathing? Then read this book! It helps you realise just how fabricated – what's more, useless - those self-depreciating thoughts are. Rei shows us how to turn the tide to live without them, restoring the powerful footsteps we are all born to walk.'

INTO THE ARMS

A DISCOVERY OF TRUTH & LOVE

ANGELICA LAMB

First published in Great Britain by IngramSpark.

This is a work of fiction. Names, characters, businesses, places, events and incidents are either the products of the author's imagination or used in a fictitious manner. Any resemblance to actual persons, living or dead, or actual events is purely coincidental.

A CIP catalogue record for this book is available from the British Library.

ISBN 978 1 0369 6618 8

Angelica Lamb

To those that never lost sight of me,

to my raison d'être,

to all that showed me life, love and evil,

and,

to those that gave life meaning. ***Everything*** is because of you.

Rei

A given name with many meanings depending on its origins and root;

Hebrew (רעי *Re`eeY*) ~ friend and my companion

Portuguese & Spanish (*rey*) ~ king

French & Latin (*ray*) ~ ray of light

Japanese (rei) ~ light, a beautiful appearance, soul, graceful, respect, the concept of zero *

* The chosen kanji character used determines the specific meaning of the name, possible options are…

麗 lovely, graceful, beautiful
霊 spirit, ghost, soul
例 example, custom, usage, usual
零 zero
玲 exquisite, clever, sound of jewels
令 rule, order, command
礼 etiquette, bow, gratitude, respect
怜 wise
鈴 small bell
嶺 peak, summit, mountain top
黎 black, dark, many

澪 water route, shipping canal
励 encourage, inspire
禮 manners, social custom, honour
齡 age
冷 cool, chill
蛎 oyster
伶 actor
苓 plant, herb, mushroom
蠣 oyster
砺 whetstone, polish
戾 return, resume, go backwards

レイ Rei written in katakana
れい Rei written in hiragana

In addition to being used as a given name in the Japanese language, ***rei*** is used to signify the following;

Bow (礼) bowing as a sign of respect.

Respect, Courtesy, Manners (礼儀) linked to the concept of *reigi* emphasising good manners and politeness.

Deep Bow (お辞儀, *o-jigi*) a deep bow in formal settings and martial arts, usually accompanied by *onegai-shimasu* (please).

Zero (零) meaning zero in a numerical context.

You are love -
what is not love is not you
unless you choose to make it so

1988

Rei had always tried hard to be a good girl. It was all she had known, all she could remember. Her long, lanky legs (great for last minute substitutions in the inter school hurdles compete) and her acute appetite for all things harmonious meant that the teachers (for the most part) liked her, or so she thought they would.

She put in a lot of time and tried really hard to concentrate both *long and hard,* on all the types of dance she had now accumulated under her metaphoric belt (ballet, tap, modern, jazz, and ballroom to name but a few) so that she didn't have to contemplate *too much* the fact that she had been sent away to school. A school inhabited by nuns that swayed and swished their pious and sexually destitute hips along the corridors and through the refectory; their habits swooshing with an eerie near silence giving them away way before they could be seen if your ears were well versed.

It needn't be told to anyone that Rei's mother only lived a few miles away in the same town. Not the neighbouring town, but...

the

very

same

one.

Maybe there is something very deeply wrong with Rei? Perhaps, but Rei manages to push down that idea deep, deep down to the pit of her core where it stays, nearly dormant, festering, brooding, perhaps multiplying subtly over time like mould on bread. Permeating her skin and every particle beneath it.

One small spot appears, it doesn't look like much. *That'll be fine.*

...And then the next day a plague of violent eruptions. Contamination. No going back. Poison of the greatest order.

But perhaps it's not as bad as it looks? After all Rei was told quite clearly let it be said, that mould was indeed only penicillin. It wouldn't harm, it's *only a little bit. Pas de problem.*

A huge unknown, condensed to a pea size problem, quiescent, in the pit-of-the-stomach-of-a-teenage-girl-sized-body.

What could possibly go wrong?

~

The crowd of other boarders with their luggage flew in at the beginning of each term, home town luggage labels (definitely not under wraps) from Gibraltar, Bermuda, China, Nigeria, Hong Kong, Liechtenstein and the like, rudely competing with each other in the house hallways muscling for *better than* status and ultimate prowess in the money stakes, their owners scanning the newly released cubicle and floor level lists, with a ferocity usually saved for leading role announcements in the w h o l e school Christmas Play.

Rei loved to watch. She would sit and observe each girl arriving on time before the 4 o'clock cut off point (Rei was never late, she always liked to arrive ahead of the game, and it would pain her if she were teeteringly close to the actual time she was meant to be anywhere, she *had* to be early) with their ginormous trunks groaning with the weight of goodies packed from their families (*with love*) to get them through the term; new clothes just because; and the latest tan from their long weekend skiing with mama and gramps resplendent with goggle lines and all. Rei didn't mind the lavish luxuries only afforded to the other girls, in fact it gave her great joy to imagine their lives and see their faces gleaming with pride, happiness and buoyancy as they would flood in to her tell her all about their weeks away as they'd sit on her bed excited to be reunited again, back at school, if only temporarily.

Rei could not disclose her *home* identity, nor did she feel safe to share with them that her parents were not together - they really never had been for long. The fact was, she was a high school *accident*. Perhaps it was a quickie behind the bike shed one lunchtime. Perhaps not. No-one really knew and no one (especially Rei) dared ask for *no-one* ever talks about such things behind closed doors and certainly not with strangers or in public. Rei had learnt to stay quiet, very, Very quiet.

A dirty secret known by, and perhaps in collusion with, the headmistress, that was never shared. Too dirty for a Catholic boarding school.

Rei smelt of dirty, lustful fornication. She could smell it on herself, it was what she was made of and from - or so she had fathomed from the secretive movements and the hushed whispers that were all she had ever known from those around her, leading her to believe it was better she was never spoken about and certainly never put in the spotlight.

Too many questions. Too hard!

So she would stay hidden out of the limelight, in the shadows, like an ornament on the shelf, collecting dust at not too fast a rate. Pretty on the eye, a *perfect* child - one to be seen and not heard.

Wow. She was a good girl!

No wonder the grown ups liked her.

But, and it was a big butt, she was also a *bastard*. A soiled, dishonest, dishonourable, tarnished word that could never be washed off. Ever.

Or so she thought, until one day it was no longer there, no scrubbing or bleaching, just insignificance. Yet another word that had been bastardised itself, laden with emphasis and conviction to the detriment of something so pure. *Another* lie that space and wisdom would later expose.

~

One day many years later, her father would come and take her out for the first and only time during her school life (Where? Rei does not remember, for sheer embarrassment).

A leafy school in the countryside far from the screeches and scrawls of urban, city life. *The Avenue,* a mile long stretch of narrow tarmac where cars could politely pass one by one at a slow elderly pace inline with all current and past images of the school and its inhabitants since their arrival from Belgium during the 19th century. This way was of course amplified in *its way* by the elder trees perfectly lining the driveway either side; they stood upright yet managed to bend inwards and touch in the middle creating a stunning living arch carrying the whispers of secrets purred within cars and carriages across the years, as all took passage this one and only regal way in.

This day was different however, the quiet, the *please do not disturb* (whatever it is we are trying to emulate here) signs ignored.

A top speed, bright red Ferrari, ignoring any semblance of hope there was for any anonymity, arrived full throttle, announcing at the top of its pre-pubescent voice (during silent, *shhh,* Saturday study time) that it was here and there was not a bloody, damn thing anybody could do about it.

Rei was sure there were sirens, flashing lights and klaxons of monumental proportions being blasted across the school campus. Every window now occupied by its owner. Piglets and their snouts up against the glass searching out their food. Jeers and titters as this svelte, young man in the tightest of tight white shorts, revealing all that young girls barely knew about let alone needed to see on a sunny summer morning, slid out from the driver's seat and stretched up (and out) in his pride of magnificence like a lion claiming his space.

Barely old enough to be Rei's older brother compared to the other fathers, Rei ran faster than she knew in an attempt to curtail his (*her* dad's) performance. To quieten the noise that although not spoken could very much be heard within her reddening ears. They were on fire. Yes, they were all talking. About her.

Being quiet and keeping stump was no longer a possibility or an option. The cat was out of the proverbial bag.

Who was this danger to the prerequisite disposition laid bare for all to see?

Rei tried to disappear into the car park floor. She'd never tried shape shifting before but wondered if it was indeed possible. There were no cars to hide behind. No rain, not even a single cloud. *How was that even possible?* It was England and it was a Saturday study time.

The sun seemed to shine even brighter, and the scene, the shiny car and the shiny happy playboy, reflected on and off of every house and classroom window possible. To make matters worse suddenly the father became nuanced in his moves. It was as if he had tapped into all that Rei could sense and was lapping it up for himself. Centre stage. An actor in their prime; a musician taking in the encore applauds; a politician well-rehearsed delivering lines, to the oceans of onlookers waiting baited breath for any semblance of...anything. Anything that would take the audience (in this case a few hundred teenage girls and a few tens of nuns) out of their everyday grey. Beige maybe. The town was certainly being painted red. At Rei's expense, but no-one seemed to care.

Why was Rei so addicted to what everyone thought about her? What everyone said? Who had taught her this?

She didn't remember ever having a classroom discussion about the necessities of morphing yourself into another's needs, desires, or comfort, yet she seemed a master at it, all by herself.
Well done.

Good little girl.

Rei felt like a prized possession, an elite hooker on the arms of a rich business man. The trophy girlfriend to the footballer's dream. She didn't like it. It felt icky. Yet somewhere deeper within, secretively (careful so not to be spotted by anyone else) she was cherishing the closeness with her father. A moment shared. It may have been abusive, perverse in truth, but Rei had missed her father's adoration.

Since he purposefully slammed the door shut with as much might as a grown man could muster leaving the house one day after a fight on the stairs with his wife (her mother), she had rarely seen him, barely spent any time with him, let alone spoken with him. A good eight years had passed.

She had to date been haunted by those last images of her parents fighting, screaming, shouting, provocatively dancing with death on the stairs with each other, with her. She had pleaded them to stop.

Anything. Just stop!

But deaf ears were out that day. No-one heard but Rei bore witness to it all her ears acting like a tape recorder picking up every nuance, every word, every bang, crash and momentary silence...*Was that a breath taken there?*

She could playback in detail every moment. That tape had been played back on repeat, re-winded, re-listened to time and time again. Every subtlety registered, analysed, considered, post-mortem'd in fact, a skill she took forward with her in life coming in handy real-time every Sunday afternoon recording The Top 40 Countdown live on air. Her ability to know exactly when to press record, when to stop before the DJ would interrupt the classic beats with their unnecessary chatter. The climax building to the announcement of this week's Number 1 chart topper, listening attentively, enthralled her body already choreographing moves that she so desperately enjoyed.

Just as Rei had seemed to see the parental separation through 4D glasses and hear it on surround sound the other witnesses that day seemed to be in a different cinema screen watching an altogether different screen show.

The pair of brightly coloured chaffinches in their ornate cage at the bottom of the stairs were not remotely disturbed by the escalating drama before them. Their sweet, distinctive song shrilling and echoing the truths of harmonious living to the bodies violently shaking in complete rage and torment at each other, not listening or even noticing the wisdom pouring forth. The gentle reminder that it needn't be this way.

Rei however noticed everything.

All of it.

Why were the birds undisturbed?

Their colourful plumage, gorgeous as always. The territorial male ready to warn off any potential suitors (not that there were any, in a cage, in a house, in a town, in a county, in a country in the continent that its species came from) doing his job regardless. He wasn't leaving. He didn't slam the cage door behind him so hard that the whole home shook, without saying bye to his daughter, who was,

right

there.

Unlike the male chaffinch, Rei's dad flew the roost, not to be seen or heard from again for what seemed like eternity to the little girl used to seeing her dad every day. There was no returning the following year for the mating ritual. It was as if he had died or had become someone else, leaving his pre-slammed-door-life a very long way behind him.

Rei seemed to have some kind of understanding of how he was feeling and perhaps would not have been saddened by it had he only looked back at her, or mouthed a goodbye, or an *I love you* as he turned to leave like they do in the movies, but no, there was no sign that Rei was any more precious to him than the next.

A piece within her seemingly died that day. She wasn't sure what part, or what it meant, but she could feel in her body that it was a piece that she would need to protect from now on. It was her five-year-old duty and her responsibility to do so.

No-one else's.

How could anyone else be expected to hold that preciousness so close and tender when it had just been shattered by the one person she thought had seen and known it, yet who had run far from it like a shadow escaping into the night?

~

Now, being paraded around the school grounds like a dressage pony with its equestrian rider on full display (albeit this one a little under-dressed for the occasion) Rei's languid tissue fibres stirred, reminding her of the depth of love her father had had and had shown her when she was a baby. A far cry, both in distance and time from what was being displayed and score-carded within this public arena now. Now it seemed the show was a spectacle for everyone else, the intimacy once shared evaporated into the warm summer's morning, it could well have been lifetimes ago it felt so immemorial.

The peacock, full plumage seemed very happy to be in Rei's company, undoubtedly for all the wrong reasons, unabashed and relishing in the momentary coupledom. The noise and the glares from the not-paying spectators, so powerful before, seemed somewhat significantly less, now that a tiny piece of that hole inside Rei was being filled. A father's love, or the desire of it at the very least.

The uncomfortableness of moving something not pure, not true, always disturbed Rei. A loud clanging in her ears, an aching in her body, signs she knew the truth, and so too did everyone else, yet no-one seemed to care, no one seemed to listen. *Did this make Rei bad? Was she the baddy in a goodie two shoes film?*

She couldn't quite work it out. From the outside in she looked the part of miss goodie two shoes herself ~ long blonde hair, blue eyes, pale yet golden skin, a clear complexion and a smile that seemed to light up the whole world both as a child and as Rei would grow old.

Her purity so evident to all.

1981

Like every Monday morning before, Rei sat at her classroom desk blank faced staring at the chalkboard, wishing time could fast-forward *just 'til break time, that should be enough.*

She could see the rest of the class purposefully scribbling as fast as they could vying for their teacher's attention. Tales of birthday invites with new party dress outfits and matching shoes; roller-skating followed by dinners at Pizza Hut; roast dinners with the extended family; a play in the park with new puppies...

It didn't matter what Monday it was, Rei never had anything to write about. There never was an occasion to describe, any semblance of a story to even half embellish.

Part frozen with a mixed amount of fear and dread, her stomach would catapult and turn topsy-turvy all by itself, knots of all shapes (stoppers, loops, bends and hitches) and sizes adroitly formed, expertly crafted within. Her temperature soaring, she felt giddy, not from excitement but a mixture of shame, embarrassment and looking disobedient. It wasn't an attempt to not do the work, she just drew a blank every time, it was not a lie.

Eventually, as was always the case, Rei would very, many hours (minutes) later raise her hand to let Mrs Potts know she had nothing to write about. It was apparent that the exercise was a way to catch any misspelled words or not-linguistic-and-articulate-enough expression that may otherwise have slipped through the net, so a repeat of the every Monday's prior work was unacceptable.

Just make something up. Anything you want. Mrs Potts quietly whispered, just loud enough for everyone to hear, the reverberations shuddering down Rei's body. Now everyone else knew she was struggling again too. An added lingering around Rei's tiny Year 1 classroom chair by Mrs Potts with a bonus insistent look over her shoulder, plunged Rei into even further turmoil.

*Please, can you give me the first sentence and then I'll be able to write…*both Rei's eyes and mouth questioned.

Every week the same response

I said Anything. Don't be silly now. Just get on with your work.

Despair.

Any part numbness that was there before was now part-exchanged for thoughts of being marched to the local prison (the head mistresses office two doors down the corridor) or for being thought of as a liar, an absolute liar, a thief of the truth.

Rei hadn't been capable of writing about her weekend. She could never bring her mind and hand in line to write about *Anything* however hard she tried, and she desperately wanted to. To fit in. To not be the naughty one. But alas, No.

A moment in time, stuck on repeat. Groundhog Monday.

Up until this point in her life Rei had only ever experienced one other looping event. It seemed traumatic experiences liked to rerun themselves like the 1500-meter race, round and round the track, unending as such for those little, growing legs.

As a very young girl before the paternal walk-out-the-front-door-and-never-look-back experience (so no such obvious trauma yet girl, *Get a grip*!) Rei would awake each and every night. Bolt upright in the darkest of black nights, soaked in sweat, screaming at the top of her voice. She would scream, and scream, yet no-one could hear her. No—one came to her bedroom to check if she was ok.

Rei realised the scream was only a silent hoarseness in the back of her throat where there should have been a voice box, one alerting everyone in her home that they were in danger, grave danger.

Rei could feel things, but no-one was listening.

She could be seen, but not heard.

Good little girl.

1989

Are you there God? It's me, Margaret was being passed from cubicle to cubicle. Pre-pubescent and pubesce-ing girls in a catholic boarding school trying their hardest to unravel the meaning of their bulging and blossoming lumps and bumps without causing any distress to the nuns (near) or their parents (afar). Each questioning young lady treating the book like they were touching evil when it was in their hands. Whispers not even shared, just secret scouring under duvet covers at night. This was a book that everyone read but no-one book clubbed. Hell, they may as well have been reading The Quran such was the level of apparent disdain and derision that all the girls feared was just around the corner.

Swish, swish.

Rei read the pages shocked and not all understanding of what was being written about. It seemed the other girls were a bit excited by what they had read, it had brought some kind of relief as their breasts were forming and there was someone at least confirming that this was a real journey they would all be embarking upon at some stage, ticket purchased or not.

Rei was unfazed by the thought of physical maturation however two years later when e v e r y o n e had a bra (or three) even if their breasts had not grown whilst simultaneously very unsubtly alluding to the fact that their period had begun, there was a sudden sense of urgency.

As she walked outside alongside the humanities wing one afternoon she too decided to ask God if it was indeed time she joined this pilgrimage, this passage to womanhood like all the others around her? Clearly still very naive about the whole thing, she willed her childhood away not thinking about the practicalities or the physical implications of such a jump.

~

It was the endlessly long and beautiful summer holiday and as always Rei and her sister were spending the entirety of it with their grandparents and their two dogs, Stardust and Cola. For the most part they spent their time, back in time, on the Suffolk coast in a tiny fishing village with an outside toilet and a sandy duned beach left unspoilt and pagan rich.

One dated red telephone box serviced the village and each week on a Friday afternoon they would walk miles there to call home, rewarded and comforted by the fish and chip van waiting for their order once ET had phoned both the mum (now at home alone) and the dad (because they should). As they slotted rather dull looking silver 50 pence piece coins into the telephone box's mouth a loud noise could be heard as it angrily and vehemently gobbled them down swallowing them whole, leaving just enough time to say hello to the voice down the other end of the line with nothing much more before the machine groaned loudly for more sustenance, demanding it, *Now*. These calls always began with unsettlement about what may be about to occur and always left with unsettlement, feeling that everything was against the clock, money included. No flow, no space. Just angry Pac-Men chomping at the bit, fingers and all.

~

By the end of the holiday as term time was approaching, they would return to London and Rei and her sister would get their twice-yearly day out up to the big smoke. They would take the Piccadilly line into Regents Street and begin with a *Meal Deal* in MacDonalds. Burger, small fries and a chocolate shake for Rei, cheeseburger, small fries and a vanilla shake for her sister, Sam. Their nanny (grandma) picking a couple of loose fries from each of the small paper sleeves as they went.

Stomachs full and fully content they would make their way to Lilywhites just round the corner, the superstore of all things sporting of its time, the stench and dread of the return to school now no longer anything but a harsh reality.

Rei had grown taller and her hockey stick no longer fitted her slender physique and its body parts, it was part of the school kit list and so it was a necessity. Walking the shop floors desperately miserable inside at the thought of returning back to school Rei had an overriding feeling to go to the toilet, an unlikely occurrence for her having done the obligatory pee-stop before leaving Maccy D's. Thinking not much more of it she entered the cubicles noticing the grey walls and the slightly dishevelled (no matter what the establishment) appearance the public toilets always seemed to have. Squatting down above the seat as taught to, she peed and wiped herself clean only to feel the smear of something thicker. Blood.

Frozen in time Rei stood, sat, squatted all at once blood draining not only from her face this time. Unsure what to do next the minutes passed by, the cubicle, its smells, its greyness becoming more familiar. The sanitary bags now highly visible where once they were not seen, like once pregnant noticing all the pregnant women on the street; the salubrious yet soiled waste bins slightly ajar beckoning the new world this way.

Rei did not know what to do.

There was a vending machine selling tampons against the wall by the sink but Rei was cashless and the other toilets were empty of people with money, she eyed up the product but they felt hard and obtrusive, she didn't feel ready to embrace them yet. Some minutes later Rei was both relieved and embarrassed (for the first time ever) to see her nanny, a beautiful woman who had aged well, who alongside her husband always looked after the kids despite having little means themselves.

Seeing an ashen Rei, she asked if everything was ok?

Met by a dam of tears and a stammering of disbelieving words she scooped up wads of toilet tissue alongside the gist of the situation at hand, and like a prevailing ninja got to work immediately, silently ushering Rei back into the cubicle to create her first hand made sanitary towel, that would be switched out later once they returned home (without essential hockey item). The uncomfortableness of the whole situation exacerbated by the wedge of scratchy loo roll against Rei's now womanly parts.

The abrupt ending to their bi-annual trip to the city meant that the final stop of their ritual went amiss too. Hamleys, the greatest toy department store in the world!

Just as Willy Wonka's Chocolate Factory was deemed the biggest and the best, so too Hamleys had earned its place. The multiple floors with never ending rows and rows of toys, games, gadgets, mechanical and electrical models never ceased to amaze little (and big) eyes; permanent displays and performances taking place enticing you to buy and partake in the fun. None of these sections had the same pulling power to Rei like the cuddly toy area. That was her one and only beeline, the rest an irrelevant passing of the time, a spectacle to be observed and enjoyed, like watching the scenery outside whoosh past on a train ride to your final destination. Grateful and happy for it, but not the main goal.

Rei had never been into girly things per se, boy things neither. She had grown up amidst the great doll wars. Barbie v Cindy - glamorous, global and aspirational v girl next door, homegrown and relatable. Neither were appealable to Rei who found the whole thing soulless and plasticky. Instead, she found comfort and solace in cuddly toys.

Each year if she were lucky her grandparents would buy her a teddy of her choice which she would take to school with her and hug religiously (there was a bit of religion in her after all) every night close to her (soon to be developing) chest.

She never chose the biggest teddy or the brightest one, it was always a well-crafted selection, often against the grain. One time a super soft full-frontal lion with a long tail who stood proudly on what would have been his two hind legs and resembled the shape of a teddy but was evidently a lion. This was Rei's favourite to date. His name was to be Leo. Leo was her only reminder and connection to anything outside the school gates and he was the one thing she felt ultimately close to, her confidante, who saw everything alongside her and whom she could share everything with.

It wasn't long before Rei somewhat regretted her choice however. On returning to her cubicle post lesson one day, she found Leo sitting on her bed staring at her like usual, this time with his tail between his legs, hairy tussle at the fore. He now had what appeared like a huge, erect phallus on full display. *Attention!*

Rei still had no real concept at this stage in her life of what a penis actually was, no-one had shared the *birds and the bees* with her, not the embarrassing book or talk that so many others had.

The closest she had ever got to any kind of anatomical discovery was in primary school in Year 2 where she sat with her best friend Kiera opposite two boys Max and Nathan. They were a pretty close-knit group of four who got on with their work and enjoyed each other's company as much as six-year-olds do.

One day during class it was decided that in turn they would each drop a pencil under their tiny tables whilst the opposite side (boys and then in turn girls) would reveal to the other side their privates. An *I'll show you mine if you show me yours* pact from very innocent explorers. Rei doesn't remember what she saw. Either she actually closed her eyes not wanting to see what was in front of her face at very close proximity or her mind carefully blocked out the findings keeping her safe from potential trauma.

Either way having never seen a penis, she was acutely aware that Leo should not be left this way with his tail cum pee-pee holding fort. It was vulgar and rude, and she would most certainly be in trouble were the nuns to see it.

From that moment forth Rei lived with another layer of nervous tension ~ each and every time she returned to her cubicle, she would worry about the state she may find Leo in.

It disturbed her that Leo was being treated this way. She knew he was a stuffed animal, but nonetheless it saddened her. No-one deserved that.

Why would anyone do that?

What had he done to them?

Secondly, she worried that the nuns may see and think it was her with a dirty mind,

Dirty girl.

The cubicles and their corridors were patrolled regularly by the nuns and someone, or some-ones, were clearly having their fun and laughs at Rei's expense.

At night times there was a sadness and fear Rei would take to bed with her, hidden, crying, silently beneath the covers with Leo in her arms. Just the two of them, against the big and often lonely boarding school world.

1998

Queueing in line at the Heathrow check in desk Rei could feel, for the first time in a very long time, her own two feet. Important and relevant here and now. Firmly grounded upon the epoxy resin coated floor. No longer flighty, waiting patiently to be let through the turnstile, symbolic of the transitioning moment between what was and what was yet to be. Distant shores had long been beckoning since childhood, but never had the light at the end of the tunnel been so close, touching, striking distance. A mere fourteen hours in the silver winged bullet flying her like a stork to a new life and good fortune. Faithfulness and loyalty in full throttle, Rei was about to jump aboard this dragon's back who would take her for the most part to her new life, one far away from that which she had been desperately trying to escape for so long.

Flying above the cotton-clouded earth in the space between what she'd so far lived and Heaven, Rei felt the most at ease she had felt in ages, whilst also feeling what she imagined a semi-boner might feel like at the excitement and stirrings of what may lay ahead.

The plane touched down, Rei was sure the wheels kissed the earth, semi-bowing with a joyful bounce at their new destination.

Destination new life.

2011

Cries, jittery and panicked, quiver through and out of her body, the reality of what she has done, what she is doing; growing, mutating the further she walks away.

How could she have been so naive?

It took everything she knew to hold it together, from running back to him, scooping him up and taking him back to the safety net and facade of money and middle-classed pompousness that had become their norm, their comfortable surrounding from which to view life.

When had she become such a snob? she wondered.

The realisation was richer than the circles they'd been moving in but it somehow stung, penetrating deep beneath the skin, puncturing it devilishly first, and then plummeting deep into the underlying tissues and deeper still into the bones.

A bite that would stay raised on the skin to be scratched, full of pus, red, angry and sore for a few days to come. A gentle reminder of what she had been moving so effortlessly in prior to their move there.

2017

As Rei edges forward in line for immigration control, fear permeates her whole as she switches on her phone and connects to the airport Wi-Fi, a message bulges and lands loudly with a grand slam on her screen despite being in silent mode.

ALL,
as in e v e r y Single penny,
of the money in their joint account has been drained.

Like a magic trick.

In England it is there, In America it is not.
Ta Da!

Rei knows this is not a magic trick that will be reversed when she wakes up back in England. It is another irreversible moment in time, the damage done. The cycle already in fruition. Revenge.

Don't for one minute think you are going to walk away from this relationship unscathed and merrily go about your life as if nothing has happened. There is damage to be done and suffering to be had she hears ringing in her ears.

Rei could read the signs on the wall in black and white, not the ones about mobile phone usage in the airport, but the bludgeoning threats being sent across the Atlantic landing real time, actioned hours ago, rudely unannounced so as if to cause further impact down the line.

She wondered if the armed guards in uniform around her could save her from herself and the choices she kept making on repeat, she seemed incapable of doing so.

The queue took an unreasonably long time. Time enough to contemplate her options. There was no point looking out to anyone else for reassurance despite having relied on that old chestnut up until this point in time. The lady in front of her didn't look like she was enjoying life much, the man behind scruffy and discontent, shifting from leg to leg in an unsightly manner. The armed guard was not there for reassurance that was for sure; no matter how hard others ahead of her in the queue were trying to smile or flutter their eyelashes at him (techniques Rei had seen before all too many times) he wasn't budging nor giving anything away.

It was obvious that this moment was asking her to go much deeper than before - to settle and to surrender. To acknowledge the choices she had made and the consequences she would bear, but that she needn't be hostage to from this point forward.

She breathed and reminded herself that she had just landed in *New York baby!*

Do not waste this opportunity.

Any moment wallowing in the past or in what would need to be attended to was not in the present. She was here now and there was work to be done, money in the account or not. The kids were being looked after and she could deal with it (all) on her return in three days time.

And so, she quietly pulled herself together, her smile slowly and gently reemerging from its hibernation cave and back out into the great old *U. S of A.*

1991

Un-arranged, un-planned and un-predicted somewhere between the lengthening expanse of Year 4 and the growing discontent of Year 5 Rei found herself struggling to keep awake. To stay vigilant, alive with life. Her body wanted to sleep day and night and all day too. Her body heavy with the weight of what she could feel around her, of what she did not want to be a part of. It seemed her body had given up before she had, although she was sure it was of no coincidence that her body was pre-empting the steps that her heart was feeling and that her mind may well have put words to had she given it the chance.

She watched the other girls merrily participating in the dance of existence, their ponytails jigging and jiving in the summer breeze, whilst Rei's hung heavy on her pillow, time slowly, very slowly ticking by. Days into weeks, into months.

Rei would heave at her body, demand it to stand to attention, plead for it to work just for that day at least. But to no avail. Dead, heavy, lead weight body parts going nowhere fast.

Silence seemed to permeate the dormitory corridors where before she remembered shrieks and calamitous noise. Time expanded where before it ran away. An appetite for anything that was before ravenous was now stunted, emaciated by her avoirdupois.

Nothing enticed, nothing inspired. Everything appeared grey around her. Lifeless like her body felt. Perhaps she was shutting down like a robot running out of batteries, slowly but evidently.

No-one really seemed to care.

Had she given up on life and pulled her own plug from the power supply inadvertently? What had triggered the disconnect?

There was nothing that seemed any more malevolent than any of the other occurrences in Rei or the other girl's lives. It had been another harsh winter of cold days and long, dark nights, running up and down *The Avenue,* a mile to warm up before the real PE lesson began; the spring had emerged with another term of swimming in the outdoor pool changing in the poolside cubicles outside, curtains blowing in the arctic wind leaving tiny breasts and growing pubes exposed for all on full display; girls *on their period* for the second time that month, teachers marking down this mysterious cyclical tendency with a blot in the registration booklet.

Rei was still too naive to cotton on to the fact that this might not in fact be what was really going on and that the other girls were already learning to play the system in their favour. The staff exasperated and infuriated being taken for hopeless fools, would take their frustration out on the few floaters or sinkers left in attendance in the pool. It seemed no-one really progressed in their swimming abilities across the years, trauma being the one recurring theme; memories and imprints of its distress guiding the body (anything but forward) rather than the positive muscle memory movements of a trained and practiced athlete doing something they loved and enjoyed.

With no obvious comprehension of the cause of her now diagnosed ME (myalgic encephalomyelitis - chronic fatigue) which had started as a case of glandular fever, Rei could only wait patiently for the symptoms to evanesce.

She scolded herself for ever kissing that boy in the darkened corner of The Hammersmith Palais.

When everyone quipped that she'd caught the *kissing disease* she feigned stupidity pretending that was a ridiculous and non-sensical idea, she didn't have a boyfriend and everyone knew it. But in hindsight and none-the-wiser she thought perhaps it was true, perhaps she had caught it from her first and only kiss so far this life, a memory she would much rather have forgotten about.

Silly girl.

~

A few of the girls from her house and others had bought tickets to go to the Christmas Ball at Le Palais. It was the kind of event that the girls would frequently go to but Rei hadn't, having never been in the right place at the right time nor having the funds or means to do so (divinely constellated in retrospection).

They (the girl's parents) had bought their daughters each a new ball gown made of silk, taffeta and organza and they (the girls) had their make-up and hair done especially for the event. Rei had found herself a short shoelace strapped black velvet dress in Top Shop for £13 on the faulty rail and breathed a sigh of relief that she had something to wear and that this time Cinderella would go to the ball!

She sewed up the small black hole with some navy-blue thread she had and counted her blessings for the summers spent crafting Mrs Tiggy-Winkles out of teasels, lavender and scraps of material with her grandmother. It appeared sewing was a great skill to have under your belt in such a moment. She could barely see the now midnight blue hole near the hem of her dress on her backside, only feel it if she ran her fingers across it so she felt content it was imperceptible to others too. *For who would really be looking there anyway?*

Having been dropped off by one of the girl's dads in his gold-coloured Rolls Royce with leather interior (Rei had never seen anything so swish) outside the front doors of Hammersmith Palace they infiltrated the establishment feeling grand but a little dubious.

Rei hadn't known what to expect but it was not this.

Complete darkness, loud music and alcohol streaming in abundance. They were only fourteen years old and although many peers could be seen, the people around appeared much older. A sixteen-year-old seemed like a grown up and an eighteen-year-old like a full-blown adult to a sprouting fourteen-year-old.

Caught in the headlights Rei looked around her looking for anything that may help her feel secure, that she could turn to. Most of the girls knowing the place having run off to see other acquaintances or to the known areas around the venue. She went to the bar and asked for some water, at which point Raquel appeared with two pints of lager in plastic cups and thrust one in Rei's hands.

Come on, get it down you.

This was the last thing Rei felt like doing and the one and only person she was not happy to see. Yet this is where she was. She pretended to take a drink letting the beer touch her lips.

There had never been any hurry or enquiry to explore alcohol on Rei's behalf especially after being caught drinking Baileys from a baby's milk bottle at school last term. Even then she had pretended to take a sip being in the wrong place at the wrong time trying to sit on the edge of a group rather than be bullied by them. Consequently, when caught by the patrolling nun on duty, they were all reprimanded, a letter written home to their parents, each having to pay a £10 fine.

Rei was (still is) distraught at the time; she did not have £10 to pay like the other girls who handed over some of their pocket money allowances, and she knew her parents would not be so compromising and find the letter home amusing like the other parents did. She sat in fear for many, many days until one evening she received her first phone call from home *ever*, from her father.

Angry may have been an understatement.

At the next available school holiday Rei was flown out to Spain and made to scrub the jet-black dirty floor of an old warehouse barn for a week to earn back the £10 to pay the money back. In the meantime, all dancing lessons were to be stopped as an immediate punishment, Rei sobbed *No, but please* down the phone, but her pleas unheeded turned into the remainder of the year dance lesson free.

Even Sister Duncan had thought this punishment did not match the crime and took it upon herself as housemistress to plead Rei's case, but also to no avail. The thought had counted however and bought huge, and most probably the only comfort there was to Rei. She knew Sister Duncan *knew* the truth that Rei was lying in front of the girls pretending she was drinking to save face and to avoid further humiliation and antagonism. She had always seen Rei for who she was and had been one of three people at school throughout the years that kept Rei from complete desperation, despair and perhaps devastation too.

~

Back in the now busier nightclub Rei felt like history was repeating itself pretending to be something she was not. Her dress, and therefore consequently her, stood out like a sore thumb, short and figure hugging as opposed to the current trend of full and voluptuous with swathes of fabric. Her long straight blonde hair striking against the fashionable up dos and bobs of the brunette brigade.

She asked Raquel *Where are the others?*

Oh, they've scored some boys - I just saw Penelope snogging some guy behind the pillar over there.

Rei glanced over to see the back of Penelope's head tilted at a 30-degree angle and her royal blue organza ball gown half tucked into her knickers, held up by a male's hand. She shuddered inside. Penelope had been by her side just a short few minutes ago. *How was that even possible?*

And the others?

Oh, I'm not sure, I haven't seen them, but I'm sure if you go wondering over there, you'll find them Raquel nods to the depths of the room's one o'clock direction.

Mimicking an urgent message delivery driver Rei scurried over to the said corner of The Palais, as quickly away from Raquel as humanly possible, the room getting darker and darker, bodies moving together in pairs in all sorts of positions and with all kinds of movements and energy unaccustomed to Rei and her youthful unwonted eyes.

She couldn't decipher one person's head from another at this point in time and turned around to see her available options and routes out of here. She could make out Raquel's figure still hovering near the bar and could also see that whichever winding route past enveloping bodies she took, all roads would lead back to Damascus. That was not an option. Looking for anything or anyone she recognised again, squinting hard to decipher any known ball dresses or hair dos, she noticed a sofa deep in the back corner.

Perfect, that'll do she thought and made her way to the now pitch-black inky nook and the empty sofa.

She plopped herself down relieved to be away from the bright flashing disco lights and the noisy speaker system, still loud but not deafening anymore. She glanced at her watch. It was still only 8.30pm they'd been there 30 minutes and Rei was already ready to go home. She'd seen enough.

Plastic beer cup still in hand she wondered where she could dispose of it. She wanted to put it on the floor tucked into the sofa as she always did with drinks to make sure they would not spill; but was fearful to as she didn't want to cause a mess and was unsure if anyone else would be on the lookout for it, so may inadvertently trip it up. Little did she realise that within the hour the floor would be a sea of alcohol, beers, spirits and even vomit as the youth got reckless and the time passed by.

Wondering what she could possibly do with the goblet full of now lukewarm brown slush she went to put it down at the other end of the sofa, the one in the corner most part of the room where it would be its safest, and as she scuttled across the sofa's cushions she found she was not alone. There was someone there even more hidden than her. It was a boy. A grown-up boy.

Rei surprised apologised and recanted her actions and what she was trying to achieve.

Actually, would you like this drink? she then asked.

Sure, thanks he responded.

How awkward thought Rei, *now what do I do?*

Staying put seemed the better of the two options and so she sat in awkward silence praying for a time travelling machine.

The guy shrunk back into his obscured corner, plastic glass in hand, beer in mouth and the playlist rattled on.

Halfway through the third song (not that Rei was counting) he asked if she wanted a snog?

Dumfounded and aghast Rei muttered something not even she could understand. In fact, she had no idea what she had said, but she knew it was some kind of attempt at saying no not wanting to offend.

In that moment of contemplation and humiliation of the noise that had just come out of her, she found a tongue lodged halfway down her throat. The crash as his teeth hit her railway-track braces, any prior embarrassment that was already off the Richter scale now rocketing to earth shattering proportions; she tried to reel herself in as she found herself floating in space trying to detach herself from the body she was inhabiting.

A couple of gurgles and swooshes around the mouth was more than enough, Rei pulled away and the guy got up and left throwing the half-drunk glass onto the floor.

Well that had all been in vain Rei thought, disgusted yet simultaneously relieved that her first kiss was now over and done with. She caught a glimpse of Frankie on the edge of the dance floor and suddenly her feet found flight.

Oh my God am I pleased to see you she blurted out like a ball explosively released from its canon, *where have you been?*

I just kissed a boy Frankie smiled, grinning from ear to ear. *His name was Rob and he's sooooooo sweeeeeet. Look he's over there waiting for me! What about you where have you been?*

Er, well I just kissed someone too Rei replied, obviously not having said many words to the guy, not only she did not have his number, but he was nowhere to be seen, not that she would even recognise his face it had been so dark.

No way! Frankie shrilled excited that her friend had got her first kiss.

…And?
How was it?
Where is he?

He had to go Rei said (that wasn't a complete lie), *his name is Alex* (a most probable lie, but he did look like an Alex in the dark she consoled herself). Ignoring the other part of the question and conveniently interrupted by a loud announcement over the speakers that the live music was about to commence. A newly formed boy band *Take That* were about to take the stage.

Yey, let's go shrieked Rei, the first semblance of excitement in her voice all evening - an opportunity to boogie on the dance floor!

The band performed their singing and dance routines like a well-rehearsed circus act; acrobatics interposed the choreography. At the end of the act the crowd surged forward to get a touch of the boys, who looked not much older than the girls themselves. Rei liked Jason of them all, she appreciated the way he moved his body it seemed much more effortless than the others. They had all been trying to lip-sync so she couldn't comment on the singing.

The performance had completely arrested Rei's apprehension about where she was, she had nearly forgotten in fact. Now there were only three hours left to go…and just like one of her favourite quotes *this too shall pass,* it did.

~

As she recanted the events from her night at The Palais ball (a far cry from the Disney princess version) a few months ago, she was pretty sure she could have caught anything!

It had actually felt like a sewer in there and that's where rats liked to hang out. She had been told rodents were notorious for transmitting diseases through their urine, faeces, saliva and bites. Everyone knew that.

Rei had seen enough hickeys that ominous evening to question what the obsession was with sucking someone's neck that hard that it looked like they'd been bitten? She personally couldn't see the attraction.

Perhaps she had gotten off lightly with the kissing disease after all.

Dirty girl.

Silly girl.

Thankfully the long spring soon turned to summer and as the grey skies turned to blue, Rei's energy riposted too.

1991

When Rei saw him for the first time her eyes lit up, her body shied, seeing him catch her eye and smile, a deep Italian smile that illuminated his hazel green eyes like stars in the night sky beneath the moon's reflective glare.

50 feet away, the connection had been made, felt and cemented. A done deal. Fate had been announced and had made itself very clear.

Rei gently turned around, trying to be as inconspicuous as any teenage girl that has just been given a warm welcome by the hottest guy on perhaps the planet can, to make sure that the silent, but all knowing, exchange had gone unnoticed by her bondage of friends.

She thought she'd gotten away with it until two fellow fair goers from the year above in school came bounding over from the other side of the park…

Did you see that?

Daniele Zanella fancies you Rei.

Oh My God!!!

Wait until everyone at school hears this.

Phoebe in Year 7 has been trying to get with him all year!

Rei tries to shrink into her skin and deep into her body. The limelight and the spotlight now firmly pounding down upon her, its heat burning with intensity.

Where? Who? Which one?

Oh My God!! He's gorgeous!!!!

Rei!!!!

Together the now sizeable group shuffled forward inline for the Spinning Cup ride. The queue whilst rapidly disappearing before them seemed to take forever under the fervent eyes of the *whole* (it now appeared) fairground.

Nothing more obvious than a gaggle of teenage girls manoeuvring their wills around their latest prey. The grown men working on the inside had had their interest piqued by the commotion building outside, each silently hoping that their colleague Daniele's magnetic pull may mean that they too may be able to cash in their chips and get a piece of the vying action from the growing harem of ravenous girls next up.

Before she knew it Rei was ushered into a teacup beside two of her friends. Rei on the inside, feeling a little safer in the dark of the ride's structure, the overhead canopy providing some kind of protection and shield from the prying and patrolling eyes around both her, and him.

The fair outside's and the ride within's music swirling in her ears, clashing violently with each other, louder than she would have wished, competing to fill the space around. An assault on her retreating body. The encircling energetic hubbub already too many decibels too loud, too fast for her liking, compounding the knowing that everyone was *spotting* her, keeping their eyes and focus on this specific Rei sized point as the ride began. The pirouetting precise and perfect in its delivery.

Rei's eye's remained shut for much of the ride, a habit of hers when she didn't like something or want to admit that something was happening; like a child putting their hands over their eyes in the belief that they can no longer be seen by anyone around them. There was a naivety in Rei that did not want to grow up. She didn't want to see or acknowledge what she knew was already happening, was already in motion.

Images flashed before her and when she did momentarily semi open her eyes, she saw Daniele and his colleague's bodies coming over to spin their tea cup faster than before. The bright lights and the loud noise nauseating with the spin of the cup, faster, louder, then faster and louder again. The two minute ride ostensibly longer this time round with no slowing down. Until, suddenly

there was a stillness,

a silence,

and time temporarily stopped.

Rei opened her eyes to find Daniele's warm smile hoovering so close to her face she could smell him, feel the heat of his perspiration from his spinning workout, and

feel

the warmth

of his lips

upon hers.

She saw him jump off their teacup and wink before getting back to work spinning the next teacup in the opposite direction, their eyes not parting.

Catching herself, attempting to wake herself from a dream, Rei glanced to the side and around for the second time this hour to see if anyone had seen.

Relieved she acknowledged that Daniele had masterfully kissed her at the back of the ride in the dark where no-one could see and when no-one was looking, her friends giddy with dizziness and excitement their eyes firmly closed and their mouths widely open shrieking half in delight and half in provocation of a dream that may never unfold.

Am I dreaming? she questioned herself for the second time in as many minutes.

The ride came to a halt and the riders disembarked, woozy from the exhilaration and the furore. The bustle congregated back in formation and moved away from the ride, all glancing back at the *Italian Stallion* now captivating every young girl's heart and dreams.

Rei walked as subtly as she could as far away from the ride as was possible, shell shocked yet warm inside. Something had stirred within her and she too wanted to turn round to check once more if it was all real. She wanted to touch her lips to see what they felt like, to see if they were still there, but she knew that was a dead give-away so resisted the urge.

Instead, she found herself wondering if Daniele had moved on to his next passenger? Perhaps it was a game for all the men working there, to see how many innocent young girls or flighty women they could kiss in a day and night's work? He who scored most, wins. But somehow there was something within Rei that knew this was different.

It was way above her pay grade, way out of her league, way beyond any knowledge or experience she had of boys or the real world, yet she was being beckoned forth to deal with it with all that she knew from within.

The hours passed away before it was time to return to school and the girls having exhausted their means and their stamina for such excitement in one day wanted to walk back past the Spinning Cup for one last look at Daniele. An image they wanted to encapsulate and carry forth with them through the next week of school. As they shimmied on past the ride Daniele could not be seen. Saddened looks shared in disbelief as if they had collectively lost sight of the target they'd been chasing the last few hours, eyes taken off the collective prize. A dazzle of horny gals' emotions dampened at the last turn.

Rei felt something, someone, open her fingers and gently close them up again, her hand tight against the preciousness contained within. She didn't need to turn and look, she knew, and she sensed somehow so too did everyone else. Like a phantom presence that silently appeared and disappeared both in the same moment Daniele had revealed himself, his identity and his intentions to Rei in full. This time no-one wanted to admit the reality of the situation. Something that had felt very whimsical and fairytale-like had now gotten *Very* real.

It was not until they got on the short train ride back to school when the coast was clear that Rei opened her fingers to take a look. She opened the now screwed up and warm, clammy handed, damp piece of paper to read the note, a note written for her eyes only.

Next Saturday. Train station.
12.30pm.
Be ready for fun.
D.

The train ride home (*to school*) was a bit of a blur, no-one wanting to talk about the elephant in the room anymore, yet everyone's minds churning out loud every detail of said elephant for the train carriage's consumption. Utter disbelief that Rei could have landed herself the county's (most probably country's) only heartthrob without doing anything.

Suddenly the fun was gone. Flirtation was pointless. Dreaming and fantasising made redundant. Another long, grey and dreary week lay ahead for most, whilst *someone* had landed themselves the catch of the century. Rei felt uncomfortable on every level at everything she was feeling. *Why did these things always happen to her?* She would rather they didn't. She hadn't done anything.

In her white jeans and borrowed check shirt (Saturday mufti - an unspoken private girls' school uniform) she thought she looked no different than everyone else in their home clothes. Her hair gently tousled from the summer breeze, blonded by the sun throughout the term's outdoor activities, her body sensitively toned from the hours of dancing and sports she loved to do. Her spirit and temperament merry with the opportunity of a day out with friends at the fair, with no sense of competition and no need to look out beyond her momentary presence. *What was not attractive about this package of abundant radiance?*

Rei had always sensed that people were looking at her and clocking her, in a way she noted others did not receive. It made her uncomfortable, it made her think she was doing something wrong, and so she tried to erase these observations from her awareness and march on forth, hardening her body a notch each and every time. This time however no matter how hard Rei wanted to close her eyes, to pretend it was all a dream, she could not. The note still scrunched in her hand was getting damper by the minute, reminding her quite clearly that there was no escaping this one.

The sense of awaiting possibility was somewhat alluring. Rei found Daniele gorgeous too. There was no denying his good looks and his gentle charm. A rose between the thorns of all she had encountered thus far in life. She didn't feel threatened instead a slight excitement and thrill that could not be shown nor revealed to anyone. Another beautiful secret that now felt dirty.

Dirty girl.

~

Mid way through the school week the girls in Year 7 swamped Rei in the quad on her way to the refectory.

Did she know she had stolen Phoebe's boyfriend?

Did she know that Daniele and Phoebe had been going out for months?

Did she know Phoebe was mad and was going to come and get her?

The disturbance unsettled Rei who had been walking alone to lunch, late having just finished her lunchtime club activity, already pressed for time, battling the silent torments of her own peer group. She had no answer and so quietly voiced *No, she didn't know, and no, she was not aware.*

She hadn't done anything wrong she reminded herself as the thoughts in her mind chided her for allowing herself to be so exposed. Again.

Bad girl. Dirty girl.

She completed her daily ritual of politely greeting nun number one at the door, collecting her lunch tray and idling herself down the queue to the salad bar. She filled her plate high with chopped iceberg lettuce before semi-sprinting (whilst the coast was clear) like the fast walkers in a race walk, one foot having to maintain contact with the ground at all times, past the hot food counters and straight to the bread baskets past nun number two. She picked up her two slightly stale brown, non-seeded, budget rolls and whilst nun number three's back was turned, coasted her way to a table furthest away from the remaining patrolling nuns on duty.

She half sat, hovering slightly above her chair, eyes open and on guard until she spied a gap in the patrolled circumference perimeter and made her way for the clearing tables around the corner.
Pretending to scrape clear any debris from both the crockery and cutlery she hadn't actually used, she placed them on a tray on the carousel ready for washing. She turned once more to smile at nun number five (or was that four? She'd

lost count there were so many) in gratitude for not having been caught skipping main meals again this time round and gracefully like a swan peddling for dear life beneath the water's surface, advanced for the back door.

The assault course was not yet over. She still had to carefully manoeuvre herself and her uniform in a way that would not give away the two pockets in her blazer stuffed full of one whole and one half eaten stale roll and a handful of squished, iceberg lettuce. If indeed she made it to the exit and released the metal handle to the fresh air outside she could indeed take a sigh of relief, her £200 for *Passing Go.*

This time she'd made it, like she always had to date, the task never any easier or any less intense no matter what the day.

Rei took a right turn down towards the dance studios where she should not be unless in dance class; the diametrically opposite direction from the turn left towards her classrooms and school house that she should be taking. She needed a safe space, a moment to gather herself amidst the *Daniele* chaos.

She sat on the step of the ballet studio where only yesterday she had been practicing her pointe work, when Dame Charlotte called her over to whisper in her ear that she had got a place in the Royal Ballet School. Rei's wildest dream. Days filled with dance. One of the only places Rei had known to date that filled her with freedom and joy, the other being the bungalow and the beach in Suffolk under her grandparents' care.

Dame Charlotte, the principal ballerina and dance expert in the county, already had a relationship with Rei prior to her starting school here, having sat in on many of Rei's previous dance exams, part of her role ensuring fair marking and grading across the examining board.

Mid way through Rei's second year at boarding school it was announced to all the dance students that someone very special and of grave importance was coming to school. Royalty, it seemed. Everyone was to be on their best behaviour and to show their best plies, curtseys, tendus and arabesques, it was important not to show the school up. Only the best was acceptable. Rei smiled when she saw who it was.

Rei had always admired the way Dame Charlotte moved. It was with an elegance, a grace and an authority that she had never witnessed elsewhere. Her movements somehow communicated to Rei that she was rich, very rich, perhaps even regal in some way, but Rei doubted it. She was a lady that commanded respect without saying anything and everyone looked up to her despite very little direction or communication between her or them. She was delicate like a mouse and always smiled and whispered to Rei that she was *magnificent* and had *an extraordinary gift*.

Rei had warmed to her from an early age but never given their relationship any thought. Like fleeting ships in the night whose paths crossed once or twice a year Rei was always happy to see Dame Charlotte, needing to be on her best behaviour as was the expectation around her but without the fear the others had billowing in their sails.

Over the years, it must have been a good ten by now, Rei under the watchful (yet periodic) eye of Dame Charlotte continued to thrive in the world of dance. Her soul alive in the secluded environs of the small dance hut at the edge of the school's boundaries, a side step away from the fight or flight of every day existence everywhere else in the grounds.

She had hoped that being here today (under different circumstances) would offer some solace, some refuge from the barrage of conundrums facing her, and momentarily it did, until Rei realised the bell was about to ring for her next class. She pulled out the welting lunch debris from her blazer pocket realising she no longer had time to eat this and checking no-one was watching, threw the contents of her hand into the bush to her right, before peg-legging it back up the hill to collect her books for English.

Dread forgotten about since Tuesday's last English lesson, reappeared ten times weightier now upon entering the classroom, taking her seat second row, two desks in from Miss Murphy's desk ready for the double English lesson to unfold.

Miss Murphy may as well have been a nun even though she was one of the few *lay-staff* at school. Everything about her gave Rei nun vibes. Her body taut and hard, her manner bitter and cold, her Irish accent harsh and abrasive. Every time she spoke a shiver ran down Rei's back and through her body, the whole double 40-minute lesson spent sat to attention in absolute fear of being pounced upon next and humiliated in front of the class. Rei was scared sh*tless of having to read out loud and to make matters worse the text today, as it had been already and would be for the rest of the term, was Shakespeare's Macbeth.

Nothing Miss Murphy said made any sense to Rei, her explanations of the text seemed more complicated than the Bard's poetic prose itself. In the silence of Rei's cubicle, the words on the page seemed to find their own rhythm, to communicate a lullaby and a sense of calm. Yet within the classroom walls a different outplay occurred, no longer could Rei understand, hear and feel the rhythm of Shakespeare's words, instead she felt jailed, imprisoned, held captive even by them.

She was scolded for her intonation, for where she left pauses in a sentence where supposedly there should be none. Everything Rei felt and was communicating out loud about the piece she was chastised for. Not casually, not kindly, but full blown demonised for.

How dare you take such a precious text, one of my favourites and blaspheme it! Miss Murphy would berate.

The lesson drawn out as always was momentarily made sweeter by the smell of freshly cut lawn outside as the gardeners swept past the window on their huge mowers circling the school grounds cutting the swathes of grass beneath and around them. But even the sweet smell could not cut the air of discontent within the classroom.

Eventually the bell rang and Rei made a swift exit to the fresh air outside and the walk back down the slope to house for the last lesson before tea.

Sticky Willys today (iced buns to other non-men-deprived humans of the world) Rei's favourite! There was a glimmer of light to this day and an end to her now rumbling stomach insight. Rei thought she felt a sunbeam smile across her face and a warmth across her body. And temporarily she had.

Frankie came bounding up beside her.

What are you going to do about Saturday? she asked on the quiet making sure no-one else was in ear shot.

The reality of the upcoming weekend looming closer suddenly landed again waking Rei up from her sweet-toothed anticipation.

There was something that felt so very true and natural about Daniele's proposition and their interaction, though short, that felt worthy of exploring despite having been thoroughly warned off by Phoebe via her mafia-esque friends. It felt like The Mitchell brothers from EastEnders had come to patrol Rei's every move. She was uncertain for sure what she was going to do, and so had confided in Frankie (one of her dear friends since day one).

Frankie although one of Raquel's minions (who could not be seen to be friends with Rei or would be party to the same bullying abuse herself) actually wished she had the guts and courage to stand up to her and let it be known that she was friends with Rei whom she felt safe and enjoyed hanging out with. Nonetheless she played the game and pretended she was poking Rei with bitchy, sly comments as she passed her by.

Both Frankie and Rei participated in this strange dance, it allowed them both to seemingly dodge enemy missiles remaining under the pretence of being within the friendly firing zone.

It was only some thirty years later that Rei would come to realise that she had had just as much say in the war games as Raquel by never speaking up and out. She had been the enabler in the match as much as any others and it had been her responsibility too. There were no victims in this life, at all.

I'm not sure Rei replied making sure her smile couldn't be seen just in case others were watching. She had to appear like Frankie had said something mean to her. *But I'm sure it will become obvious, I kinda want to go, it feels like it would be fun.*

And with that the girls both smiled within, silently, their bodies giving nothing away, and went about their ways, excited for the soon-to-be taste of Sticky Willies on their lips once more.

1998

It's Wednesday, the second afternoon of the pre-Japan assembly, and Rei glances up at the escalator coming down. She sees him smiling at her, bronzed, blonde and handsome. *Cute* she thought as he smiles coyly at her, and off she walks to the assigned hotel reception room to gather the next load of information about her new job and where she will be stationed.

It had only been a couple of weeks since she had finished uni and she already had the next couple of years sown up. A job in Japan teaching English in a small town in the middle of nowhere. Her degree on paper said Economics, International Relations & Japanese, although by any stretch of the imagination her linguistic proficiency in this area was basic. Nonetheless the promise of a good pay packet and lodgings far away from home (whatever and wherever that was) only boosted her knowing that this was exactly the adventure she needed.

She found out she would be stationed in the northern island of Japan and would be the only *gaijin* (foreigner) around for miles. None of the other attendees were positioned anywhere near. Many seemed to be in larger towns and cities in closer proximity to each other, which could have triggered some kind of anxiety but did not. They were told vaguely about what they could expect upon arrival and before they knew it this information session was drawn to a close. Rei felt not much the wiser, but perhaps the reality of the situation became a little more tangible.

She walks back out into the foyer with the surge of others, a bobbing head in the crowd of excited players, her eyes glancing to see and her ears to the ground, on the lookout if there was anyone else going anywhere near her. She watches groups congeal and coagulate forming entities and exchanging telephone numbers of their new local governmental departments (the only thing anyone knew for sure and had had officially assigned to them).

It was a pleasure to observe them all, to listen to their back stories, to witness the chat and the allure of what may unfold. Somehow watching this screenplay unfold before her settled her. Rei had never been a nervous person and there were very few times that she felt unsafe or insecure and times like this she couldn't have put it into words, but she appreciated even more that she was very apt and capable of doing things by herself.

She turns to walk away having got all that she can from the event and he is there, right before her having exited his information room next door.

Hi. Did you find out where are you going? she asks. The words tumbling out of her mouth.

Yes, to Hokkaido he replied, Rei's ears pricking up. *Me too!*

The names of the places could not be pronounced and meant nothing geographically to them at this point in time so getting out their newly assigned maps emblazoned with red dots they each pointed to their allocated towns sharing a smile as they did. They did not need to know much Japanese or be able to speak it to realise they were nowhere near each other. They were a good day's drive from each other at best with a ferry ride too.

Ah cool! Rei said *You're on an island.*

Yes, I asked to be he retorted. *Shall we exchange our numbers?*

Sure. Rei wrote down her name and recently designated number and handed it over delicately receiving his, noticing he had nice writing for a boy. Also noting that perhaps that had been from the trying she had witnessed as he slowly formulated the swirls concentrating out loud as he jotted down his number.

Have fun Rei booms. *Hope it all goes well!* and turns back to the only other people she knows who have now joined them in the foyer.

It was time to get out of there.

1992

They are (she is) sixteen when they officially sleep together for the first time. Official not in the sense that they had done it elsewhere at another moment in time, but official because it was not a spur of the moment thing. Not a randy, fumble and stab in the dark occurrence that Rei had heard about from most of her friends. They were experiences that Rei was glad she had not been a part of.

James's parents had sat him down and spoken very directly to him about what he could and could not do, how he must and must not treat a woman, what it meant to actually sleep with someone, with Rei. They had bought him a pack of condoms and given him explicit details about what could be expected, what the boundaries were, but perhaps most importantly that there was space, no rush, no pressure and that they were there for them both, whatever.

As James relayed what had been shared between his family at the kitchen table the night before she felt embarrassed that they had been talked about like that, whilst also reassured and slightly pleased that this seemed like a moment when *a problem shared was a problem halved*. Talks of candles, gentle music and zero expectation seemed both prudent and comforting at this point in time in their relationship right now.

His parents left for their afternoon out and Rei and James went upstairs to his attic room like every other time before. Smiling and talking about anything and everything. Despite never having fancied James, Rei loved being with him. He was gentle and kind, never bolshy or needy, and that his parents embraced her fully into their arms and home was beyond incredible. For the first time ever, Rei felt part of a family and it suited her very well.

The family motto was *Shame To Waste It* and they lived this in abundance. Laughter always, games, study, food, hugs, adventures, sharing, debates, you name it, nothing went by without exploring it in full and in detail.

They lived in a picture-perfect cottage tucked away down a country lane behind a petrol station on the byway. An unglamorous location, but one which you were wholly unaware of once turning into the hedge lined lane. Pale pink in colour with roses at the front and a beautifully manicured lawn both front, back and sides; a garage with two nice (moderately expensive) cars, full to the brim with outdoor sports equipment and a freezer full of handmade food ready for consumption; everything looked delightful and inviting, and it was.

Rei was never made to feel anything other than one of them despite her self- (and other's) professed *inadequate* background. She had been worried that given the usual first meet questioning they might rebuke and rebuff her…

Where do you live?
What do your parents do?
Do you have any siblings?

Most others adults Rei had ever met sounded surprised at her answers, having never met someone outside of their normal circle before, with huge undertones (overtones) of judgement and subsequent spurious inferences.

Oh! I see. Really. That's fascinating. Their minds made up and silence ensuing.

As Rei and James arrived upstairs they looked at each other awkwardly for the first time ever. They knew it was time. They were the last of their group of friends to lose their virginity, not that it had bothered them, but it still hung in the air around them, everyone waiting for the shift to occur, for them to be able to join the *after*-gang

Like a cloud edging slowly, so very slowly on a still summers day casting cool shadows in front of the beating sun, the fact that they had been in no rush to join the group seemed to niggle and nark the others. Perhaps more so because they wanted to hear details to comfort themselves that their own clumsy and often graceless encounters were the norm and not just their own.

James looked outside the window to check his parents were still out, lit a candle and chose some music, they laid down together, not on his usual double futon but on the single one at the side of his room. Rei realised it had been carefully prepped for the moment no doubt overseen by his mum; she could feel the care and sensitivity.

They didn't look deep into each other's eyes but neither did Rei close them. The bright daylight streaming upon their naked bodies a strange sighting, she had never even contemplated sex in the daytime. Any stories she'd heard had been of night time escapades, of darkness and not being able to see anything. This was completely different. Their bodies pale in the sunshine every nuance spotlighted. There was no hiding.

It didn't hurt like she'd been told, nor was it fantastically amazing as others had disclosed. There was no blood to clear up and no emotions to mop up either. They lay wrapped in each other's arms, the sun through the dormer window delicately maintaining the warmth of their bodies. A buoyant content shared between the pair. Nothing had gone wrong. The condom had not split. The house was still all theirs and there was no mess to clean up.

Together they went back downstairs and out into the garden to play croquet, drinking fizzy water with cucumber shards and freshly squeezed lemon, music playing from the incredible sound system playing effortlessly inside.

Thankfully at the dinner table that evening they did not have to relay the afternoon's events for all. James discreetly shared with his folks on their return that they had partaken in the action and that all was well. When Rei went up for a bubble drenched bath that evening, he stayed back and confided with them more. They were relieved and happy for them, nothing more ever said on the matter.

2000

As soon as she starts to feel sick at teaching college Rei knows unequivocally what is up. It is only a few weeks in, having landed back in the UK after two years away in Japan. They had been inseparable since her return and had booked themselves in to get their teaching qualification in a six-week intensive academy program in London. This would ensure their continued safe passage out of England away from everything they were still running from (themselves) - this time the chosen destination was India. Heading, Kerala.

Landing in London via a stopover in Hong Kong Rei steps off the plane and out into the sea of faces at the arrivals gate. Ethan was there waiting for her, happy to be reunited after a month apart. Rei was not sure she was feeling the same way. She was not unhappy to see him, but her time away from him had made her realise how happy and content she was and that perhaps her life ahead did not involve him at her side.

She had felt a freedom this last month and had felt a growing sense of herself for the first time ever. And it felt grand. However, they had made plans and Rei was not one to let people down. They had not considered the practicalities of what or how they would navigate the next couple of months before their departure to India, but they knew it was a necessary means to an end and so both in their own naif ways bumbled on with their half-baked plan.

The tube out of Heathrow would indubitably pass by her grandparent's house, it had to, so Rei joyfully suggested they go surprise them. If she wanted to see, and had missed anyone whilst she was away, it was them.

They arrived at the pale green front door, faded by time and sunlight Rei noticed, and knocked. There was no bark from the dogs and the house was still. Rei realised immediately that they would be away in Suffolk, it was the summer and so there was no one home.

For as long as she had remembered her grandparents had stashed a spare key to their home in a tin in the garage at the back of the house. She had seen her Uncle Pete perform the fence jump on many occasion so knew the drill and she thought she would recognise the appropriate tin if she saw it. It was worth a try. Hesitantly she began the obstacle course, feeling bad that she was breaking and entering her grandparent's home, but also realising there were few other options right now, no cash or credit card in hand and tired from the journey, suitcase in tow, this seemed like the perfect pitstop to gather herself and start afresh tomorrow.

That evening, inside, having contacted her grandparents to let them know and apologise that she had broken in but also to ask if it was okay to stay the night, she snuggled up in bed, now tired and ready for a rejuvenating night's sleep. The warmth and closeness of Ethan's body seemed comforting in the bleary haze of being reunited with the country she had spent two years happily far away from. Before dormancy overtook her body they slept together, her first night back in the country. It felt different than usual, markedly so, but in her heavy-lidded semiconscious state she put this down to the whole day being very strange as she looked around her uncle Pete's bedroom in disbelief she was here and fell into a deep slumber.

She had been dreaming of motherhood for a year now but as her periods had dried up without trace and with no current explanation from any of the doctors she had seen in Japan any dreams had been parked and instead replaced with real, heavy, dark days of sobbing at the thought it may never happen.

Rei already had a strong sense of the parent she *didn't* want to be alongside a knowing that she would be a fab mama, and although she had wished this moment to come true for months now, the timing all seemed wrong. She hadn't realised pregnancy was a process. She'd only dreamed of the actual kid part. She certainly hadn't accounted for what it may do to and with her body.

How naive.

Silly girl.

Ethan visibly shell shocked by the announcement could not and would not believe the test results.

But you haven't even had your period! How is this possible?

On their first day off at the weekend they visited unregistered (making matters even more excruciating) doctors and clinics nearby to ensure this was as real as Rei's body was communicating.

Rei was happy, deeply so, although watching Ethan's reaction to both her and to the news she began to reconnect to the feelings she'd had before returning to the UK, that perhaps they were not meant to be together. It seemed harder having to navigate his processes and reactions to events as well as her *all day* sickness (there was no *morning* sickness about it at all).

He went out drinking with his university friends one evening after college to return home late, a mess, in tears after a friend had slapped him round the face telling him to *wake up and smell the coffee*.

Rei knew better than to ask for the full story, Ethan was struggling not only with the idea of a child but most definitely with the reality that she was no longer able to fulfil her previous role of general manager, PA and night and day entertainer for him, it was taking her every breath to stop being sick everywhere all of the time, they were four weeks into their course and exams were coming up soon, she needed to do the work, stay awake and show up without puking everywhere.

The tiredness, fatigue and the responsibility became too much to continue the daily ten-mile cycle both in and out of central London to their course and so Rei opted to take the tube. Ethan reluctantly relinquishing his fitness regime perhaps not out of duty, care or respect, but because without her he would quite simply lose his way.

As the tube bustled about, swooshing through the tunnels, after eight hours of teaching, Rei could feel the vomit rising. She thought she should be used to it by now, but each and every time was afresh and equally as horrific as the last.

Desperately, she urged her body to the door grappling with the other bodies in her path on the sardine-canned carriage. As the doors thrust open at the next station and the myriad of rush-hour commuters scrambled to alight from the platform, Rei's mouth spewed forth like a lava fountain volcano erupting at full force. The doors closed again and Rei stood there in shock her mouth still full of tephra and crater debris, her invincibility levels at an all-time low.

For the first time ever, Rei wished she had a large bump visible so as to assure the other travellers that she wasn't just disgusting and bad mannered, or ill, or drunk as their eyes narrated, she was a 24-year-old girl who was pregnant, credulously so; unsophisticated, inexperienced and simply so.

Silly girl.

2001

As the weeks turn into months Rei & Ethan find themselves living with Ethan's mother, Elizabeth, in a small town on the outskirts of Banbury, a far cry from the India they had imagined themselves to be living in. Ethan still makes Rei laugh and they enjoy their time together but there is a part of him that is closed off from her. He voices his concern that Rei will no longer love him when the baby is born and Rei responds (naively)

I will never love anyone like I love you.

You will always come first.

Her response seems to appease Ethan's growing discontent, his itchy feet. Yet as Rei's belly grows, he withdraws all the more.

Their once burgeoning sex life waning, Rei asks if he is ok? Having consoled and reiterated to him on numerous occasions that no harm would be done to the baby inside her she fears there is more to the story than he is letting on. *Perhaps he is disgusted by her now? Perhaps he is worried he may inject her with a poison for the second time in a row?* It was possible of course; it had happened once already.

As usual as a lack of familial communication was to Rei, she realised that Ethan's family were *same, same, but different*. His parents had slept in different beds in separate bedrooms for as long as he had known. He thought that was how it was. It was only after he had left Cambridge University aged 22 that they shared that they had been living a lie *for him*. His dad had been having an affair with his secretary for many, many years and now that his son was old enough (at 22) to hear such things he had moved out and in with his new wife to be.

Rei couldn't understand how Ethan could not have known, not have sensed anything, but again she knew not to question or probe anymore, it was fruitless, but she understood that just as she did not want to see the world around her, Ethan had a cast iron blindfold on through which no light could penetrate.

It had not been easy for either of them, or indeed anyone, meeting the prospective families for the first time announcing a completely unplanned pregnancy and a never before met partner. The questions only aggravated the narrative. None of it seemed plausible to anyone and eyebrows were dancing.

Perhaps it was a culmination of all these things and more that Rei was sensing, but it did not feel good; she was not a welcome member of the family, in fact she knew Liz was positively furious at her for *taking* her only son from her, every move communicated it.

The only comfort for Rei with a distancing partner in an uncomfortable house where she clearly was not wanted, was the growing baby in her womb whom she loved and adored dearly and whom she would do everything she could to protect from harm, including negative thoughts and emotions, this she was sure of.

As she rolled over to kiss Ethan that morning before he left for a job he hated he muttered that he was *exhausted* and *didn't feel like it*. It had been the same all week. Rei was disheartened and she could feel that it was beginning to affect her. She felt captive in a grey town with no friends around her and nothing to call her own, she had regressed from her own lovely space, and freedom to move as she chose, to this.

She knew this time she couldn't let it pass, if she did it was a slippery slope ahead and she wasn't prepared for that life for her unborn child. She had vowed and made a promise to herself since young that she would *Never* put her kids (when she had them) through what she had been through. *E v e r.*
She manoeuvred herself out of bed, belly protruding yet perfectly formed and gorgeously proportionate on her womanly body. She took a deep breath before entering the bathroom prepared to have an awkward conversation with Ethan about the necessity of them working together as one, as a team, letting nothing come between them.

She heard the shower running and thought perhaps she should wait until he came back to the bedroom but something told her it was ok to go in and wait on the toilet seat for him. He may actually appreciate that she'd made the effort to do that for him.

She turned the handle and stepped inside only to be confronted by the back end of Ethan naked on the bathroom floor hand firmly caressing his penis back and forth, back and forth and a porno mag propped up in front of him, her legs and breasts akimbo.

Rei hadn't been sick for a couple of weeks now, yet here, now it was back in an instant. She gagged, silently retching, whilst sloping away into the morning light trying not to be heard and not to disturb anyone, including Ethan.

She scurried back to bed shaking, unsure what any of this meant, but knowing deep inside she was sickened to the core.

A few minutes later Ethan returned smile upon his face to get dressed and leave.

How was your shower? asked Rei.

Great. Hot but needed Ethan lied.

Rei knew he hadn't even set foot in the shower but had splashed his face with a handful of water droplets perhaps in an attempt to set the scene.

See you later he said as he left the room.

Rei's life shattered.

Any vague hope she'd been holding onto of a life of happy families came crashing down firmly to the ground. Too stunned to do anything she lay there and thought of her commitment to their baby, her baby.

The sadness turning to anger at herself for neglecting all those moments she had felt and known before that had told her and communicated to her that Ethan did not truly care for her but only for himself.

Why had she got herself into this situation?

How utterly stupid. She only had herself to blame.

Silly girl.

Rei went back to the bathroom, the only bathroom in the house, to investigate.

Was this a dream? A nightmare? Where was the evidence?

She got down on her hands and knees and opened up the cabinet beneath the bathroom sink, at first glance nothing, but on closer inspection behind the lotions and potions sat conveniently next to the cleaning products was the porno. Not one porno magazine, but many, a stash, a collector's albums worth. The sick instantly returned but this did not prove a problem as she was already bent down next to the toilet. She wretched and she heaved; puke first and then just motions and movements. Rei thought if it carried on any longer she may give birth to the baby by mouth. That would be a first, a bit like its seeming immaculate conception.

The deceit hit hard, the enabling, the knowing.

Oh my God even Elizabeth knew - about them, about him and was sanctioning it all.

Rei puked air some more, her stomach raw and her body yearning for respite.

It was snowing outside and icy beneath the fresh fall, she knew it was not safe to walk, she may slip and she would be being hawk-eyed by Liz.

Her beloved racing green, walnut clad Mazda convertible that she had imported back from Japan with her, lay protected from the weather in the garage. She saw an exit strategy and decided to make a run for it. She wasn't sure where to, she hadn't got that far yet, but she needed some space and some air and she wanted to run as far away from the mess she had created as she possibly could.

She tip-toed down the stairs trying to hold back the tears that were now streaming, falling from her face. She felt disgusting, dirty, ashamed, embarrassed and many more hideous things that she was unable to yet reference or compartmentalise.

So as not to disturb the un-mother-in-law she sidled her way around the hallway so her reflection could not be seen in the mirror as she entered the kitchen where her car keys were kept.

Up until this point in time any sight of Rei would ignite a smoke-filled conversation of sorts with Elizabeth as she puffed her way unapologetically on the cigarettes between her slightly yellowed fingers. Today Rei could not be sloppy about this, under no circumstance could she be seen, especially now, snot streaming from her face merging as one with her never-ending tears. She had to be silent, any sound could disturb the sleeping lion, it was too risky and too dangerous to not be anything but. A globule of snot fell to the floor silent enough to not be detected but obvious to the visual eye and any house-proud member (which both the women were, they shared that and the man-boy of the house in common).

She entered the kitchen relieved, a step closer to some fresh air and some space and hopefully an alleviation from the compression and tightness she was feeling all around and on her. She opened the kitchen cupboard reaching for her keys to find an emptiness where they belonged. Sudden panic and a burgeoning fumble for her ticket out of here.

As her head was as far into the kitchen cupboard as possible whist leaning over a counter laden with child, the door behind her banged shut too loud for comfort.

Are you looking for these? chided Elizabeth.

How the hell did she get here? What are the chances of that? Why is everything conspiring against me? thought Rei her face now a mush of mucus and phlegm, her clothes sodden from undulating sobs - there could be no disguising the state she was in.

Rei tried to remain calm and walk towards Liz to collect her keys without lifting her head, with no eye contact, in a last attempt to get away with it. As much as Rei seemed so different than Elizabeth in so many respects, she knew she had met her match for someone who detected *everything*. Not only did Liz *know* but she was also someone who made it their business to *know* everything about everyone *all* of the time.

Rei reached out her hand to take the keys from the dressing-gowned silhouette, keys in one hand, ciggy in the other. As she did so the hand retracted, fingers closing tightly around the keys, Rei's keys.

Where do you think you are going? she asked, confrontation in her voice.

For some fresh air Rei stammered *I'm not feeling very well* she too now lied.

I don't think so, not in that state Liz retorted taking Rei's keys and herself back up to her bedroom locking the door behind her.

Rei slumped on the kitchen chair barely able to get in, her bump was so large now even the table seemed to be distancing itself from her.

She sat in disbelief, grey dubiety, motionless, empty, drained, exhausted, and unable to go anywhere. She had noted that Liz had taken all the sets of house keys with her too.

Rei and her unborn baby were trapped - it was either prison in the warmth that she knew, or potential freedom in the freezing cold middle of nowhere. It did not seem much of a choice. And so, Rei made none. Her body incapable of movement at this stage.

And so, in her given-upness her reluctance to not cause a scene, to stand up for herself, she was in fact choosing their fate and sealing the deal on what lay ahead.

1987

On the first term at boarding school each pupil was asked to vote for a class prefect. Everyone was new having entered the school aged eleven in Year 1 and it seemed a preposterous challenge. Given a list with everyone's names and asked to tick the select six of choice for all the appropriate merits and attributes needed for a year prefect of such a fine and exemplary establishment, it seemed quite a difficult task unless you were going to do a lucky dip selection.

The votes were in and Rei had unanimously won prefect status receiving votes from over 90% of her year group. The tutors and house mistresses were beside themselves wondering if the vote had been rigged, commenting that no-one had ever received such a landslide success. But looking at the sweet and innocent eleven-year-olds before them they knew it had not been.

Here was a girl who had won everyone's heart by not doing anything in particular.

2001

As the weeks turn into months Rei's tummy finally begins to show. At six months the baby was still not visible to most and her energy levels had not waned, she looked like a regular twenty-five-year-old sexy blonde high on life.

Her determination and passion to create a loving home for their child kept her busy most days, but perhaps behind this lay a drive to be out of Liz's home as soon as possible and into their own space. They had bought a basement flat together in Oxford with the financial help of Ethan's dad and Rei had found a steal on the open market at the time that needed work doing to it. A nice little *doer-upper*. She was only teaching English a few hours and days a week now so all her spare time could be ploughed into the project.

Ever since she was a little girl, she had had a very natural love of spaces and homes, her mum had a keen interest in antiques and anything French and although they had a simple home with little money to spend on it, it was carefully curated. Rei's mum would often come home from work to find Rei had moved the furniture around, no doubt perplexed and annoyed, but it was something they shared in common, a knowledge that their home and how it was maintained was important to both their mental and physical wellbeing.

Rei designed the new Oxford flat's reconfiguration, organised the workmen, bought the furniture and decorated the interiors whilst attending to the garden space at the back. She was in her element and was thoroughly grateful for not only the project but also the opportunity they had been given and indeed gifted. It was such a comfort to know that they had a home of their own as the baby was soon to arrive.

Although not knowing for sure, Rei had always had a strong sense that the baby was a he, so much so that it was a contributing factor to their sudden departure from Portugal and their previous teaching positions there. The thought of a son of hers, any son in fact, being called for military service was not one that sat well with her, and alongside Ethan's recurring bouts of anxiousness and his inability to settle in their new home even a few months in, they called time on the contract and returned to England, but only after having fully embraced their one bedroomed apartment above the mortuary (given to them as part of their relocation package), decorating and painting the walls and wardrobes with murals to brighten it up. Rei would never leave a space without adding more love and enrichment to it than which she was given or found it. Never.

~

It was early morning when Rei first felt a contraction. Her newly met friend had given birth only eight weeks prior to a baby girl and had had a long and arduous birth that spanned three days across her visit in hospital. So, Rei was prepared for the long-haul.

Originally, she had relished in the idea of having a water birth at home, she knew the hospital setting felt too clinical and not intimate enough for her and what was needed, but the more she looked into it, the practicalities of a birthing pool appealed less and less. Their one-bedroom flat was not large and the whole thing seemed too many steps away from simplicity for Rei.

She appreciated the fact that Ethan had no strong opinions during her pregnancy about the baby, the birth or moving forward. She wasn't entirely sure if that was because the whole thought scared him too much that he didn't dare go there, or whether he didn't actually care (potentially both) either way it was perfectly convenient for her this way too. She knew exactly what was needed and so Ethan's non-committal behaviours avoided any future conflict or confrontation. Rei took control and led the way almost singlehandedly in all aspects.

It worked well this way. Rei liked looking after someone, and Ethan liked being looked after. A perfect arrangement that suited them both. Problem was that by not really discussing anything of any great substance together, they conceivably aggregated an accumulated gross scale problem across the ensuing years, the sum of its minutiae parts.

As the contractions grew stronger and came more quickly and more frequently, Rei called for the midwife who came to their home pretty sharp. The pain was unbearable and the pacing around the kitchen table and up and down the corridor (as instructed) did little to relieve not only the pain but the feeling that she was about to give birth to the whole of her insides. She wasn't sure gravity could handle that. To add to her already peaked self-consciousness, she couldn't be sure if she was actually pooing everywhere too, the pressure bearing down on her made her want to sit on the toilet and never leave, *what if the baby came at the same time too? Down the toilet?* she pondered.

She couldn't be sure where the front, the middle or the back of her began or ended at this point in time. The midwives (there were two now) told her not to worry, she could just let go and if she pooed they would clear it up. Rei recalled the curry they'd had last night and was now regretting the choice to do all the things possible to speed up a baby's birth. She had drawn the line at driving over speed bumps at great speed, that sounded both potentially painful and dangerous to her, but a mega hot curry had sounded, and tasted, like a good idea. Until now.

The midwife suggested running a bath, which sounded like a grand idea, a compromise on the missing birthing pool. The idea of a floating turd seemed somewhat less obtrusive than a cow pat on the bathroom floor. It made no sense, but she rolled with it.

It would relieve the pain they said.

Like hell it does! thought Rei as she suddenly had a loathing for water anywhere near her skin. There was nothing mermaid like here, more a whaling massacre. The upside Rei noted was that they had not spent out on the birthing pool, that would have been a complete waste of time and money. *Every cloud!*

Rei felt even worse as she attempted to lift herself out from the narrow bath, the water feeling heavy on her body, but the midwife assured her that it would not be long now, she was 7cm dilated,

We're nearly there.

The women asked Ethan if there was any sugar or toast, anything really, that Rei could take, as she could see Rei was getting tired and her energy levels were depleting. Rei explained she didn't eat sugar or gluten, or dairy, neither did she drink alcohol or caffeine. Between screams and sweat building up on her clammy skin, she told them both about their time in Japan and how she felt so much better for not eating these things. They tried to persuade her that it would potentially be in her best interests to do so right now, as she needed her strength for this next stage of the delivery. Hearing this Rei complied and directed Ethan to some of the honey he loved that she had in the cupboard for him. She took a teaspoon full and felt nauseous but perhaps a little stronger too.

Ethan looked paler than ever, the colour draining from his perma-tanned face with each of Rei's crescendo-ing wails. The midwives assured him too it wouldn't be long now; they jokingly offered him the gas and air that Rei had flatly refused and he took some, on repeat.

The potential threat of a secondary casualty that the midwives had had on their hands a second ago now looked less worrying.

To keep him present, focused and engaged the midwives asked Ethan if he had a camera ready to take some photos of the newborn. It was as if a light had been switched on.

Oh!

Trying to get Rei to come out of their pea sized bathroom and into the lounge a mere meter or so away was a task too large. Rei could not move or be coaxed off of the bathroom floor. She had curled herself tightly around the toilet bowl beneath the sink. The midwives took their seats on the floor outside the fully opened bathroom door, so they had a full and clear view of Rei, without having to look down the neck of a toilet basin themselves.

Seconds later Ethan came and stood hovering above Rei looking into the bathroom mirror. The midwives asked very gently and uber politely what he was doing, suggesting that perhaps Rei needed the space around her to breathe. He replied that he would not be long he was just bleaching his hair ready for the birthing photos.

The small fan in the even smaller, windowless, bathroom was working overtime to extract the dye fumes stinging and piercing the vacuumed air. Rei thought she heard it splutter, coughing up the toxicity. The midwives stunned into silence at what was unfolding could not contain their body language or disdain for long. Rei observing it all unable to contribute, embarrassed by the spectacle, and again feeling like she was watching the whole thing from above, outside of her body, groaned as another contraction came and went.

As the time passed Rei could feel herself weakening, she hadn't known a pain like this but thankfully she only had to remind herself that she was about to meet this gorgeous, precious being that had grown inside her over the last nine months.

Anything was possible.

And with one final push out he came.

The midwives acted quickly and professionally and congratulated Rei and a recently, hot to the touch, blonded Ethan and their newborn baby before letting them know that an ambulance would be outside in the next ten minutes. Rei had done a grand job and the baby was fit and healthy, but he had come out with his hands above his head and in the process had scratched open Rei's insides, she was bleeding heavily and needed to go in for surgery after all.

Whilst they waited Rei would need to give birth to the placenta too. Thankfully this time she agreed with them, *it wasn't half as bad.*

Rei remembered the epidural needle entering her spine and the irony of it all did not go by unmarked. She had tried so hard to avoid being in the hospital for the birth, yet fate had bought her here in the end anyway.

When returned to the hospital room post-surgery she was (rei)united with her son, his mouth to her breast and for the first time in a very long time Rei felt very, deeply happy, a settlement that things were exactly as they needed to be.

She had found her place.

1998

As Rei was growing up, she never really fantasised about getting married like the other girls did. Doubtless part reaction from the dissolved parental marriage she had witnessed and part having a very arms-length relationship with any men at all. From an early age her father would jocularly remind her (on repeat) that neither should she ever bring home a black man, a man with an earring, one with long hair, nor a man without work. The boundaries had been set. It was not up for discussion, more of an underlying threat covered up with a smile.

A *joke* is what it was called.

It never made sense to Rei. There was nothing in her that saw or felt any distinguishing factors between a black man and a white that warranted such a dramatic (if any) rule to be laid, but it was clear. She wondered if this would be *where her dad and her would cross swords later on in life?*

She couldn't imagine finding long haired or ear-ringed boys attractive so that part was easy to imagine. Even as an eleven-year-old she knew that much, yet she did wonder about the rest.

There was a distant dread within Rei that somehow her pool of future husband opportunity was being shaped by the world around her, not remaining free and open to all of the elements. She knew it couldn't *really* be like that. No-one *actually* had that kind of control in this day, age and society that she lived in. *Did they?* But she was also aware that there was a part of her that did not feel quite strong enough to stand up against this netting, this capping around her and her future pathways.

She was acquiescing from what she felt, the truth of what she knew, passively, reluctantly. It wasn't a deliberate agreement having contemplated and weighed up the pros and cons of such actions (or non-actions) and what they may mean to her life ahead, more a silent withdrawal back into the shadows, where there would be no kickback and no short-term confrontation. It seemed the safest way.

So far, she had only experienced a relationship with James which had been loving, gentle and kind. In their 5.5 years together they had never argued, never had a disagreement. There was only one incident that had been out of character, but they both chose to close the chapter, turn the page and never look back on it.

~

It had been a Saturday night one half term.

Rei had gone home to see her mum for the weekend before she would spend the rest of the week at James's family home as was now the norm. It was about 7pm or 8pm and Rei suddenly felt an impending doom in the pit of her stomach. She wasn't sure exactly what it was but she knew it wasn't good.

Her mum noticing the instant shift in Rei asked if she was ok? Rei shared that she had a bad feeling about James and it was making her feel sick. She knew he was at a party that afternoon and evening with his friends. She had never felt worried about that sort of thing before, and hadn't even today, until now. Her mum said not to be so silly.

James is a good boy (which he was), *you'll see.*

Rei reprimanded herself and told her ego that she was being silly, all their other friends did stupid things, but not James.

Silly girl. Why did she have to make a fuss out of nothing?

She took herself to bed berating herself for whatever it was she was feeling. It was powerful to say the least; she really needed to give herself a good talking to to settle down for the night.

Eventually she did.

It wasn't until 11am (later than usual) the following day when James rang to arrange their plans for the day as promised, that Rei allowed the stomach curdling to be felt again springing back into action, this time on high of its own accord. Like the binary fusion of one bacterial cell, asexually reproducing under the conditions of the situation; a handful of insecurity here, a sprinkle of doubt there, some self-loathing and now some self-bashing too as a cute multi layered topping; it was a potent concoction.

Rei had never heard or felt James like this. His usual strong and lively manner and presence diminished, waif like and pathetic. He didn't know how to tell her, how to let her know, that something awful had happened and he wasn't sure how. He had got drunk with his friends and had ended up kissing (snogging to be clear, more than once, in fact, twice) Pamela. Rei's stomach already viscid and soured dropped to the floor with a thud, heavy as leaden weight.

When? she asked desperate to know.

Last night whimpered James down the phone.

Yes, but when exactly?

I don't know, I wasn't looking at my watch.

James realised he was in no position to be holding any cards at this juncture in time and retreated back to the recounting of how the previous night unfolded, step by painful step to Rei's ears.

Pamela wasn't even nice or particularly attractive in her eyes.

What was the pull for him? Was she really 'that bad' that she was worth cheating on with another? ...with Pamela?

She tried to compartmentalise the emotions from the facts and listen out for what surprisingly was the only relevant and pertinent information to her at this stage.

It must have been about 7pm or 8pm he said, silence falling after the maths had been done.

Rei felt a sense of relief above all else. She hadn't been going mad after all. What she'd felt had been pinpoint accurate. Everything else was now music, slow, muffled, drowned out music to her ears. It was as if James was talking to her under water. It was comparatively irrelevant.

Rei was able to catch through the dampened squelchy discourse a sense that James was devastated. He was ashamed this had happened and only had his appetite for alcohol to blame.

Rei observed that the other trigger for her in this was the unsettlement with the fact that it was Pamela. She couldn't understand the attraction, it felt like a personal insult, an attack even, and it was one she wasn't taking very well.

She wrestled battles in her mind, scouring past meetings, past conversations, anything that may shine light on why Pamela was better than Rei.

She knew no-one was *better* than another and that wasn't really who she was to be going down this kind of rabbit hole, but there was something that had disturbed her, had her by the short and curlies, piquing a hidden something within that had been dormant for a while, lifetimes perhaps and was now not showing any signs of being ready to go back into hibernation.

She asked him if he *liked* Pamela, to which he honestly replied *yes, I quite fancy her,* the sting stung a little fiercer now.

He was unsure of what had really gone on and what would play out but he was sure he had not wanted to hurt Rei. They were like brother and sister and they did everything together. Feeling the depredation of guilt and upset across the telephone wires was small consolation to Rei but she could feel it none the less.

Rei said she needed a bit of space to process this all and so they said goodbye (perhaps their final one) to each other in tears, both gutted not knowing what course their lives may take next.

~

Plausibly Rei could have listened to Janet Jackson's album *Janet* one too many times in her top floor uni flat, bedroom over-looking the back end of the stunning Georgian architecture surrounding her. The front facade grand, elegant, symmetrical, regal even, the backside for the servants, given little to no consideration, a hotchpotch of styles, floors, openings and architectural materials. Much like society, Rei had come to realise more and more. A front of polite niceness and smiles, the back end a more earthy, at times vulgar display of emotions hidden from the naked eye.

She could still hear Janet's sultry melodious chorus

Like a moth to a flame, burned by the fire
My love is blind, can't you see my desire?
That's the way
That's the way
That's the way love goes…

She wondered whether she had actually become Janet from the song having listened to it so many times.

Was this possible?

Could the music be subliminally telling her something, morphing her into someone, something else?

There were definite signs of it being so.

What was this desire, almost reckless attraction to be drawn to someone despite the obvious, potential for pain or harm?

Like a moth drawn to a flame?

Where did it come from?
Was it retaliation on a deep sub-conscious level to not being able to choose a husband for herself, but only from a pre-prescribed pool of candidates?

For although her past few dates weren't black, didn't have an earring or long hair, and actually did have a job (in fact they were all positively gorgeous) Rei was left thinking that they were just all *too nice and boring*! She wanted someone with a bit more of an edge, a bit more rugged.

2024

Rei and Gabriel marry in Old Marylebone Town Hall in early December. It had always been Gabriel's dream to get married there and it seemed like the perfect venue, a few minutes stroll down Baker Street from his (soon to be *their*) flat. From the time they got together in June to the time they wed was 25 weeks exactly. A seven 7 (2+5). And it was Saturday the 7th. An abundance of 7's.

They had known they were married from day one. There was no getting to know one another, no let's see if this might work trial run, they just were.

One.

Together.

By week three they had spoken very openly and candidly in great depth about their personal finances, their wills, their kids (7 of them between them), what they wanted and what they didn't want. There was nothing of any great consequence that had been shelved for a later (never to come) date, everything had been laid on the table, warts and all. It was in fact very liberating and hugely refreshing.

Post dinner one night week one, Rei stood in awe and deep appreciation of the conversation they had just had. There had been no reactions, no rebuttals, no recoiling, no fallout to what was normally a very sensitive subject where the game players would tread carefully around each other proceeding gingerly, cautious for stepping on eggshells.

She looked at Gabriel with a tender care that he so deserved and told him so.

The steady and stabilising feeling she felt in her body for the first time in a very long time continued to permeate through her body. A deep settlement and knowing that this was it, how life could be lived. They hugged and kissed gently and tenderly beside the oven, the extractor fan silently removing the faint redolence of the salmon they'd just eaten lingering in the air and on their lips.

They had originally planned to get married a year to the day of their first car trip down to the country party together, but as the previous couple of months had rattled on by, they both felt a pull and lagging feeling in their bodies. When they realised that they just needed to get on with what had been given to them it was super simple, and they were responsive to it.

Some friends had just been round for an early supper and midst clearing up, they looked at each other and the clock. It was 5.23pm.

Their guests now gone, Rei looked to Gabriel and asked *What time does the Registry Office close? Could we make it?*

Gabriel eyes wide open said *Let's take the car and we'll be in with a chance.*

Putting down washing up brushes and tea towels from their hands they took themselves to the car with no rush, only a purposefulness that would carry them swiftly to the Town Hall. They pulled up outside at 5.29pm and looked briefly at each other, a silent acknowledgment that whether or not they would be served with a minute to spare before the doors were closed for the weekend would determine the fate of their wedding day date. They had looked online earlier and seen there was one appointment left but having already made an appointment for later the following year they had to go in person to amend the date. Being Old Marylebone Town Hall there was always a huge demand and therefore wait list to marry there - the establishment prided themselves on the celebrities and royalty that they wed.

Neither Rei nor Gabriel had an attachment to the outcome but they knew they were being obedient to the undeniable impulse. Rei jumped out whilst Gabriel stayed with the car. It was Baker Street on a Saturday in the run up to Christmas, it was heaving with shoppers and Christmas parties. The stunning festive lights adorned the trees, the street and the shop windows all around. It was the first time Rei really appreciated how pretty Christmas could actually be. She smiled deep within.

As she entered the building the doorman smiled, a genuine beam, not the welcome she was expecting from a man stood out in the freezing cold about to clock off for the day in one minute's time. Rei recalled her time working in a country pub on her year out where last orders were 9pm. All the customers present would be in the last moments of their meal, sitting with their bill and credit cards at the ready, the kitchen tidy, everything more or less packed up and ready to close for the night, and barring none, each and every Friday the same couple would without fail come in at 8.55pm to place their order. Not only would they order a three-course meal but they would proceed to take the longest time eating it, savouring every moment, blissfully content in their own little bubble. It was only when the pub closed for good at 11.30pm that they would collect their coats and leave, never leaving a tip.

It was an interesting lesson for Rei at the time, she felt caught between two thought processes. She appreciated that the couple were well within their rights to do exactly as they did each week, yet the fact that they showed no empathy, no awareness of the fact that they alone were the reason the four restaurant staff members could not go home got under her skin. There was a level of entitlement that wreaked and oozed through their every move, and despite however graceful, amazing and wonderful she or any of the team members were they never gave them even a hint of a smile, any conversation at all or any word of acknowledgement, it was if they were working scum neither to be seen nor heard.

Whilst the other team members wanted to spit in their food, Rei tried harder and harder to break them through kindness, to crack their hard shell. A fruitless, futile and dysfunctional exercise that served no purpose than perhaps to pass the time.

Ever since that lesson many years ago Rei was always acutely aware of the people around her, what jobs they were doing and whether she was interfering with them or their schedules. She was by no means a slacker, work was important to her and she knew it was a responsibility, all the same she never took anyone's service for granted and always thanked them for their time.

So, as the doorman smiled, Rei couldn't help but smile her sunbeam smile back in return, in deep appreciation for the loving welcome she had received on this cold winter's evening, twinkling like the stars already out in the sky. She entered the main office to find the receptionist equally jubilant to see her.

Wonderful and perfect reflected Rei.

The woman had shown them round when they had gone to see the Town Hall initially to see if this really was the place for them to tie the knot. They had got on well and she remembered Rei as if it were yesterday, asking

Why the sudden move forward of date?

They giggled that Rei must have been pregnant to cause the gunshot wedding knowing full well there was no chance. This future wife was near fifty and her future husband older still. They had already had the conversation with her previously that they were done with the childbearing this lifetime at least. In another life they'd find each other earlier on and start a family together.

Rei explained the real reason in detail not holding back, in the absolute joy of it all. The receptionist completely at one with her, she didn't care that it was going home time. Rei tried to excuse herself for coming in at such a late hour,

This has been the best part of my day so far, I don't care how long it takes. I want to hear it all! the clerk beamed.

They spent what seemed like a very merry Christmas time together, the new date booked, yet when Rei got back to the car and glanced at the clock on the dashboard, she noticed it was only 5.39pm.

Time had slowed and expanded for them, no one was left short or compromised only enriched, strengthened and unified. Rei and Gabriel even more so now.

2019

There is a heartbeat betwixt rousing and slumber each day where Rei forgets the reality of her situation, she doesn't remember dreaming much if at all of late, but sleep each night is a comfort, a place of respite where the days, the pain, the memories, the actuality of it all fall momentarily to a seeming state of non-existence.

In the juncture between eyes closed shut and eyes wide open there is for just a millisecond a moment of aliveness where Rei simply is.

Then it all floods back

in

and

through.

A dam, an Iguazu Falls of her past actions, hundreds of individual cascades from all directions, encapsulating every aspect of her life grabbing every past moment and carrying it from the trickle it once was to the stream, to the river, building momentum as it flowed, culminating in millions of litres of water streaming to the waterfall's mouth (and downwards) each second. The force pummelling her body and her head, the pain in her body excruciating and real. The desire to move, to fix things, to get back up (*She'd always been a fighter*) powerful but insubstantial. Her frame defunct from its previous capabilities, now could only enjoy her gentle breath, which alone seemed hard enough.

There was no longer the option to keep her eyes closed (as she often had throughout her life) and to pretend that by not opening them she would not have to face it all head first. She'd always shrunk from and evaded confrontation, but she knew that was a different life, the one before her procedures. The one she went back to after operation number 1, the one she still held onto after operation number 2, and the one that was nothing but a distant memory after operation number 3, 4 and 5.

It had taken that many attempts to call an end to, to pull into check, her wayward habits. This was the beginning of a new cycle. Parts of Rei that had run havoc and amok with her life before had been arrested and other parts previously in the shadows had come to the fore with an absoluteness that was now unshakeable.

Where previously she had not wanted to see, she immediately wanted to pull back the curtains and let the bright light in to reveal it all, to rip off the Band-Aid no matter the consequence, for *How much worse could it actually get?*

Unable to do so physically from her bedridden position, she metaphorically and energetically did so, to everything. No more time could be wasted.

Her sensitivity was boundless after the surgeries, whilst her fleshy physical capability bordered around the zero mark, nothing was as it was before. She had nothing to fall back on, no money in a savings account, no job, no role as mother, no friends or family nearby or able to support. She was delicate, sentient, raw and fragile. If she'd had the mental capacity at that stage she may have likened herself to a newborn baby coming into the world helpless needing other's support to function for her basic needs, but she hadn't so didn't.

A few friends came to help, each meaning well, wanting to assist, to encourage, to facilitate, but Rei could feel the energy behind it all and it was too much for her body to handle. She could just about be with herself let alone anyone else with their expectations and their own agendas. Most wanted to know what had happened, the story behind it all; an exchange ~ let me feel relieved and pumped up by your story (perfect gossip fodder, if only for their own ears) and I will help you this one time. For it became apparent that the day-in-day-outness, the no-end-in-sightedness of the situation was too much for anyone with their own busy lives to attend to.

In past times Rei would have accepted the aide from anyone if it were helping her out in some way, shape or form, getting her where she needed to be, but it was not even a possibility now. Her body screamed at the energetic imposition trying to manipulate its way back into her life.

She asked a friend who had travelled down for hours from London to leave three minutes into her arrival. The niceness was smacking Rei like a wet fish slapped hard across her face on repeat and it stung. Her friend astounded, shocked, horrified and mortified all at once looked at Rei as if she were mad and gave one of those *Poor Girl* looks, so condescending, so patronising, so self-righteous that Rei nearly combusted. Thank fully (for the friend) Rei did not have the energy to argue, retaliate or respond to anyone or anything. Her breath was her saviour. Breathing she knew she still had a chance of making it back through this all, for *This Too Shall Pass*.

There were no longer any *Silly Girl* musings in her head. There had been a very real and loud acknowledgement of the downright stupid things she had done, the so-called mistakes she had made, but above all Rei could not bring any more self-flagellation to this body, it might crack her open, shatter her for good. She knew she had been presented with the greatest gift on a plate and she needed to humbly accept it for what it was, an offering to move forward on this journey without a pre-packed, pre-determined, laden backpack. She could let it *all* go. None of it in truth had served her thus far.

She was also acutely aware that so deep was the physicalness of it all that there was only one option - to fully respond to what her body needed and to what it communicated to her at all times.

She had always, for the most part, looked after and taken an active role in the preservation of her body, her temple, but she had often been quick to dismiss and neglect its messages. She had chosen and taken the hard way.

It was yet to be seen if she had learnt from it.

1997

She finds herself lain on the super king-size bed with them both recounting their days work. There was something about the pair of them that made Rei slightly uncomfortable but she couldn't quite put her finger on it. He was spectacularly handsome and she was an English beauty yet somehow the fact that they were married both wouldn't and couldn't quite register, compute in Rei's mind, she wasn't sure they matched and they were both *so young*.

As the rest of the team congregated around the room in the eaves overlooking the kitchen below, the light lessened as the sun finally began to set. It had been a long few days setting up equipment for the tracks, hundreds of people through their hands *team building* their way to success in the real world, and tomorrow they would dismantle and pack it all back up again.

Rei had found this job through one of her uni housemates and she really enjoyed it. She got to travel the country, be active and outside, be with lots of people, have fun and get paid! *What was not to like?*

Over the past couple of years, she had got to know the team well, different members for different events, depending not only on their skillset but on their schedules, each bringing their own unique flavour and background to the melting pot. Not all these were people she may have gotten to cross paths with otherwise, some she may have, or at least people like them she thought. Rei loved it. It was the first place she'd worked where everyone just pitched in to do what was needed, together, all hands-on deck. It felt like her new family. Since splitting from James, she missed his family and the jolly, wholesome support she had had from them for the past five and a half years. She understood why her mum had said the hardest thing splitting up with her father was losing his family, they had become her family. The sardonicism noted. *It ran in the family*.

Ten bodies, same uniform; navy blue shorts and tanned legs splattered with mud from the fields, a team shirt fresh with the day's odours; all ravenously hungry after their long day in the sun. It was their last night together for the summer, there was only one gig left next weekend and only a few of them were working it, so tonight they would make the most of being all together. They were all going to crash at Steve's one bedroomed studio-esque house on the floor, in make shift beds, wherever they could find some space. It was already 10pm and they had to be back up and out at 5am so for the few hours of sleep it felt possible this once.

They'd ordered a take away from the local Indian which they were told should arrive within the hour, and so in the meantime the music went on and people took their place of comfort around the room, on the sofa, the armchairs, the floor and the bed, every gap filled. The older men, peeling off to drink a crateful more beer than the two tinies they'd already downed, each lit a spliff down the other end of the room and seemed happy enough. The younger crowd of four down the other end chatting about life and enjoying getting to know more about one another, or at least that's what Rei thought was happening.

Whilst deep in conversation with Rob, a minute or so later Rei felt a hand up her tee upon her left breast, she looked around to see it belonged to Tori, the English Rose, Rob's wife, her freckles freckling in the diminishing evening haze, an uncanny smile on her face.

WTF!

Rei had thought perhaps Nick had gotten on the bed without her noticing and was trying his luck, but no, it was Tori.

WTF!! WTF!!!

Have you ever been with a girl? Tori asked.

What about Rob? stammered Rei unable to formulate coherent words in a sentence (distant memories of *The Palais* flooding back in) more concerned about the fact Tori was doing something against, contra to Rob and to their relationship.... *And* in full view of him! Rei wasn't really asking if Rob was ok with this, merely a concern for *why Tori was*? Although she hadn't put them together as a couple, she certainly didn't want them apart, they had become friends and she liked them both. In their own ways, they made her laugh.

Don't worry, he asked me to she half smirked.

In disbelief Rei turned back to Rob, the hand remained, firmly, caressing her breast.

I fancy you, we both do he retorted, not remotely disturbed or perplexed by the occurrences.

We have an open relationship. Its ok, just go with the flow. And with that he leant over and kissed her, Rei, passionately.

Rei tried to pull away but she was pinned down beneath the two of them now, flanked on both sides and from above. She didn't try very hard, she didn't want to make a scene, to alert the other guys at the other end of the room.

What would they think…that she was trying to break up the happy couple's marriage? To create an issue when there was none?

She was mortified, and more than anything she couldn't work out what exactly was happening. She could make no sense of it, these were two stunningly gorgeous, well off, married youngsters and they were playing with her, in *so* many different ways. The overwhelm drowning her, distorting her reality. The smell and smoke of the six bulging spliffs now all around them adding to the haze. The beer and its merriment added extra bludgeoning, devastation.

As she tried to comprehend the situation, to think of a plan A, B & C out of here, Rob unbuttoned her shorts and began to kiss her belly moving downwards at an alarming rate.

Plan Z it was.

Her car was miles away, parked up where they were working in a field in the middle of nowhere, they had all bundled into two cars instead of bringing ten. No-one was fit to drive anymore and this was pre mobile phone and internet times. She was where she was. More than anything she didn't want to make a scene.

God, why was this such a prevalent theme in her life? she wondered.

She spied Nick out of the corner of her eye imploring him to come over hoping his presence may break up the menage a trois. He could see the pleading prayer in Rei's eyes and so joined them on the bed, but before he could do anything, Tori was upon him. At which stage Rei heard the other men in the room cheering *Wey, hey!*

Oh

My

God

Rei had never been so mortified. She had shrunk before in her life, but tonight in this moment she had contracted like an erect penis fresh out of freezing water. Her body's blood vessels perhaps constricting themselves in an attempt to preserve any semblance of dignity Rei had. There was no sexual arousal right now, no greater blood flow, no expansion of tissues, in fact she no longer even found Rob attractive.

With only one body atop of her now she managed to sit up and catch her breath, as too did Nick, stunned mullets together, they must have looked a right pair. Rob and Tori not remotely perturbed by the rejection of their advances began to undress each other and proceeded to make out in front of all, whomever wanted to watch. Rei slunk into Nick's arms craving some kind of protection from it all. He gave what he could although Rei knew she was protecting him too, equally so.

Saved by the bell had never been such a powerful or relevant expression. They had been rescued by some chicken korma, onion bhajis and peshwari naans. Indian food had never tasted so good. Rei ate as if she had never eaten nor would she ever eat again, her appetite handsome (unlike her co-workers who were becoming less and less attractive by the minute). Shovelling food made for ten at an accelerated rate down her gullet gave her momentary relief from everything she was feeling. Thankfully the guys were too stoned now and had lost their appetite so Nick and Rei had the feast to themselves. Rob and Tori were nowhere to be seen. Upon realising this Rei began to calm down, to slow down, to actually chew her food, at least once, before swallowing it.

It was really late now and they had work to do tomorrow. Rei felt safest sleeping in her work clothes on the floor beside the bed where there was no room for extra guests.

Nick at her feet, them both curled up foetus like, leaving the bed for the married couple.

Although she had her eyes closed Rei wasn't sure she slept that night, it certainly didn't feel like it. It appeared she had the worse hangover of them all by the morning. She guardedly looked for Rob & Tori afraid of what the daylight may bring but they were not there, they had not been for the rest of night. A mixture of relief and of looming trepidation permeated her body. She knew not what lay ahead.

Thankfully, as usual the group of co-workers were already in full swing, laughing out loud, enjoying each other's company, and Rei was able to partially park her apprehension. They all (ten minus two of them) were gathered in Steve's kitchen for an early breakfast just after 4am. He was cooking them all bacon butties ahead of their action-packed day. As they all sat down hovering around to eat the feast together, the news flashed on the TV interrupting the white noise that had been carrying on in the background, no one interested, listening or paying attention before.

Princess Diana was dead.

The room fell silent and back came the malignant taste of dread. Metallic in her mouth, heavy in her heart, and racing in her body.

Rei wondered if her actions last night may have caused such an impact. She had never been a royal fan as such but the death of Lady Di somehow felt significant and for a moment the whole world seemed to stop.

Any chance of ever forgetting this night was now gone.

A moment in time that you always remembered where you were when something pivotal happened

...the day Princess Diana died.

2019

Rei speaks with her dad every so often. There is nothing wrong with the calls per se, but the tension of what is not said is significant. It had taken its toll over the years until Rei could take no more.

Having given birth to her first born she was determined to make sure that there was nothing in the way of her living completely clear of any emotional trauma or hurt, effectively of loving him with all of her.

She wrote her father a long letter, pouring her heart out, describing in full everything she had been through, all she had felt and had never shared with him. She hadn't thought about what the consequence of that would be, she just knew she had to do it. Arguably it may have changed everything, in actuality nothing.

She told him about the boarding school Christmas Play an event that had haunted her to that day. It was (and would be) the second only time he had visited after the infamous weekend school pick up in tight, white shorts and a very loud, red Ferrari. *How could that ever be forgotten?* Forever written in the sands of time.

Rei had been so excited so proud that someone from her family would be there, at school, at the play. She was usually one of a handful of students in her 200+ year group whose parents did not turn up to events, the other three kids were the Chinese students who parents Rei never recalls seeing at school.

She was feeling a little apprehensive too, he had said that he would be bringing his girlfriend (now *fiancé*) with him and that said fiancé's best friend *knew* the deputy headmaster. Rei had learnt enough by this stage in life, as naive as she was, that *knew* was code for something, she guessed perhaps they had been girlfriend and boyfriend. How naive she was.

Rei had quite a large part in the play and had written a song for it, her name was even written on the program; her dad would get to see it, and would be proud,

of her,

for the first time,

Ever.

Truth was she hadn't written it herself; she'd part cribbed it, adapted it, from her friend who'd written it a couple of years ago at primary school. Memories ripping through her, she stopped herself short of pining for her old school and old friends knowing she just had to get on with it. She was embarrassed she'd stooped so low, pretending it was her work, but thought that perhaps it would be worth it, to be seen, to be recognised, it may even stop the bullying.

She vowed never to do such a thing again, already she knew it wasn't worth it. Rei was not a liar, and the heaviness of this untruth so far was a lesson well learnt.

Her father had said he would get there early before the play began as they would have to shoot off immediately afterwards to a party. Rei had read between the lines (her lines) that he was saying that he would definitely get there early to make sure they could spend some precious time together. Rei (thought she) understood and made sure she was ready and waiting in her long, pale blue dress, hair tied back neat and tidy, standing to attention in the lobby, the designated meeting area.

The nerves were already kicking in, the parents were arriving, the school chapel already full to the rafters. The whole school was present, the choir dressed up in their Sunday best robes, organ at the ready, the clouds on the (Cistern Chapel-esque) ceiling seemed a little plumper and fluffier than usual, there was a buzz about the place. The *swish swishes* of the nun's habits out in full attendance were there but had taken a back seat role today, fading to a distant background noise amidst the hum of happy family re-unions and the excitement of the students expressing in their multi-lingual mother tongues. It was lovely to see the corridors alive like this. Rei loved the fact that she'd met so many people from all around the world, from places she'd never heard of before. She'd already picked up all the swear words in most of their native languages; that seemed like the cool and only thing others were willing to share, so she took it. She'd even been taught how to say *Go f*** your mother* in

Chinese. She couldn't imagine a time where she'd ever need, or want, to say that in any language, but it rolled off her tongue now should she ever need to impress. Sometimes she found herself saying it under her breath as she sprinted (silently and stealthily) up the back stairs when she should have been taking the main ones at the front of house, walking in an orderly manner as she was meant to like all the really good girls did.

She checked the clock on the wall, yes it was 6.27pm now, 30 seconds later than the last time she'd looked. They were meant to meet at 6.20pm but they were nowhere to be seen.

Perhaps she had got the time wrong, perhaps the wrong place?

There was no other plausible explanation. Her dad was always on time for everything.

What had she done? Why couldn't she remember? Silly girl.
S i l l y girl.

By 6.38pm Rei was a mess inside, the nerves in her throat gyrating violently and obtrusively, her stomach churning like a spin wash on a fast cycle, she was desperate to pee but didn't want to miss her dad.

By 6.39pm she had to go. She made a conscious choice to run, she meant walking fast of course, she couldn't get in trouble, especially not today, to the toilets at the back end of her house, the ones under the stairs.

Diu lei lo mo. The Chinese words now falling quietly and effortlessly from her lips without any hesitation.

She reasoned that although a little further away she would make up the time by not having to wait in queue for the toilets elsewhere.

As she pushed through the door eager to get in and out as fast as she could back to the meeting place for her dad, she came to a grinding halt. On the floor was Raquel and three other girls. They had a Ouija board and a Voodoo doll with them and were intently playing. Rei didn't know much about this stuff but she knew what it was, she'd overheard others talking about it. It felt dark and creepy to her and the thought of sticking pins in a doll and commanding evil actions upon others was not something that seemed like an enjoyable hobby to her. She contemplated running back out of the loos, but with the pee nearly half way down her legs and not wanting to spoil her dress, she ran into the third stall on the left, locked the door shut and relieved herself.

Although her bladder was now empty her heart was beating faster than usual, her mind filling up with worry. As she flushed and went to open the door, she realised the girls had barricaded her in, she could not get out. Raquel proceeded to ask the Ouija board at the top of her Irish voice, to not only put a *curse* on Rei but also demanded the spirits to *kill* her.

Being at Catholic school Rei's every morning was filled with religious doctrine, she was hugely aware of hell and of what would happen to sinners. Every day she felt not good enough and wasn't sure she ever would be. She didn't belong here with the others, she felt like an outcast on every level. She tried to be good, but there were always others that were *better* than her. She already felt cursed, but *was that really worthy of death itself?* she questioned herself.

Raquel's commands and maledictions now echoed around the toilets as the girls chanted in unison, shaking the stall's walls as they did.

Kill Rei!

Kill Rei!

Kill Rei!

It was nothing short of a horrific Ku-Klux-Clan scene. Rei was petrified she was about to lose her life to a Voodoo God listening from on high, that some thunderbolt would come and strike her through the toilet walls, that she would never be seen alive again.

Oh my god! her dad would be waiting outside for her; *he hated people being late.*

Not sure what she was more scared of, the girls on the other side of the stall door or her father waiting impatiently for his daughter that didn't turn up at the right place at the right time, she cursed herself now too.

Silly, Stupid, little girl!

Rei used her body weight to try and push open the door but three against one was no fair match.

She pleaded *Please let me go my dad is waiting for me.*

To which the girls laughed and cackled even louder.

Poor Rei won't see her dad. There, there!

The bangs on the toilet stall doors were getting louder and louder, the chants faster and more melodic. Rei was sobbing, tears streaming down her face, her whole-body trembling in fear, with cold-blooded fright.

Rei didn't have a watch but she knew time had passed. It had already been close to the start of the performance at 7pm when Rei left for the toilets at 6.39pm goodness knew what the time was now? She did know that as a major role in the play she was meant to be in situ by 6.50pm at the latest where register would be taken and all final checks performed. She felt sick to the core. Now the whole school would be waiting for her, it would all be messed up *all because of her*, and everyone would know it.

Rei didn't exactly remember or know what happened next. Conceivably someone opened the toilet door, stopping the girls in their tracks; quite possibly they themselves realised they would invariably be in trouble if they took this any further and took a step back; but either way half stunned, soggy with emotion Rei made a run for it, this time running as fast as she could down the maths corridor, into the lobby and into the arms of her father.

He was busy in conversation with his *fiancé* and the Deputy Head, doing that grown up laugh thing that made Rei cringe every time, champagne in their hands looking very *la-di-da* with themselves. He barely flinched despite Rei's thundering entrance which was completely out of character, an absolute give away that something was up.

Trying to control herself, to hide her face which she knew would be red, blotchy and swollen, as it always was when she cried, her eyes bright green instead of the usual non teary blue, she shuffled from one foot to the other in an awkward, uncomfortable way, hoping no-one could see her if she stayed silent, eyes to the floor.

As the conversation broke at a natural point Rei's dad looked down to her (finally) and asked if she was ok?

Yes, I'm fine strained Rei, in-convincible to even her lying self.

Are you sure? he asked for reassurance.

Yes, I'm just nervous lied Rei, her body convulsing within, tears welling up in her eyes, her voice shaky, her hands trembling, knives stabbing in her back.

You'll be fine he replies, patting her on her back as he always had, and returned to his grown-up conversation.

La di da.

Rei bowed out of this *menage-a-puke* even more distraught than before. She thought that he would have offered safety, support, encouragement, a listening ear, a shoulder to cry on. Well, she didn't really *think* any of these things, she wouldn't have been able to categorise them as such, but she did *know* that she now definitely felt an emptiness within, a lacking, an isolation and a despair that she hadn't known existed until now. This was an all-time low. Another part of her died in that moment, no goodbye in sight. Invisible and un loved, she made her way in the shadows along the side of the chapel to her teacher, and the waiting crowds.

~

Rei wasn't looking for any sympathy when she wrote to her father about this, or the other incidents in her life she penned, but she wanted to voice it. To say the things that she'd bottled up inside. It wasn't about him and what he had or hadn't done, but about what not expressing, not telling the truth, had done to her. It had disfigured her, it had led her to make subsequent choices in a certain way, and they had harmed her.

She realised if she didn't start changing things up it would be like a cancer that slowly spread through her body. She didn't want that, it didn't belong, it was ugly and it was getting in the way of the purity and love she had and could only feel for her son and also now daughter. So, she didn't hold back.

He called a few weeks later to say he had received Rei's letter and was shocked at what she'd written, he hadn't realised she felt like that and he was sorry she did. The conversation was pleasant enough, nothing ground breaking or deep and meaningful, the job had already been done when Rei had picked up her pen, she felt a little lighter and a little less strained than before.

~

Today she was ringing to let him know. To share the news. She had evaded his calls and fobbed him off with WhatsApp messages for too long now, it was unsustainable. There was nothing he had done at all, she had just been shirking her own embarrassment for too long.

Are you ok? he asked. This time unlike the one some thirty years prior, she did not lie, she told the truth.

I'm sorry you haven't heard from me in a while. I was pregnant and I lost the baby at 12 weeks. I had to have an operation to remove it whilst I was abroad, then when I flew back to the UK I had to be taken into A&E as was haemorrhaging whilst staying in a hotel with work.

Still unable to tell the WHOLE truth, she omitted the parts about how dank the hotel was and that she was only there because it was no longer safe to return home, the police had told her to take the kids and get themselves to a safe house, that she was running out of money to pay for it so was wearing herself thin working to make ends meet, and yes Jack had stolen all the money from the bank accounts again (despite her dad telling her to get one in her own name after the last time this had happened and to not sign her home over 50:50 to him as he knew she was doing).

Then when I got home to the kids it happened again and I had to go in for surgery for the third time.

She too chose to omit the part where the doctors were so concerned themselves that they flew a surgeon down to perform a triple surgery on Rei, and that Rei for the first time ever thought she might die and had re-written her will on the hospital in-patient day bed on her way in.

The doctors say I might not be able to move for at least six weeks, maybe longer.

This bit was true, Rei didn't believe it herself, not for one minute, she was a fighter, always had been. Six weeks seemed like a ridiculously long length of time under anyone's watch. She'd be back on her feet in no time!

Oh, you'll be fine, they always say that kind of thing. You'll be back up on your feet in no time he said.

Rei smiled at how similar they actually were sometimes having really spent no time together in life.

But I'm sorry to hear that Rei, I know that's hard.

Rei knew he did; she could feel his sincerity.

What it was to lose a child.

1992

Perhaps if she'd know any more about any other religion other than the Catholicism that had been all around her since she was young and that was now being rammed down her throat, water tortured directly on her temples at school, she may have wondered if she had been a Buddhist in a previous life. She contemplated and wondered why she didn't have the same pre-disposition as everyone else to absolutely wreck her body? For some reason unbeknownst to her the nuns hadn't taught them that *Your Body is a Temple* despite it being in the bible. It didn't make sense even at the time not knowing it was a colloquial phrase that simply everyone knew. Whilst everyone around her wanted to drink and smoke, take drugs and sleep around, Rei on the whole felt no attraction to any of these vices. She'd tried smoking an incense stick on the school playing field to see if that was something she could join in on, but it proved way too much effort and it was cold and dark outside, she would rather be inside in the comparative Social Room warmth.

It was break-time and Georgia (from the year above) called her into her cubicle next door. She was beyond excited. They sat on the bed together as she proceeded to tell Rei about what had happened at lunchtime. She had gotten together with one of the kitchen staff and he had taken her round the back field and *gone down on her.* Rei wasn't sure exactly what that meant and so asked wondering if she'd lost something and he was trying to help her find it? At the same time, she was trying to picture how and why she would be with a member of the kitchen staff, *surely this was dangerous?* They were grown men, and they were pretty ugly and quite frankly scary to Rei. A mixture of the overweight, toothless, burnt-out prison inmates you may see in a horror film. Rei had noted from day one that it was a particularly unattractive group of people, but thought nothing much more of it. Later on, she would think it was a clever tactic of the nuns, and it may well have been. But not on this day.

You know, when he licks and sucks your vagina and it goes all squelchy and wet! You know?! Oh My God, it was a-ma-zing!
I'm going back for more tomorrow it was sooooo good. He just kept going and going and I was all giggly and screaming and then I sucked his willy….and…and….

Rei nearly barfed. She'd never heard anything so disgusting in all of her life. And she was fourteen years old now, that's a lot of years. She sprang up off of Georgia's bed fearing she may already have caught a disgusting lurgy from such filthy talk.

Oh My God what if the nuns had heard? What if they thought she was a part of it?

Was what she was hearing even real? Even a thing?

Rei very sub consciously decided that she would stay as far away from Georgia as possible (even though they slept and breathed only a partition wall away from each other). Taking the long way round, down the front stairs, to and from her cubicle to everywhere else on campus was now the only option. The backstairs past Georgia's room seemed too perilous, she was a clean girl and would not be dirtied by such tempestuous talk.

She would keep her head down and pretend she had not heard a thing.

Nothing.

2013

It was another warm September morning; the kids had just gone back to school returning after a long summer break. The renovations on the house could be ramped up now the working flow and traffic systems were back to normal; their team of workmen were in smashing up the foundations to the original building as the wooden beams were rotten to the core and needed replacing. The building propped up with makeshift builder's joists, the floor now fallen away beneath them, soil to be seen beneath the couple of plank boards propped up as walkways between the doorframes. To walk through you had to wear a hard hat, a mask and protective goggles. It was a mess, a consummate building site.

They had known they were taking on a big renovation project but neither of them had realised it would be quite this large. A home to a princess when it was built in the early 1700's, later turned to a doctor's surgery and then law offices it had not been lived in for hundreds of years, everything needed dismantling and rebuilding but only in strict accordance with the local government and their specialist Listed Building departments. It had been a challenge but they knew they were up for it and with their skill set together it could be a breeze.

As Rei walked from one building door to the other, the short gangway between their place of work and where they were living, she would at first catch her breath taking off the mask being able to breathe free from plumages of dust and then gently sigh at how difficult it was actually living like this.

They had what would have originally been the horse's stables as their current place of residence. Two adjoining partitioned rooms upstairs and two separate stud-walled rooms downstairs, one of which they'd made into their kitchen-diner, the other a make shift bathroom come tool supply lock up. Upstairs the two rooms consisted of one king-size bed in the walk-through room and into a room with five single mattresses squished together in a line, wall to wall, directly on the floor, in the other. All office equipment, furniture, storage units, fluorescent strip lighting, manky carpets, swirly wall paper, etc had been removed. What was left was decaying chip board as flooring, and half eaten walls.

At first it had seemed novel, six weeks of *glamping* in a building site until phase one was complete and then they would be able to relocate to phase two, but with the unearthing of the dismembered foundations another few months in situ seemed ever more likely.

Rei placed the mask down on the kitchen table which was currently masking itself as a *working design and plans station* to look for her next job for the day. She was expecting a call from the carpenter so was surprised to see her dad's name come up on the screen. It was a sunny day and she saw the rays stream through the door as Jack walked in, signalling to him to hold on and keep quiet whist she answered the phone. It didn't matter which of the four rooms you were in, it was if there were only one and you were all in it together. Jack disappeared from sight into the room next door either looking for the next tool to be used or for a pee, she wasn't sure which, but knowing she would hear and be able to work out which within the next couple of seconds.

She answered the phone excited to be receiving a call from her dad. It was a rare occurrence, but a welcome one.

Rei didn't recall the exact words spoken but she felt every fibre of her body recoil and felt every chord in her body wail like the loudest whale breaching, the most deafening cougars screeching, and the most meretricious racoons mating.

She felt like she was giving birth again from her heart out. She wasn't sure she could hold it in at all this time. It (her heart) was trying to jump out of her, to fall flat on the deadbeat floor just as it felt, dead, heavy, lifeless.

As too was her brother,

Now,

Dead.

Hung by his own hand.

Dead by rope.

1992

He gives her a watch, an aqua marine green, water sport kind of a watch. It's clearly expensive as it comes in its own case which lifts and stands up all by itself, with a cleaning cloth inside too.

He is clearly very proud of the watch and is hoping Rei will be. Rei feels bad. She hasn't got him anything. She feels *really* bad now.

Still clearly mortified by his previous alcohol induced actions prior, the three weeks apart had bought him closer to the truth that he definitely wants to be with Rei. That wasn't what she was expecting. She thought he said he fancied Pamela. She thought that's where he was at with it all, where *it* was going.

She smiles and takes the watch case from him saying it looks lovely, as he gently removes it from the loops holding it in place and wraps it around her tender and delicate wrist in a befitting manner. She silently gives him credit. It looks good.

I knew it would suit you he says.

Yeah, you got it bang on she says and gives him a thank full hug in return.

Rei couldn't bring herself to tell him everything about her summer apart from him in The Alps. She recounted swimming in Lake Geneva, about playing Masterpiece with her sister and mum, about walking down to the boulangerie every day for their daily croissants and hanging out in the Salle-de-Jeux.

She omitted the part about falling for Francois the local stud whom she saw every day and hung out with nearly every early evening or about the equally dashing but more mature Luc who drove her home one night and kissed her in his car. She didn't want to hurt his feelings; to ruin the situation at hand, it was kind of awkward enough as it was. And so, she remained mute to these truths, locking them in a vault.

The same lesson back round to re-learn, she could never lie like this again, the burden was too much.

1990

When Rei was about thirteen or fourteen her mum worked as a bilingual secretary for a law firm in Brussels for a few years. One holiday Rei got to *fly* home like all the other students and she felt mighty grown up doing so (even though she had to be escorted on and off the plane as an unaccompanied minor by the airport staff. She kept her head low for this part).

Her mum's studio apartment was something else with a mezzanine floor overlooking a brand-new city with bright lights and an historic past. Rei was beginning to embrace her teenage years at this point and appreciated the slightly more grown-up things life had to offer. As they walked along the streets, Rei looked in the artsy side stalls for a postcard she could buy to put up on her cubicle wall on her return, tired of seeing the same repeat Athena posters on everyone else's; Slash & Axel from Guns & Roses (same pose different filter); a black and white photo of James Dean leaning against a wall, leg half bent, striking up a match; a fluffy kitten; a dressed up dog. Rei's wall was usually a miss match of photos, ripped out Vogue magazine pages, some artsy hand written quotes and now a new-to-be postcard from *Bruxelles*.

They walked a few steps further to the crepe stand, to buy and then devour *une gaufre* (or most probably two). It looked much like an expensive patisserie version of a Birds Eye potato waffle, *they're waffly versatile!* yet tasted nothing like it, the warm, sweet batter cake base topped with molten sugar, absolutely delicious. A sense of Christmas in the air (no matter what the season) as it touched their lips. The fact that they were called *Gaufre de Liege* in Brussels was not un noted. It seemed Rei could run from school, but school could not run from Rei. The young girl's school she was in attendance at had been originally founded in Belgium offering an otherwise forbidden Catholic education back home, but it (the school) and its students had had to flee back to English shores during the French Revolutionary Wars. It seemed Rei was doing the journey in reverse. Fleeing to Brussels to escape the Catholic education and then flying back when her time away was up. She had always been disturbed by the fact that as students they were called *fishes*. A code name nuns used at the time to conceal the fact they were smuggling students across the Chanel. It was bad enough to be known as such but to publicly announce it too seemed both silly and ludicrous to Rei. Teenage talk of sex and bodily parts spoke of girl's vaginas as being smelly, like fish. *Fishy fanny this, fishy fanny that*. Rei always shuddered on the inside and shook on the outside when hearing this. She had no experience of this herself but the expression was rife everywhere. So degrading, so humiliating, anything other than honouring or respectful.

Gosh how embarrassing. To be a girl even.

A,

Silly little teenage Girl.

1985

Rei remembers walking into the forest clearing heading back towards the picnic blanket, back to her mum and dad. It was a summers day and the sun was shining, huge swathes of light streaming in through the windows of the trees. She had just found her sister for the umpteenth time at hide and seek and was getting hot, desperate for a drink of water.

It was not a usual day. No conventional run-of-the-mill Saturday.

Her mum and dad were never together; in fact they positively hated each other. Since he had left, life had been visibly tough for her mum and she had found it hard surviving on her own with two small girls, although perhaps Rei only recognised this the more she matured. Thankfully Rei could be relied upon and by the time she was eight she was already preparing and cooking the meals, walking her sister to and from school, and doing whatever shopping was needed. She could turn her hand to pretty much anything; the washing, the sewing, the baking. Living on a shoestring budget meant they had to be resourceful and they were. Her mum tired from her working days and the constant stress of money (or lack of), suffered from intense migraines and would shut herself in her blackened bedroom for days, the girls fending for themselves.

One evening, frustrated, her mum *needed* a fringe cut in her hair, and she needed it *now*. It was late, there were no hairdressers open and no money to pay for one, so to control the approaching rage Rei stepped in kitchen scissors at the ready and cut her some bangs. She did a grand job, and thought she could always be a hairdresser if nothing else ever transpired. A new string added to her developing bow. As a little girl Rei had always dreamed of being an air hostess, of seeing the world, its people and perhaps of flying somewhere far, far away. She had experienced enough poverty to appreciate it was not a nice place to be living from and she knew deep down she loved the world the world over.

Her mum kept a notebook that she would write in religiously every day, every pound spent, every penny accounted for. There was no room for error, no margin to overspend. The food shopping duly rationalised and scrutinised each week, if there was a spare 89 pence then it would undoubtedly go towards the funding of an own brand Coffee & Walnut cake. The girls would get a small slice each and watch suspiciously as the cake length dwindled moment by back turned moment, too scared to say anything but devilishly hungry for more. Perhaps this was where Rei's slight possessiveness of food began, she often pondered. She wondered in later years why she was one of those people who if they opened a packet of biscuits had to eat the whole packet and not just settle at one? The entirety eaten in a flash, no crumb spared. Every last morsel hoovered up. She wasn't quite as bad as the Oliver film she'd been sure, but it seemed her body was on a heightened protective lookout anytime sweet things were about. It was a *now or never* approach, *all or nothing*.

Her piano teacher years down the line did not help matters by placing a large red, open box of Maltesers a top his piano for the duration of his lessons. The forty-five minutes were arduous enough as they were without the constant allure and enticement of a sweet treat tempting you to be naughty and skip and dance your little musical playing fingers into its open sleeve.

Rei had day dreamt ways to turn his head so she could steal a (just one) chocolate covered honeycomb ball. She pined at the thought of it. Her body longing for one (more) she could taste it already. Yet her beady eyed maestro clearly looked like he'd eaten all the previous contents of last week's Maltesers box and the weeks before that, and the week's before that. She didn't stand a chance, and so she would sit, back straight, an air of chill at her waist and perform, mediocrely at that. As the lesson came to an end, she was allowed to take 1 Malteser, 1 solitary Malteser.

This was torture and Rei immediately realised was worse than having any. It left you wanting more, desiring more, needing more, hungry for more. Sometimes she thought she would sit through another forty-five minutes with him just for one more. But she didn't. The resentment brewing, knowing that at some time in the future whenever she was able to buy her own packet of Maltesers, she would be able to sit there and eat the lot, by herself, should she wish to.

That one day came, and indeed she did, on repeat like the maestro of her childhood lessons, but this time it was not a box but a family pack.

Get in my belly!

~

Rei could see the clearing ahead, the spot where her parents had been left, and half still in quiet mode from hide and seek, she ran surreptitiously to them. She couldn't see them anymore so slowed her gallop to a canter, to a trot before drawing an immediate halt. She could make out beneath the speckled light her father's hand upon her mother's naked breast. They were smiling and both clearly enjoying themselves. Rei lost her breath and her legs buckled beneath her giving way to her now heavy frame. She didn't understand. This made no sense.

No. Sense.

What.

So.

Ever.

~

The week before Rei, as usual, stood holding the phone receiver at one ear, the other finger tight in the remaining ear, trying to block out the sound coming from one end of the line, stopping it from landing at the other.

*Tell your mother she's a f***ing bitch.* Transmission Number 1

What's the bastard saying? Transmission Number 2

Moving the mouthpiece close to and as tight into her chest as possible in-between transmissions so as to muffle and mute any sounds almost puncturing her lungs in the process, Rei looked at her mum,

Dad's asking what time he can come pick us up on Saturday?

Well, is he actually going to turn up on time this week does his majesty think, or take the piss as usual? Selfish prick! Transmission Number 2

Mum said 12pm is fine Rei replied.

Tell her she's… Rei didn't listen for the rest she'd heard it all a million times before. It never got any easier to hear.

Dad said he'll be here at 12pm she consoled her Mum.

Ok, bye Dad, see you on Saturday she placed down the receiver able to breathe again now the weekly phone call was over, her connective tissue within already preparing for the subsequent blasphemous attacks between the two of them the following week.

~

This was but a couple of days ago. It made no sense. The hatred, the vitriol, the spite, the anger, the devastation, the hurt, the frustration, the envy, the jealousy, the suspiciousness, the loneliness, the insecurity, the burden, all deeply felt in the quick-fire rounds between one end of their daughter and the other.

Rei was learning, quickly, to morph into the background, to retrace her steps back to the shadows, away from the light. Like a chameleon the pure crystals within her were changing rapidly as her nervous system took a hit. Hormones played no part this time but perhaps as she grew older, she too may adapt these *(ab)normal* behaviours being exposed to her at such an early age. Abuse. Comfort. Abuse. Arrangement Abuse. Sexual favour.

Hours later they said goodbye to their dad as usual and by the following week it was as if nothing had happened, it had all been a dream.

Rei wondered sometimes if she was psycho.

It was either her or the whole world.

Odds were it was her.

2024

Their wedding day was fast approaching. From the time of booking it, to the actual service was less than four weeks away. Both were working full time and some. Rei was flying and presenting on stage for a world-famous lifestyle brand, plus teaching and giving consultations - she hadn't had a busier month for some time, yet time expanded.

Nothing had been pre-planned or thought through, they'd just responded to what was given and run with it. They weren't living together at this point so extra hours were spent travelling between one home and the other in between work events.

They decided that the guest list be absolutely only those that both parties said 100% yes to. Only then could they make the preliminary list. They'd been looked after this far and so it seemed pointless to try and work it out themselves from this point forward.

It helped that Rei was a Celebrant, she had done this many times before but when consulting the Town Hall to check in she realised it was actually quite different than the free reign she was afforded as a Celebrant elsewhere, she had always been able to tailor make the ceremonies to each couple. The Registrar and their ceremony here however were to follow a specific script and format.

The first thing they did when they got home was choose their wedding songs. Gabriel had a few ideas and Rei had some too. They got the speaker out and Rei played the three she felt suitable in the order she felt they should be played. They already had *their* song, it had been *theirs* from about day three, and Gabriel regularly listened to it on his way in and out of work. It was a dance music number that felt like the stars twinkling in the night sky pulling you home, deeper and deeper into space and beyond, it would be the perfect way to end the ceremony - an explosion into and of the universe.

Song Number one was a beautiful piano instrumental that unfolded, solid from the start, inviting you in to a deep surrender and settlement before slowly taking you on a journey growing in an understated but clear and simple way. Gabriel had never heard it before but instantly fell in love with it. He may have found his new favourite song. It fitted perfectly and matched symbolically too. Easy peasy, two songs done in just as few minutes.

The third was up for debate but when listening to the contenders it became apparent immediately which it was to be, there was no choice.

It was all already written for them.

It was now just gone 6pm. Within the past 30 odd minutes they'd legged it down The Town Hall, booked their wedding and confirmed their playlist. *What was next?* At this rate they'd be ready to marry before work began tomorrow.

Over the course of the next few days whilst Rei was abroad with work and Gabriel was immersed in the city, they worked out the guest list between themselves. There were thirty people on it including themselves. It seemed like not too shabby a number considering the fact that they thought it was just going to be the two of them plus a couple of witnesses.

~

Rei's daughter had known from the start this was *the one.*

Mama I've got tingles she said when Rei told her about him. She had distanced herself from anyone of the male species that her mum had gotten to know over the past few years, having seen more than her fair share of trauma. She never understood why her mum was so great at everything. Everything except men; she seemed both extremely and exceptionally inept in this department.

Bella on this occasion was behind her mum all the way. Both Gabriel and Rei knew that Bella was to be invited to be one of their witnesses, the other their joint friend, Olivia. It was on the car journey down to Olivia's daughter's birthday party earlier this year that Gabriel & Rei had actually felt the beginning of something between them so it seemed not only apt but truly befitting that they should be there too. Olivia's presence had been instrumental to both of them as individuals and under the circumstances they couldn't think of anyone more perfect for the role. They knew she was a busy woman and so late in the day it may not be possible for her to attend, but they would ask all the same.

When Rei asked Bella to be their witness, Bella replied but *what about the boys?*

I wasn't sure they'd want to come replied Rei.

What do you mean? she asked *Of course they'd want to come!!*

Rei wasn't convinced but she also knew how wise Bella was knowing them all better than perhaps anyone else. Rei presumed this was another sneaky attempt of her own subconscious to keep it all low-key, to not be in the spotlight and perhaps to not be in any obvious or true celebration of their marriage. Deep down she wasn't sure her path or journey here was really worthy of celebration and still believed she needed to stay undercover. She recognised both her and Gabriel were being slowly urged into the limelight. Their guest list expanding by its illumination.

2013

She takes his royal (sunshine) blue Pull & Bear hoodie that lays trailing between his wardrobe door and the carpeted floor and holds it close, smelling it as if it were him. It feels like to take it would be to steal a moment in time. She didn't want this bit captured but the everything that was that came before it. She wondered if it was evidence, evidence of a young man, lost. She looked around the room and could see nothing out of place, nothing untoward, nothing screaming out signs of *Help me, I'm dying here, in this place!*

She looked to the Velux windows for sign of life outside and found none, a grey sky with transparent clouds, motionless. Looking upwards she saw the wooden beams holding up the room, masterfully crafted and erected hundreds of years before. *Did they know how strong they were, how they would be used in years to come?* she wondered.

A time and a place for everything.

She looked closer, squinting her eyes, for a strain in the wood. She guessed there must have been one. To carry, the weight of the world, weighty in its encumbrance. To hold it whilst it passed between turmoil, suffering and agitation to the next; the burden seemingly lifted, the baton passed from the strain of one person to everyone else left in the slipstream behind, heavier, more significantly tainted now, with greater aplomb than perhaps considered. Rei had heard that suicide was *the* most selfish act before, and she'd understood it in her mind. She didn't for one minute ever think it would be something she would have to experience in her body. Since the phone call with her father, she still could not compute that this was real, it made no sense. Perhaps if it had been her sister, yes, but not Olli, he always seemed so grounded, so down to earth, the one who would always be having a laugh, keeping things real and keeping it light. No matter how much she wanted to pretend it wasn't true her body had clearly told her otherwise and it was only now she realised what it was.

About 7pm the night before the call she'd been folding the laundry upstairs, everyone gathered around on their bed under the eaves watching the Arsenal match. Suddenly Rei asked the kids to move across quick, she felt like the blood was draining from her, a wooziness she'd never felt before. She explained it exactly as such to the kids who were looking on worriedly at her, anxious at her demise asking what was wrong.

Again, she replied *I don't know, I just feel like the blood is draining from me.*

She did know…

…just as she had known when James had kissed Pamela.

There was nothing to be seen, no proof as such, but the body, her body had communicated it to her, very clearly. There was a connection out there in the ether that was very real.

Her whole life she had felt things, sensed things, but the world around her seemed determined to undermine her, to tell her otherwise, to disprove her and she had let them, but not now, this was too big, too real, a moment that would never be forgotten no matter how hard her mind may try to, it was a physical memory imprinted in her body forevermore.

~

They sat in the lounge, a makeshift family on a makeshift day, there had been no party the night before but the hangover, the aftermath was being felt right now. The policemen looked on, hands cupped in laps, sharing that it was a very common occurrence, especially for young men, suicide being the highest rate and means of death these days. Clearly, they'd delivered this message before, sharing the facts as means of compensation, of relief, of some kind of comfort, of support, of alleviation of the terror and pain; an attempt to jump in and strangle the knot weed (of ensuing guilt) already taking shape. Every moment she'd ever shared with Olli was suddenly relived on I-Max playback.

Had that moment contributed?
Had the next?
Or the previous one?
Or the second to last one?

Had that smile, that laugh, been real?
Or was it a cover up?
For something?

Of something?

The hidden detective out to play Cluedo.

Everyone knowing it wasn't Colonel Mustard in the Billiard Room with the Candlestick.

It was already written. It was Olli in The Bedroom with The Rope.

The question now hung in the air just as morbidly,

But why?

She had been feeling slightly feverish all day but was deeply immersed in her work, which took the edge off slightly. Her client was sharing her life story with her and the importance of the task in hand was obvious. They had three days to downsize their large two bedroomed home to a camper van for life. The real, full-size husky was staying.

Rei would often impart her own learnings (when called for) to her clients, it settled them to know that they were not alone, that they weren't the only ones in such a mess. Rei had seen a lot already this life and if there was one thing she was sure of it was that these experiences *of hers* were there to serve others, not just for her own evolution. *Did everyone really have to burn their hand to know the oven was hot?* She was sure not, although the determination and intrigue proved too much for many; another hand scorched and blistered, unnecessarily so.

As they ploughed their way through the Lego sets, the kitchen cutlery, the jewellery from her client's ex and the dog basket, tears, anger, frustration and a slow realisation arose from her client and then dissipated like dew on an early morning lawn. Rei listened and moved effectively and attentively as always, her client mesmerised and in awe, of the magic unfolding, the impossible, possible now.

As they approached afternoon tea Rei had to speak up, she was not feeling 100%. Her 99% felt like she was running on a mere 1% and she was embarrassed and ashamed, it felt so glaringly obvious to her; it always did. Everyone else always said they didn't notice any difference, but to Rei she felt poisonous when she wasn't bringing her A-Game. The fact that someone was paying her for this made it so much worse.

I just want to apologise she said. *I'm not feeling that great. I'm fine but I feel a little feverish, so please don't take it personally.*

Oh, my goodness, are you ok? No, no, you're doing a great job. I couldn't be more thank full. What you've done, what we've achieved together today, already is far more than I could ever have imagined possible. Do you need to…in fact please do, take a rest? You can go lie down on my bed.

Rei contemplated the thought for a millisecond and then jettisoned it to the *you can't possibly do that* pile. For although she was a master on many levels she still was yet to fully let go of the perfectionist, do it alone whilst looking great persona, she'd carried and managed to cling on to so tightly so far this life. This job, along with the next was her saving grace right now. Two birds, with one stone. Money in the bank and her accommodation for the week paid for and sorted. She had to make this work. There was

No

Other

Option.

They worked through the art sets, every poem ever written, every song ever sung, through the ill-assorted duvets and the dishevelled towels, through the attic, through the garden with its deflated footballs and half eaten cricket stumps and it was only when walking down the stairs, craft box in hand, that Rei knew there could be no more.

I'm sorry, I've hit a wall she said. *Let's leave it here and I'll be back tomorrow. I'll come in early or stay late, whatever works for you, to make up the time.*

It was 4.30pm she'd done well to get this far.

Perfect, I'm feeling a little exhausted myself. It's been a long day, thank you. Take care and see you in the morning. Shall we say 8am again?

Absolutely, if anything needs to change, I'll let you know Rei added.

Rei left closing the door gently behind her happy to be in the fresh air, the sunlight on her skin, no longer needing to put on a brave face. She felt like shit, her fever piquing just a little more fiercely than before, letting her know it was not safe to relax *just* yet.

She glanced down at her watch, her constant reminder of her grandmother (which and who was with her always) a mother of pearl face with a small diamond set at each of the number time placements. It always made her smile, bought her some reassurance that she was not alone.

4.47pm.

She looked at the Uber app and it now being rush hour in central London the journey would be long and costly and Rei could not afford either. Walking it was. Every penny counted, and who knew, perhaps the movement may do her good, she may feel better even.

She followed the blue line on google maps showing her the quickest way home, to her dank and pretty grimy hotel. She thought they'd missed the 'S' out. A *hostel* was a very different preposition to a Hotel (capital H), and a more realistic one at that. Rei usually stayed in nice, comfortable places, but given the circumstances she'd opted to take the hit with a lesser quality ho(*s*)tel for a couple of nights and put the cash in the bank instead.

~

They'd been living away from their home for over a month now, a backpack of clothes each, nothing else. It hadn't meant to be that way. When Rei told the kids to *Grab some things for the night, we'll go and let him calm down*, she thought it would be just that. Little did she know they would never be back.

Thankfully her astute capacity to pack all the right things for the job in hand meant that Rei's handful of clothes had seen her through the past few weeks. Her dresses carefully selected to cover any signs that a new life was growing within her. She was on high alert all of the time, she had seen what energy could do to a person before and did not dare think of what reaction it may trigger this time if the truth were known. She was no longer treading on eggshells or skating on thin ice, she was pissing on the third rail, skating down the edge of a razor blade, she'd already licked the frozen flagpole, her time could be up at any moment and she knew it.

She knew she was tired, she'd flown back from Italy yesterday, still in shock and most probably belated trauma from the DNC a few days before, although her *can do* attitude kicked in at the airport gates knowing there was only forward, no going back, she had created this and she had to get on with it. Part relief that she could apply herself to something she was great at, it felt like it was a step forward in a direction, she wasn't sure which direction, but it was a step at least, *one small step, a giant leap for mankind* and all that! She'd collected her car at the airport and driven into central London a long and taxing drive at that time of the day. Her day had already been long she was now on the twelve hours travelling mark, which for a seasoned traveller like Rei was nothing but post operation, this time it all felt different.

The past three days she'd woken up at 1am snuck into his lounge and lay on the floor foetus like, sobbing. For hours. She wasn't thinking about the baby that no longer lived within her, she had felt it disappear the week before, the connection, the beating pulse absent, just like that, without a trace, without a goodbye, just gone, like a thief in the night. Perhaps it had triggered her own old childhood trauma, of knowing something so deeply, and then having to watch it disappear out of your life, silently, no looking back? She wasn't aware of this, but perhaps it was true. After a few hours weeping, the well, well and truly dry, she would sneak back into the bedroom and into the bed, next to João, who was completely undisturbed and unaware of these night time occurrences. He didn't seem upset, not to her at least. Rei didn't want to disturb him, he had work in the morning. She was still too *something* to say how she felt. She wanted to be there for him; make sure he was ok.

Good little girl.

~

She arrived back at the ho(*s*)tel some 50 minutes later having walked right past one of her father's old mews houses, and had texted him as she had. She marvelled at the constellations of life and how at nearly every corner there was something asking her to question, contemplate, reason, consider, ponder on life beyond the three-dimensional life as shown. The smell of damp hit her before she even entered the building, the darkness heavy on the summer's day. Had she not felt quite so bad she would have stayed out longer, but she'd decided on an early night after a bath which would hopefully rejuvenate her body and set her up for a deep sleep ready to jump up and out of bed with a spring in her step the next morning, ready for another day of the work she loved. She ran the bath trying hard not to notice the brown water marks staining the tub, pulling back the plasticky, sticky, shower curtain that would have contained the showers of who knows how many travellers. She was trying really hard not to give any of it any emphasis, to not consider that she could have been in her own home (*her* home) with her favourite Reverence Aesop hand wash, her Epsom bath salts, and her L'Occitane lavender bubble bath in the beautiful new delicately thin stand-alone bathtub she had picked out a few months prior. Those days were long gone. As she swished her hand around the lukewarm muddied water spluttering pathetically from the bath tap, she emptied the remnants of her travel sized shampoo squeezy bottle into the tub pushing and scooping the water between the palms of her hands trying to create the bubbles she was both missing and longing for.

Swish, swash.

She lay in the bath and stared up at the ceiling contemplating the day and thanking God for helping her get through it; it had been touch and go.

She was grateful to be there, in warm slightly discoloured water, with a smattering of bubbles who'd failed in their attempt to stretch and enclose the air within, limp like her body. She registered the yellow rings on the ceiling above her and pretended she was interested in their history. She contemplated how long they must have been there. Smoking had been banned indoors since 2007, twelve years ago, she couldn't believe the ho(s)tel hadn't had a facelift since then, the disgust now re-registering in her body.

It really was that bad.

The thought was beginning to take her down less of an upbeat path than she wanted to go so she decided it was probably time to start moving and get herself out of the bath towards bed. She stood up and gently manoeuvred herself out of the bath the blood rushing to her head, surprisingly so for such a tepid bath she noted. As she reached down to pull the plug out, she felt a whoosh between her legs and as her glaze turned, she saw the puddle of blood on the floor and half way down the side of the bath. The ho(*s*)tel's unsolicited facelift was taking a turn for the worse, the whole room now looked fresh out of a murder scene.

Well done, Rei!

The red paint job didn't seem to want to stop. She half sank to the toilet pan beside her, shaking, the blood still flowing. She tried to catch her breath to think, slowly, rhythmically, but stars, little glistening yellow stars, were spinning around her and all she could smell was the impending loom, damp and dark.

She had a flashback to when Aaron had fallen over as a young child, his head slamming down on his tongue splitting it wide open, the blood gushing, never ending. She'd ended up putting a tea towel up against and partially in his mouth in an attempt to catch the deluge as they drove to the hospital. She wondered who could bring her a tea towel and escort her right now, she was feeling like a small infant herself.

She tried to think where her mobile was. *Oh yes, it was on charge beside the bed!*

She grabbed the towel, clamping it between her legs hoping not to make a mess across the ho(*s*)tel floor as she walked half debilitated, disabled by the bloodstream and the nauseousness.

She really did not know what to do, who to call, she had backed herself into a corner and there was no one to fight her ground. She tried 111 speaking to the lady on the other end of the line who seemed surprised that Rei was waiting for direction.

Get yourself to the nearest hospital immediately. Now!

I'm not sure where that is? stammered Rei suddenly aware she had no idea of where she was, other than in her ho(*s*)tel bedroom.

Where are you? What's your address?

I'm not sure, I'm in a hotel, somewhere near Shepherds Bush… maybe? said Rei unsure herself, the downside of following a satnav and not using your brain anymore like the good old days. She looked around the room for the usual hotel paraphernalia; excess signage, a bedside pen with notepad that was usually adorned with the hotel's name, address and signature, a food menu, a spa selection, but lamentably no. None of these items existed here, they clearly did not have the budget or requirements for them. All she could see was a manky *No Smoking* sign that looked as if it were yellow from nicotine, half peeling from the wall.

I'm really sorry, I don't know Rei apologised feeling more and more stupid by the minute. *I can try and look up on my emails for the booking!* she spurted out, finally happy that her brain had come alive. *I'll have to put you on speakerphone. Bear with me.*

Ok, in the meantime let me take your details said the operator *and I can get you logged in the system and let the hospital know that you're on your way…once we know which one that is. Name, address, date of birth?*

Rei quivered inside. She gave her name and date of birth without hesitation and then she paused. *I don't really have an address at the moment; I'm in the hotel.*

Yes, I appreciate that, but what's your home address dear? came the voice down the other end of the phone, twinged with sympathy and slightly patronising, condescending tones Rei registered.

I'm not stupid, and I have not lost the plot Rei thought,

I just don't have a home,

At

All.

I can't give my old home address as it is just not safe to do so, and I have been out of the Airbnb for over two weeks now, I don't know where I'm going next, but I know tonight and tomorrow night I'm here. That's ok for me, can it not be ok for you too?

She pondered if that might be too much information to give right now?

Are you still there dear? came the voice.

Oh yes, sorry, it's complicated, can you put the hotel down as my home address please? Rei asked as she bought up the booking reference on her phone. *I'm here* she said giving the postcode and name of the ho(s)tel. Her home. Dark, damp, yellow, brown and now blood stained too.

Wherever I lay my hat, that's my home ringing in her ears, a Sixth Form of Paul Young now stinging her eyes.

Hold on dear, the ambulance will be there in no time, it's on its way, please stay on the line.

Ok, I will said Rei now back in the bathroom where she felt safe that any mess she may make could be cleaned up the easiest for the cleaners. If there were any.

Good little girl.

2024

She tells him everything. Not the usual paired back, polite version for prime-time audience ears only. The real one.

He had *only* asked her *When was the last time you were loved for who you truly are?*

And in response he got the truth, without restrictions, unrestrained, gloves off.

As soon as he had asked, she felt the string being pulled from within her, unravelling something that had been wound up and protected for quite some time now. The process occurring before she could even put words to it, which she did. She told him how it felt, how she felt. She had nothing to lose, no reason to hold back. She needed nor wanted anything from him.

They had known each other for nearly ten years now, seeing each other maybe once or twice a year at mutual friend's birthday parties or the like. One dinner she had been sat across the table from him and he commented on her watch. He'd picked up on its exquisite detailing which she appreciated, no one else had ever noticed the finer parts before now. It wasn't a loud obnoxious watch, but in the delicacy and space if you looked closely enough you could see how precious it was. To her anyway.

~

As she told her story, gave the reasons, the tears flowed tenderly and graciously from her eyes, down her cheeks, building at the edge of her jaw before plummeting to their final destination. There was no emotion in it, but it was clear it was a release from deep within. The tears fell some more.

I can love you. He piped up.

Rei disturbed by this sudden declaration, retorted, *I don't need anyone to love me out of sympathy, or duty!*

That wasn't me that said that he replied, *that was The Heavens* he implied.

Rei could feel the truth of his words and they stung. She'd reacted in her usual protective *I can do this alone* way; it was obvious that was neither needed nor necessary right now. She apologised and told herself sternly but lovingly to reel herself back in. And she did.

She sat humbled by it all. The piece of string still unravelling at an alarming rate yet with no end in sight. The tears still falling.

ばらばら, ごぼごぼ.

Bara bara, gobo gobo. In pieces, gurgling.

The singular moments turned to singular minutes, turned to plural groupings of 60 seconds. Time was time travelling itself. It was as if they were still moving but the world around them was frozen. Rei could feel what she was being held in and she knew well enough by now to surrender.

Gabriel held out his hand as any friend would, and Rei took it, the tears still falling, as did the silence around them. There was no awkwardness, only Oneness.

The rest of the journey they sat in the stillness that cradled them both, speechless but full, in the tranquility of the Universe.

2019

Rei has always gone out to see João, that's how it began, her working for him. Two weekends booked to do a wardrobe edit, and then a home edit, with some interior design thrown in too. She loves her job, the many different angles of heaven that stream forth each one supporting the client from all sides, in all walks of life.

It was not an intentional match, but looking back on it Rei realises it was inevitable, to jump from the depths of abuse into something *better*, into the arms of comfort and illusion (delusion). He was tender and gentle and kind; he appreciated the same things as Rei and loved the finer things in life. Rei knew he would never raise his voice, he wouldn't attempt psychological jeers, he wouldn't be jealous, all the things that had become her everyday despite knowing they needn't have been.

~

She remembers the first time Jack had asked her to do something that didn't feel quite right to her, to not go to a dance that evening, something he knew she enjoyed. He asked so politely letting her know that he wished she wasn't going, some kind of reverse flattery that Rei lapped up, like a new born kitten nursing on her mother's milk, hungry for the feed. The starvation of being wanted. She hesitated a few times and then gave in to the quiet, unassuming demand. The door had been opened, the floodgates opened. An opened pack of cookies, one gone and then they were all gone. *Give an inch, and they take a mile.*

Gradually perhaps, but over time deceiving herself of the frequency of events as the patterns of behaviour built. It wasn't until a few months later that the next incident occurred.

Jack had been taken into hospital and had been kept in for a few days with a rare neurological disorder. It had been a shock to his system and he felt gravely disappointed that his children had not come to see him there. He was angry at the world for this apparent set back in all he wanted to do and achieve, angry at his ex for not bringing their kids to see him, sad his kids weren't fighting to see him.

After being discharged from the hospital ward the first thing he wanted to do was ring them, Rei could hear his voice rising from the room next door. She went in to see what was happening, to divert the situation, something she did oh so naturally, metamorphosing into and around her environment, the path of least resistance. But it was too late, he slammed down the phone then picked it up and hurled it across the room. It shattered into pieces to the left of Rei.

*F***ing bitch!* he yelled.

Words and a vibration Rei knew well, transported back to her eight-year-old self caught between two divorcees and their slagging match down the phone. She caught a glimpse of the world outside, sunny, fresh, vibrant and moving forwards, different to the stagnation she was feeling within her body, her home, which was suddenly pulling her backwards. She saw the silhouettes and heard the voices of three people she knew outside, two close friends and shuddered. *What if they heard?*

Since young Rei had tried to protect people; protect them from themselves, from others and perhaps from the world around them. She always saw the best in people, always saw them for the stellar souls that they were. She didn't like the way people would focus on the negative and run with it, create and distort stories, embellish them for their own use. And so, for a host of so many reasons most still yet unbeknownst to Rei she would distort the reality, hide the truth in a subconscious attempt to not give fodder to the flames.

In a movement that may well not have occurred on a different day at a different time, she ushered herself forward into the firing line, jumping above and around the detonated bomb in an attempt to smother the impact, contain the debris. She cared what people thought, more than she cared for herself. Their opinions had formed what she thought of herself, she now saw through their eyes, through their lenses.

Jack could not be silenced that easily but the upcoming deadly crash collision had been averted. Worried that her friends outside may have heard something, may want to knock at the door and see if everything was alright, Rei ushered herself and Jack upstairs out of sight, where she could pretend that she hadn't heard anything should they come knocking. There was a running commentary going on, silent, yet substantial enough to be heard, persistent in its endeavours. She knew this was wrong, so deeply wrong, yet there seemed no other way out, not one that she liked the thought or implications of anyway.

It all felt so exposing, so brash, so violent.

Why couldn't people just get on? she never understood.

1993

Rei had seen it often enough in those around her, orchestrating the final scene so they would be the ones leaving, not the ones being left. In some it came with a tinge of drama so as to be the centre of attention, in others a sloping into the background as if they were irrelevant, insignificant. Whichever way she saw it, it was obvious, the deep abandonment being played out again, any tens of years later. Grown men, old women, young girls, pubescent boys, it mattered not, but there was always a silent cry of *Run, before you get hurt!* She could see it in their eyes, the way they looked, searching for any sign to tell them it was ok to flee. Any excuse not to stay, so it could be anyone's fault but their own.

They were protecting themselves.

Protecting themselves from their own sphere of evolution.

~

As Rei came down the back stairs from the attic room to the kitchen, she heard screams and bangs. Running to catch what was going on she opened the door latch to a kitchen knife in her face. Of the finest Japanese quality, razor sharp, clean cut as a gyuto should be. Its owner had learnt the art of cordon bleu cooking in London in previous years and had become pretty nifty with the blade so it seemed. Before Rei had chance to think what was actually going on there were two. Two knives, two bodies. Two voices, two spirits vying for attention, trying to kill each other. Prophetically so. Aggressively with vigour, not so much trying to protect their own life from the other but more so trying to kill the other as if their own life depended on it; on killing them that was.

Rei screamed *Stop It!* but her voice fell to the floor, silent, deadly, cold, there was no carpet to catch it, to soften the fall, to comfort the landing. She tried again *Stop!* in case she was imagining the sound, in case it hadn't left her voice box the first-time round. As she did her body lunged forward between the pair of them, coming between them and their brandishing swords.

Swoosh, schwing.

She didn't have much care for her step mum but without a shadow of a doubt two people should not be behaving this way, *Ever*. She screamed again. *Put the knives down!* tears streaming down her cheeks.

Hearing the knife shatter on the kitchen counter and screech to a halt as it collided into the tiled splash back, she was momentarily grateful and relieved that her pleas had been heard, she wasn't mute after all.

She was invisible.

A Le Creuset pan flew across the kitchen island at great speed, groaning from its own weight mid-air before landing splat into the wall, missing its target by a centimetre at most due to a last-minute dodge.

The saucepan stand once resplendently full of Volcanic flame orange cast iron stone ware was losing its totality. The completeness of the set, forfeiting its stature to the wills of the pair performing a merry dance of abusive attack around the scullery.

Rei thought of ages passed, of Tudor times, burning stoves, boiling cauldrons, in the hub of the house, the cookhouse where the servants would convene. As a child she had dressed up once for a school trip, taken on a tour to a place such as this, a grand manor house in the middle of the country. One wing for the family, the other for the servants. A different entrance and exit, separate lives under the one roof. She ran back up the stairs carefully not to slip on her tears, up to her sister's room, the part of the house she shared with the Filipino nanny, the one away from *the family,* her family.

She was tripping over herself, over her words, slurring over her tears, nothing could come out quick enough to relay the events to her sister now thirteen. Rei felt less than thirteen at this point, she felt eight again, not the eight and ten she very nearly now was, a so-called adult.

Her sister more than unamused or disturbed by the narrative, purred *What's new?* and carried on with her homework, the pans smashing against the walls below them both clear to hear.

From their side of the house anyway.

It seemed neither husband nor wife were playing the usual game of quitting whilst they were ahead, of running before the other ran. They were playing chicken, the last man standing.

And the stakes were high.

All in.

2007

In the garden was a small cast iron tub collected from a car boot sale for next to nothing. Placed under the outdoor tap the kids would play for hours here splashing with their buckets close to the mini orchard, nine trees of mixed plum and apple varieties. The chickens Susie, Lola and Daisy running around between them. The cockerel, Bert, mute since his 5am wake up call.

Today there was a film of frogspawn covering the tub, bunches formed and obvious in pattern and shape, yet breathing as one on the still water. *Ogres,* Aaron smiled overjoyed at the potential of more than one this time. His first pet as a child had been a large frog, *Ogre* (his beautiful way of pronouncing the tailless amphibian word), who lived at the bottom of the garden stairs, alone, but there every day communicating to and receiving communication from Aaron. They could sit for hours in each other's presence completely mesmerised by one another.

They gathered around the water pail and inspected the developing progeny. Thousands of embryos swelling in jelly like clumps reflecting signs of life and growth, a new cycle in the early days of the year.

Excited, Aaron rushed inside to find his nature picture book that explained the growth formations, finding out that their mum would have only come there, to their garden, to lay her eggs needing water for them to grow. After they had matured and developed the spawn (by then frogs) would find their way to the nearby damp woodlands and beyond.

Wow she came such a long way and to ours! he said beaming with joy and pride. *That's really special.*

Indeed, it was. They watched and monitored the hatchlings day in day out, proud parents revelling in the growth of their children.

On day six they went out for the day to the local farm. It turned out to be a surprisingly glorious wintery spring day the sun beating down on their pale snowy skin. They ended up staying out all day their thrown together sushi and edamame bean picnic seeing them through 'til the farm gates shut at the dusk of day. As they pulled back into the driveway Aaron pleaded *Can we go see the tadpoles first before we go inside? Please?*

Rei's body retracting, the horror upon realising they had not topped up the tub with any water for a couple of days now.

Umm… Shall we go inside and wash our hands first? she recommended hoping the slight delay may change the already pre-determined outcome.

Okay said Aaron, yes, we don't want to bring them any harm or germs, do we?

No said Rei *Absolutely not. You're amazing* she beamed, loving them all for their gorgeous ways, aware that their lives may well about to be shattered just as hers had been by her own childhood dead chickens. Only this time there was no fox to blame, only herself.

She walked across the grass watching them sprint and then come to a complete standstill in front of the iron tub, a mass of sunburnt crisped debris before their eyes.

Rei didn't see this as nature's failure, of a mother frog's poor judgment, or of the consequences of the day's weather. She took it on as her own oversight and she felt horrid; both sad and bad that she'd let *everyone* down.

Again.

1999

That Monday morning, after the weekend away where she'd got alcohol poisoning, she vowed things had to change. She had let things slip, *get the better of her.* She knew there was something she wasn't dealing with, for why else would she be so loose, so erratic? Why else had she quite naturally taken a swig of cheap Suntory, plastic, screw bottle top red wine before going into work for the day, to teach a group of thirteen-year-olds? None of it computed or made sense. She still didn't even like alcohol, never really had.

The dawning or re-awakening some might say, occurred over the toilet bowl of a Yakumo hotel. Barely able to walk, talk or focus. She had drunk a lot that day in the company of friends that she began to realise could not really be that friendly, happily laughing as she spiralled downhill into the basin of a bog.

She had always been in control, and if there was any sign that it would not be that way, then Rei would act accordingly. Right now, she was not in control, of anything, and no stern self-talking to could change that. Her body was speaking and communicating to her on her behalf, reminding her of her purity and her responsibility in life. She was sweating, vomiting, unable to breathe in her own breath, her own rhythm. She tried to feel her pale, discoloured looking skin but couldn't be sure if she was touching what was beneath her hands or feeling what was in her head, she felt confused and embarrassed. Unsure if she was awake, semi conscious or passing in and out of both states, she was aware that this was the first time that Ethan was fully awake in life, he was worried and it was clearly visible. The shock of seeing Ethan this way, shook Rei to attention some more, called her back into the responsibility she knew and thrived on so well. She crawled to the motel bed, dragging her body across the floor, disgraceful and pathetic, and managed to pull the duvet around her, wrapping herself up as best she could. She would sleep and the whole thing would be gone in the morning.

~

By Monday the whole event was ever more present in her mind. The night's endeavours reverberating and echoing through her body. Horrified she had let herself get that way she emptied the half-drunk bottle of Suntory delicacy down the drain. *Never* would she let herself get like this again. It may have been a one off, but it was *once too many* she chided herself. And so began another chapter of Rei's life, one of complete control. The pendulum had swung.

The escape to Japan hadn't been everything she had hoped it would be, for sure there was so much she was loving and enjoying, so much on offer that she was taking both by the horns and riding, but deep inside there was still an unsettlement that was gnawing away at her, leading her down a back alley. It was time to get herself out of this gutter. She began running in the very early mornings before school began, a few steps at first, to ten kilometre and more runs in no time, through the hills and mountains that surrounded her. She would put her mini-disk player on full volume and run. *Run Forest, Run!* It was not a leisurely run, although she tried to sell it to herself as such. It was part punishment part brutality. An attempt to rein in the loose, unwieldy aspects of what she thought was her character, not realising it was a part of her that did not belong, that wasn't even hers to begin with. She wanted to be seen, to be heard, to be loved and yet here she was compounding everything she despised one heavy body weight transferring thud after another. To wile away the time she perpetually gave herself maths equations working out how much she'd run, what proportion she had left, how many minutes it may take. It occupied her mind and gave her next to no space to actually feel what was going on within.

Her body was toning up, she felt fitter and stronger than ever before and she had a vitality she hadn't previously known, but she was hardening herself emotionally and psychologically. Just as quickly as her capacity to run long distances fast increased, her capacity to menstruate, living as a sacred young woman shrivelled up, ceasing its natural, organic existence.

And with that too, her hopes and dreams of motherhood.

1999

It was an inevitable love born from the unexpected. They had met and liked what they'd seen. The silent boxes had been ticked. *What was there not to love?* Her time in Japan so far had been fruitful enough and her Japanese boyfriend and his family utterly delightful but Rei knew she could not settle down here, this could not be her life. It was not what she was destined for.

When he rang out of the blue to ask what she was doing for Christmas she told him she was travelling to the Philippines to Boracay for a week or so whilst the schools were closed.

Can I come too? was all she heard.

Part not sure, and part open to the idea, the words *Of course!* tumbled from her mouth, ever the one to not make anyone feel uncomfortable. She contemplated the consequences and decided it could be a good thing traveling with someone rather than going solo. She wasn't expecting anything from it, other than a sunshine break to a beautiful unknown island.

He turned up handsome, laid back and gentle, a happy-go-lucky charm about him that was endearing from the outset. The romanticism of the trip playing heavily as background music as their boat danced across the ocean's crystal-clear azure waters to their destination from the mainland.

Rei had bought him a teddy as a Christmas present, she knew everyone else just *lurrrved* Christmas and she wouldn't want to ruin that day, or any for that matter for anyone just because of her own personal persuading. She felt a bit silly when she gave it to him, clearly a one-way gift (itself not a problem) which she found herself apologising for. *What was that very English habit of apologising for anything and everything?*

You stepped on my foot = *I'm sorry…*
It's cold outside = *I'm sorry…*
They (not you) are late for your dinner date = *I'm sorry…*

Was she really sorry she'd carefully considered someone and wanted to give them something gorgeous for a potentially special day? Was she sorry she'd made a special trip into the city and chosen something she thought would hit the spot not needing anything back in return? No quite frankly she wasn't, yet here again, as always, the phrase somersaulted from her lips and found solace in the waiting ears.

The sand was as gorgeous as she'd heard it would be, white and silky beneath their feet. It was like going back in time, back to basics. The rain plummeted from the sky drenching them as soon as their feet hit the ground off the boat, bewildered and exhausted they looked at each other and laughed. They hadn't signed up for a wet t-shirt contest, but they'd got one, there was nothing much left to the imagination, whether they liked it or not their bodies had been revealed in full.

As they stood catching their breath between the inundating cloud bursts, they decided they could be waiting for a long time if they waited for the torrents to cease so they should make their move to find accommodation. First stop straight ahead. They ran into a young girl in a garden with some chooks running free amongst the verdant tufts, not camouflaged but completely at one with their surroundings. Rei signed a question about lodgings and the girl signalled to wait. Out came a spritely old woman who whisked them away round the back of her house and up some wooden stairs outside.

It was as simple as that.

A room with a view of some hens and a backyard of the ocean, rippling to the shore.

2001

Rei would take Aaron with her everywhere, there was no time they were not together. She had tried postpartum to go for a run around the block, a smidge of that drive still within her, wanting her body to return to its svelte, waif pre-pregnant ways. She needn't have worried too much as her body was pretty much back to good within the week, this time accompanied with blossoming breasts, full of milk for her newborn.

She left him holding him, and him holding him, not sure how this may pan out. They were standing at the kitchen window looking up into the world as they watched the woman of their lives leave (for the first time in 4 months). She closed the wrought iron gate behind her and waved, smiling, feeling the fresh air upon her face, and ran.

The last time she had run was in the hills of Japan, the lush green forests and the spring flowers neatly manicured around the villages. Today she was running in the grey, between the cars. She took a left up to the canal, passed the ducks searching for food in the reeds, past the dog taking a crap on the lawn, the owner smearing the poo into the grass in an attempt to collect it in his purple poo bag which he'd just pulled from his newly acquired poo bag holder.

The rain was just beginning to fall, ever so slightly and Rei was beginning to feel slightly uncomfortable. She took a left down towards the railway track and made the U-turn towards home, towards them. Part of her had enjoyed these few minutes of freedom, to herself, on her own, and part of her could not wait to get home to him. He had become a part of her. A slight anxiousness beginning to rise.

She smiled relieved to get back to the gate and turn down the stairs, pleased that actually she was still alive and could vaguely still run, but more importantly that she was back quicker than suggested. She'd said she may be half an hour but it turned out to be thirteen minutes. Perfect.

She looked into the window expecting to see the two of them smiling in each other's arms, just as she'd left them. Instead, she saw panic, mayhem, tears, the cries escalating the closer she got. Her pace quickened as she opened the front door feeling the distress within.

Where have you been? he scolded.

As if that was even a question thought Rei, grabbing for Aaron, red faced barely able to breathe.

He started screaming as soon as you left and hasn't shut up... Until now!

He trailed off hearing the silence deafen the room as Aaron landed back in his mother's arms.

Great! He has thrown up all over me, all over the kitchen floor. What were you thinking? Don't ever leave me like that again.
Rei's face fell to the floor. Flabbergasted. Stumped.

Aaron was quiet now but still trying to catch his breath, regulate the inhalation and the exhalation, his body still in shock, still in trauma, sobbing from deep within, his baby suit soaked, half tears, half thrown up regurgitated breast milk.

That was the last and only time Rei would leave him.

Her colleagues try to belittle her, to make her feel like she is doing something wrong calling her a *'flight deck floozy'*. Her crime to talk to the pilots, to have a laugh, to befriend them, to act normally with them. It was not *standard procedure* although it should have been, instead it showed them up for how they behaved, putting hierarchical structures, names and badges above the person, projecting, needy, and all too often longing. Rei wouldn't let it disturb her; she knew the truth. For the first time she felt happy within herself.

They'd just moved home to Slough, home of Ricky Gervais and The Office. Anyone that she told she had moved there from Oxford had apologised to her on their behalf.

Oh, I'm sorry, as if she was mourning the death of one of her children.

No don't be, I love it! I live in Heaven Rei would reply.

The recipient unsure not hearing the expected sarcasm in her voice would usher *B, b, bu…but…why?*

I have an apartment literally given to me by heaven. Its brand spanking new, stunningly gorgeous, not damp, warm, the sun streams through the tall ceilinged warehouse windows, it's close to work, has a concierge, gym, cinema, roof top terrace and the rest. What is there not to love? I can be in central London within 15 minutes and straight onto the motorway to get back down to Oxford when needed. It's everything I could possibly ever want or need. Rei gushed unapologetically about her home. Everything she said, she meant from the bottom of her heart.

Each and every morning since moving there, upon waking each day she would wander into the kitchen, turn on the kettle, prepare her fresh mint leafed tea in her cafetière and sit on the luxurious velvet sofa, feet up on the footstool, staring at the mural on the wall in front of her. The stork taking flight evoking times past in Japan, the pink cockatoo, still and observing the world around. Without fail each and every day the tears would fall. Rei had never felt so held in all her life. The green leaves around symbolic of the bushes she'd passed through, the weeds she'd slain and the fresh life ahead. Never had she been so appreciative of everything she had and that she was, than right now. It had been a tough few years to say the least. It was beyond her wildest dreams and expectations that she could be anywhere half as decent or gracious as this. It was nothing short of miraculous, and there was nothing that could take this gratitude away. It seemed to deepen every day.

Talking to her colleagues it stood out how much she loved her home; how grateful she was. She had come a long way in just over a year.

When she had started out working there (at the airport) she had had to pull over, half way down the motorway on her drive to work exhausted already having driven some fifty miles in the past hour. A twenty-minute nap was not enough to stave off the fatigue, her body not used to anything much outside the mile radius she had grown accustomed to.

Since her operations nearly five years ago now she had worked her way back to health and a fitness of some sort. She started out with a four hour a day graveyard shift in a large department store, she felt it was a safe way back into the world. She had longed to be back in the throes of busy city life amidst throngs of people and this was her golden opportunity. She revelled back in the work place and soon found her feet whilst there, her previous managerial position in retail paving the way. Desperately overqualified but having pleaded with the interviewer that this was exactly what both she and they needed.

Every morning her body screamed at her as the alarm clock went off, sore, desperate, aching, still riddled from a traumatic past. Her body cursed but there was not a moan to be heard from her, it was a step forward into a whole new world. By the end of her fifteen months there she firmly had enough energy to cover the role which had become a front facing customer position moving to prime-time customer hours. She had built up the stamina to face and serve thousands of people each day in the busiest store in Oxford and she was thriving from it. She moved on to another store in town working full days but ad hoc on a zero-hour contract so there was no pressure whilst her body readjusted yet again to longer hours, again as she stepped up to the role so too did her body. They loved her there and within weeks she was asked to be store manager of the Banbury branch having transformed their regional sales and their store.

She had applied to work for the airlines a few months back after a sixteen-year-old Bodhi said *Mum, you should do something you want to do, you've looked after all three of us singlehandedly for what, twenty-four years now?*

She appreciated this from him, it was very grown up and mature and despite the hard time they'd been through, she loved and admired the amazingness that all three of them were and that they showed and shared so openly. She had always wanted to be an air hostess when she was a little girl, and now that her travel with work had dried up post covid and with no money to traverse the globe it seemed like it ticked all the boxes. She had sailed through the interview process and it was now in the hands of the vetting gods. She was glad it was taking so long as it gave her the chance to get physically stronger still. Eventually they rang to say she was ready to begin and gave her a handful of dates, one of them being her birthday. It seemed like a fitting way to begin the start of a new year, a new cycle. So, she worked her notice in the shop, prepping for the next adventure.

It was an intensive six-week training course up near the airport and there was no way she could travel up there and back each day, she messaged her friend Gabriel to see if she could stay with him as he lived nearby. The last time she had seen him was at the August garden party on the river. She'd caught wind of the get together and messaged him to see if she could come along too.

He said *Yes, of course.* Having recently renovated the house he knew she would be interested in seeing it.

As the party was packing up, he reached out his hand to take hers, showing her the way upstairs to the refurbishments, a natural gesture noted but nothing more. A harem of woman followed to take an eye preying look too. One of Rei's friends later commented that they would make a great couple.

No said Rei, *we're just friends.*

She was unable to stay with Gabriel; he was going through a tricky break up and needed some space so she spent five nights a week at the local Holiday Inn preparing her food in advance for the week and packing it with her before her long trek up the motorway.

~

Now some year into the new job she was frequently working twenty-hour days on her feet across the skies, through the nights and into the next days, traversing time differences, with little sleep and disrupted circadian rhythms. A far cry from where she had been two years prior. Every single day she appreciated her body and what it could do. She still felt relatively weak and incapable but there was absolutely no denying mountains had been moved.

She was coming back, clearer, brighter and potentially very much stronger.

2016

High above her head to the right she could hear a voice she recognised. They were half way out into the ocean, sunlight on their faces, the cold water on their skin, respite to the heat and to the storm they'd just left behind.

Jack had lost his rag again, and it wasn't metaphorically. Shouting was an everyday norm now, no topic off topic, no item too small for the agenda. This time his kids, their kids, had chased down the stairs and managed to crack the glass balustrades, hundreds if not thousands of pounds of damage done in an instant. Rei mortified at not only what had happened but also at the prospect of telling her father that they (she) had wrecked his home.

Herself and her kids had been there every year for the past ten years and never, not once had there been anything go wrong, no cracks, no scratches, no wear and tear, and now this, the most devastating colossal damage possible done in one moment. His kids, their kids, didn't even stop to notice, stop to say sorry. Rei had seen this before, it was a common theme.

~

The first time Jack's kids had been invited round to Rei's home with her kids they had gone into Aaron's room and played heavy handedly with his Lego figurines he'd delicately created and had displayed in his room. They didn't care, had no awareness to the fact that they were someone else's possessions, not that Aaron was overly protective or one not to share. Rei's kids had been bought up to respect their belongings, to tidy up after themselves since birth, if there was something out it had to go away before the next activity came out to play. It wasn't a chore, it was a way of life, no questioning, no arguing, it was just how it was. Done.

Rei delicately spoke to Jack about it, traversing the slipstreams of potential reactions; protective parent; unaware parent; don't give a shit parent. She knew not what was behind his inability to not only not say anything to his kids but apparently not to see the damage done by a pair of bulls in a china shop.

She could tell Aaron was upset inside, they'd never had friends round that would behave in such a way, it was all new. All three of the kids had grown fond of Jack, but Jack with his own kids was a different kettle of fish. She whispered to Aaron that she would sort it out and so she was doing just that. She hadn't accounted for the impotence to see what was so glaringly obvious to her, she tried to explain as gently and non-threateningly as she could.

Oh, they don't mean any harm, it's just Lego for heaven's sake! It's meant to be pulled apart and rebuilt, get a grip. They're just going to have to learn to all get on together. Simple as.

Rei wasn't so sure. This didn't feel right to her. My god she loved her kids, she loved the way they looked after each other, the way they were there for each other, never an argument or a fight, no competition, no comparison. The four of them lived very beautifully together, harmoniously. Now there was a tornado, a hurricane in her house and she'd invited it in, opened the door to it, then trapped it inside closing the door behind, sealing any chances of any natural escape. The wreckage was extensive, she wondered if she would be able to collect all the pieces up or if some of them had been thrown, jettisoned too far?

She could hear Jesse J's *Price Tag* blaring through the open kitchen door from the neighbour's house,

We're paying with love tonight.
It's not about the money, money, money.
We don't need your money, money, money.
We just wanna make the world dance.

She'd heard her neighbour come home in the early hours of the morning and wondered if he was still up drinking or passed out on his living room sofa unaware of the weather report next door, this song, *his* song, on repeat as he leaned into the words; a promise of love, happiness, and authenticity in life away from the material world and all its trappings…

She was praying for the hours to pass quickly without further agitation and suggested they all go out for a walk, hoping the space would do them all good and guessing no more damage could be done.

It proved a wise decision.

Rei reasoned that she needed to give them all space, space to learn to adjust to each other and to be able to communicate. Just as she was learning to find her voice, she could see that her kids needed to do this too.

~

As the months turned into years, she found herself here in the Canaries on holiday, all seven of them, together for the first time.

Her dad had been surprisingly welcoming to Jack when he had met him the first time and her mum was pleased to see her daughter be treated, to flowers and a man that wanted to be with her. She gave words of encouragement *That must be nice. You deserve that.* And Rei supposed she did, it wasn't something she'd had in a long time and here was someone who wanted to be her partner, not another child.

~

They had got through (not over) the hurdle of the broken glass balustrades through much shouting and screaming (his, not hers). Rei's morals and values neatly tied up inside her now. Tongue twisted in knots in her stomach.

They didn't mean to do it. Get a grip. No, I will not say sorry, it was an accident. No, I will not pay for the damage, nor offer to. You do it, it's your dad. He's got enough money.

Rei slunk downstairs to her father's house to apologise profusely for the damage, her dad firing questions at her *What happened? What do you mean they just tripped? That's toughened glass, thicker than most, meant to withstand a fall. They must have been swinging from the bannisters not walking down them…Monkeys, Buffoons all of them! Where were your kids? Did they have anything to do with this?*

Rei knew they didn't as she knew her dad knew too, it was his polite way of reminding her that she was with a scoundrel. *Bob the Builder* as he liked to remind her, the cartoon character predictable and inept at the same time, reacting awkwardly to situations that should not be difficult to navigate with a professional head. Rei promised to pay for the repairs from her own pocket knowing full well she didn't have the funds to do so.

I'll sort it out huffed her father as Rei shrank a little more, the five remaining days seeming longer every second. Rei knew she now not only had to stop one volcano from erupting but two. She was walking on hot coals herself and her feet were getting burnt. Consequently, she'd suggested they all go down to the ocean play park for the day, a bouncy castle in the water with an assault course too, that should keep him, and his kids, busy and hopefully out of trouble.

~

As they swam out to the aqua park she had to do a double take, she was sure it was James. She'd spent nearly six years of her life with him; she knew his voice inside out. *But here on the other side of the Canaries in the abundance of marine, on this day, what were the chances?* She looked around searching for James and instead saw his wife.

Rhiannon! she shouted. *Rhiannon!*

She'd only met Rhiannon once after James and her had gone their separate ways over twenty years prior but Rei had that special ability to see a face once and know it for the rest of her life. She had never been so good with names, but give her a face and it would never be forgotten, locked into the vault forever. *Rhiannon!*

Rhiannon turned to see Rei's head bobbing up and down, treading water as fast as she could, waving ferociously so as not to be missed. Her face meaning nothing to her, another face in the crowd.

Rhiannon! The words kept gushing from Rei's mouth, *It's Rei, James' ex!*

Noticing, their kids (his, hers and theirs) had all stopped now to look at what was going on.

Rei suddenly feeling the piercing lasers burning in her back realising she'd poked the bear. The hibernation period was over. Both James and Jack swimming over to the scene to investigate. Rei suddenly deeply uncomfortable all round.
She knew there would be trouble.

BIG (capital T)

Trouble.

She also knew she had done nothing wrong but that meant nothing in the grand scheme of things.

James super excited to see Rei, absolutely dumfounded at the coincidence, introduced his wife (again) and his kids to Rei. Rei turned to do the same by which time most of the five kids were swimming off realising there was nothing to be seen here. However next to her, dangerously close to her, was Jack, ever attentive to Rei knowing or being with anyone, particularly a man, other than him.

The way the ocean sloshed upon her skin next to him gave her a heightened alerted slap with every wave break…*Be careful. Don't be too friendly. Don't smile too much. Don't give anything away…*It (the sea) punched, clouted and whacked against her delicate frame, a not so gentle reminder of the playground she was now within.

What should have been an incredibly gorgeous moment was not. Rei shrunk, not wanting for one moment to introduce Jack as her partner, embarrassed of the relationship she had and of the (no longer isolated) movements that had occurred just an hour or so ago. Yet she knew she had to. *This is Jack. My partner* she nuanced, Jack edging closer, chest inflating, arms bulging, his whole body like a puffer fish blowing in James's unthreatening presence trying to deter this so-called predator.

Rei couldn't wait to wrap the conversation up, to help the magma stay as far away from the volcano as possible, to keep it dormant. She wasn't ready for another eruption yet; she'd barely recovered from the last. Its thick ash collapsing glass balustrades, disrupting relationships and peace on the island, causing respiratory problems to its inhabitants, she was sure.

Rei was the only one she thought who had the power to navigate the storm, she would do what she could. She had created this monster, so it seemed, it was her mess to clear up.

Bye! she waved to James, a jaded and downhearted smile, head hung low and gobbling salt water, deeply sad within that this was her life now unable to even speak to her nearest and dearest.

2018

She sees him turn his glance away from the ocean, away from them, in deep contemplation wishing he was somewhere else, and she knew.

This one turn of the head, one lowering of the eyelids, one breath out of sync signified everything to Rei. Staggeringly loud and simultaneously extraordinarily quiet the end of a relationship had been seen and observed by the onlooker, by her. The finale already told, already written in stone.

It had been the most glorious day, her birthday at the end of January always cold and melancholy, the radio repeatedly blaring woes of blue Friday, the most miserable day of the year. This year the kids had all taken the day off school something they never did, but today in unison they'd made a pact to celebrate their mum. Perennially, as prosaic as it was, Rei chose to go to the beach. It was always her go-to, her happy place and although it was the middle of winter that was still destination of choice.

It was grey outside, damp and cold so they wrapped up warm; boots, coats and jackets piled high in the boot, the two Frenchies nestled in amongst them, and set out on the car journey south to the coast. Two-and-a-bit hours later, song'd out, gamed out, and in high spirits they pulled into the car park usually teeming with cars and ice creams, soda, shandy, ciders and dogs of every shape and size, including the hot dog variety, and drove straight to the front, to the cliff's edge. As they pulled into the imaginary car parking space the clouds separated, the unseen (for months) blue sky appeared and the sun emerged bright, potent and glorious. It was biblical, bringing them all to a complete halt. They sat there watching the rain droplets dissipate from the windscreen, the steam beginning to peel across the windows from within as the heat from the sun pounded down upon the car.

Happy Birthday Mum, even the sun has come out to celebrate you!

And what a picture-perfect day it absolutely was. The dogs jumped out first needing no encouragement, followed shortly by Rei and the kids (her kids) and with a slight spring in his step mirrored Jack. They ran down the rocky limestone slope deciding to opt for just one of the layers of jacket or coat now the clouds had parted company, enjoying the space that was never usually there.

The Jurassic Coast and Durdle Door in particular had become a Mecca point for the masses, squadrons of pelicans congregating for feeding time, the world famous stone arch attracting instagramers *#chasingsunsetsandgoodtimes.* Today there were none, there was no stampede, no jostling for space, just them, an expanse, the cosmos of the universe. Their boots met the stones beneath their feet, crunching like fresh snow newly walked upon for the first time, the water between the rocks and pebbles drying up in the heat of the gleaming sun's rays. It seemed like a ludicrous idea in the middle of the coldest season having just driven through wintry wind and icicled rain, but Rei felt drawn to take her shoes off, to feel the earth beneath her feet like she did as a child, sand between her toes as she touched down in Suffolk on each occasion. She felt like a minor, free, able to take it all in, everything around her, in the full appreciation of it all. They picked up the stones and threw them into the water's edge seeing how many times they would skip along the surface before disappearing into the depths below. They launched pebbles far and wide seeing how far they could hurl them into the ocean, how deep their sling shot. They laughed, belly aching, smiles creasing from the fun they were having, clothes were removed as if it were summer time on the beach, jumpers now wrapped around their waists, hats and gloves shoved precariously in coat pockets as they ran between goal posts made from rocks in their hand made Olympic Games courses. The sun shone stronger, the heat fresh and raw upon their ghost-like skin.

Rei noticed the subtle withdrawal, the smiles with a tinge of fakeness that lingered a little longer than a natural one, she wondered what it could be, knowing full well what it was. Sometimes the possibility of doubt entertained the desire of something else, the semblance of another way. Rei had learnt this on many an occasion and had seen the play out yet could not bring herself to cut the movement, the momentum of it. She didn't always want to believe the truth of what she was feeling, what she knew to be true. Today was not one of these days. There was no questioning of what she could read before her.

To her it was the most perfect of days, everything in its peak flow, everyone full, glowing, zestful. The sun showing no signs of fading, and not a cloud in sight to play peek-a-boo behind. They took a stroll across the cliffs to the neighbouring Lulworth Cove and stopped for lunch sitting outside on the benches, the seasons having changed just for them. The food was exquisite, the best they'd ever had there, but still Rei could feel the disturbance and sadness within Jack, a longing for all that was not there, a focus on everything that was not. Rei gently encouraged an appreciation of the what was, the gloriousness, the magic and the wonder of what they were in at that moment, but she may as well have been talking to a brick wall. The words fell short of the six-yard line. The walk back over the cliffs unbearable and relentless in its truth, each footstep compounding the inevitable split, the end.

This was it; it was over.

For good this time.

Once

and

for

all.

2001

It was a year of closeness, a year of Gemini, a relationship in harmony with its two parts working together as one. Rei and Aaron didn't need words (not that as a baby he had any) but every movement communicated was responded to. As soon as he would murmur Rei was on it, they may as well have been one, twins cut from the same cloth.

Rei couldn't understand the other mums around her who would let their kids scream in their buggies, on the ground, in their arms. It was as if overnight she became a baby whisperer, she knew what each one needed often before they did it seemed. A pre-emptive call and response quality. The mums around her would watch as she would attend to Aaron and their babies in play groups not understanding the *how* behind this powerful ability to calm and truly meet each and every subject. Likewise, Rei could not understand the disconnect between mother and child, it seemed easy to her.

I need my nappy changed,
I'm hungry,
I'm tired,

Basic commands and requests that if met allowed a smooth running of the minutes, hours, days and then years that became of the beings in their lives.

~

Once Rei remembered losing her calm. Aaron screaming and writhing like never before. She'd been feeling the building energetic exodus as Ethan removed himself further into his own studies, a convenient excuse not to participate in the life going on at home that he hadn't really asked for, hadn't really signed up for, and definitely did not want the responsibility of. This life so far, he had wandered aimlessly dodging accountability of any role, self or otherwise assigned. Like the littlest hobo, he played the hippy part well, it suited him; good looking, eloquent, long (bleached) blonde hair, tanned skin, chiselled body, surfer vibe, *freeeeeeee and happyyeeeee* (or at least that was the vibe).

Rei wasn't sure exactly what culminated in the ferocious feelings of that day, but all of a sudden in that moment she felt rage, isolation, frustration, sadness and a deep despair. She didn't know what to do, how to make Aaron stop crying, she even screamed at him to stop, begging him to stop. Eventually he did, and at that very same time Rei swore to herself that would and could never happen again.

Ever.

~

Most days Rei would take Aaron to the local pool, they'd taken out membership at the closest hotel and spa that was a five-minute walk around the corner from their basement flat. It was more like an exclusive members club than the usual leisure centre establishment she was used to but they had been given a great deal on the price and she deeply valued being able to go there each day taking Aaron to be in the water. She would hold him close and walk up and down the 15m length pool, both enjoying the stillness and serenity around them. If another member were to walk by poolside it was often only to use the hot tub, very few used the pool itself.

Everyone to date had always commented on Aaron, his gentle, very smiley ways. It didn't matter how old, how young, what race, what nationality, whoever would pass him would stop to smile, to say something, or even to just acknowledge him, it had been the same day in day out for these first six months of his life. Today however as they got out of the pool and into the changing room, they came across an older lady changing into her swimming costume, sunglasses at the ready, hair neatly coiffed (ready to come into no contact with any water at all). Despite having to ask them to move slightly across to access her locker immediately next door to theirs, there was nothing. No exchange, no commentary, no smile, no *nada*.

Rei surprised, yet also not, laughed within and chuckled at the fact that Aaron had had his first knock back aged six months by the infamous Joan Collins.

2017

The conference was over; it was time to go home. Three days with incredible people from all over the world doing something she loved, something she was passionate about. She'd barely slept with the long hours of the certification course and with the knowing that back in the UK her bank balance still read zero and she still had an uphill struggle ahead of her.

She'd called off their wedding and their relationship ten days prior to her (their) trip abroad to the USA, the recurring yo-yo of abuse too much for her otherwise unfluctuating way of living; settled and not in doubt. It hadn't been received well, but surprisingly it had become more matter of fact and less emotional between them, something Rei could deal with. There was of course the usual slinging of insults and accusations, blame and insinuations but each landed and was dealt with suitably. His flight was cancelled and refunded on claims of sickness, his half of the hotel bill paid back into his account, now it was just the reality of her being away without him. He would not look after her kids now he would be home but neither could the friend that Rei had organised to help whilst they were away, stay either. *He would be sleeping in their bed from now on, no one else.*

Rei reminded him that he had plenty of other options of places to stay that weekend and please could he let this arrangement continue, getting this qualification was a big deal, she knew it, he knew it. They both knew that right now he had the power. Suddenly seeing his kids was no longer important to him, the thing that had most probably driven them apart currently within the palm of his hand. Instead, he opened up his fingers and blew away the prospect, like a candle in the wind. Free, careless and wishing it so. The course now set rushing in to fill the space where before there was none.

Rei had forewarned her friend, given the kids strict instructions, packed her bag and gone on her way. The energy, the one coming through him, would not win. Not this time anyway.

~

She woke early and walked The High Line before the course commenced, she had exactly 90 minutes to explore the urban oasis and had worked out a loop that could work. As she waited for the gatekeeper to open the doors to the steps above and beyond a young man asked her for directions. He was American but not from *these parts,* his accent was unknown to Rei, it had a sweetness about it she hadn't heard before and as quickly as their conversation had begun, they found themselves knee deep, immersed in conversation walking the high-rise path together. Their conversation flowed like the lush vegetation grew; he was great company a perfect addition to the emerging and beautifully bloomed flowers and branches along the way. Rei appreciated her new companion and he was ecstatic at meeting Rei, he was open to all she had to say on life and everything she had to offer, it seemed her experiences in life thus far were there to support him at that precise moment in time. As Rei turned to say goodbye making the detour back to the offices he asked

Can I have your number? Would you mind if I took it in case I ever needed some support again? You've changed my life, literally; I cannot thank you or God enough.

Of course, Rei said, who still found herself shocked each time anyone professed to, or even spoke about God openly, and entered her digits into his mobile thinking nothing of it, waving to say goodbye.

~

The course had ended at 5pm and she had had to take her wheelie cabin suitcase with her when checking out of the hotel that morning. She had a few hours to kill before her flight home and she was determined to not give whatever was about to come in the future any space until such time she could actually deal with it.

She had met up with her dear friend from her Japanese days with his wife and friends the night before for dinner and they had recommended a restaurant nearby where Rei could hang and get a good meal inside her before her long trip back. Rei had gone easy on the details of her life situation with them but nonetheless they'd sensed she had a bit of a battle ahead and Tom offered to help her out should she need it. They had a close connection over many years now and Rei felt assured knowing there was someone, albeit it in a different country on the globe, that could help her out if she needed, knowing too it was pretty certain she would ever ask.

She walked up to the bar, suitcase in tow and asked if there was any chance of getting any food, she appreciated it was early but she had a flight to catch and could do with some good food before she left.

Of course, replied the barman, *what would you like?*

What do you recommend? she asked.

The oysters followed by the burger piped up the young guy propped up at the bar beside her.

He would know chipped in the waiter.

Oh really? asked Rei as the young man moved open the stool for her to take a seat beside him.

Thank you smiled Rei ordering the oysters and the burger, the exact same recommendation her friends had shared with her the night before.

As she waited for her food to arrive the conversation between the three of them flowed, it transpired the guy at the bar was catching the exact same flight out to London in three days time. He asked for recommendations of things to do, places to go. It seemed he was a bit of a party goer so Rei wasn't really the one to ask, but she offered what she could.

She was going to be in London working a couple of the days he would be there so they shared numbers in case she thought of or came across anything for him to do in the meantime. Unlike the guy from the previous morning Rei could detect this one flirting with her ever so subtly, not obviously, but she knew if she'd have made the move he would have been all over it and her. Quietly inside she was enjoying the fact that someone actually still found her attractive, appealing, exciting, delightful. Jack had told her on repeat that…

No-one will ever love you like I do

…and part of her had questioned whether he was right, perhaps they would not.

This moment in a New York bar reminded her that Jack's prediction wasn't necessarily true, she may not be in a relationship with someone, but there were people out there in the big, wide world that were open to being with her that could see the joy and love that she bought to the planet and that wanted more of it, not less of it. It didn't need to be contained, or mitigated, or censored even, just left to be the exquisiteness that it was.

~

She arrived home to the UK and the welcome was less disturbing than she imagined, the money still absent from their account, but any obvious bodily rage contained, like a Jack-put-back-in-the-box. Formalities attended to, Rei's focus was the kids and checking they were all ok, and that together as a unit they were solid.

Jack & Rei had already navigated the reality of having to still share the same bed at the moment with no spare rooms in the house and Jack's resolute standpatism on moving on and out meant that Rei and the kids had to work with and around what they had. The kids were heading into their final term and years of exams and there was nothing around on the rental market that supported them as a possible home. Besides this was *their* home.

As the evening drew in sleep was beckoning, not jet lagged but a body ready for regeneration, Rei undressed, perhaps putting on more clothes than she had worn during the day wanting to feel protected as best possible, and entered the bedroom. Jack was there awkwardly, standing, his frame enlarged by the window's light behind him; he had a habit of puffing out his chest and standing straighter than usual when he was trying to prove his part in it all, in this space, here and now. The garden behind looking formidable in the twilight, the shadowed frame before it a mere distraction from its beauty. Rei thought that she had got away with it, made the clear run, the passage from the bathroom to the bed without disturbance.

So how was it? he asked, a slight derision in the delivery.

It was really good, thank you Rei replied careful not to give away too much of a sense of the enjoyment she had in fact felt, she didn't want to incite any unnecessary aggravation.

How was your weekend? Did you manage to see the kids? she asked genuinely interested but also aware that she was walking a fine line and needed to appear interested but not invested, separate but not distant.
She didn't like this role it was exhausting, but she had lived with this tip toeing for years now, feeling so much, navigating the stormy seas taking refuge and respite when the winds dropped and the seas calmed before the next cyclone hit. Large waves and strong currents had become her norm, she was aware as swells surged and she knew the signs, could spot them well in advance, but nothing ever prepared her for the eye of the storm.

Did you meet anyone? he asked a little more inquisitive now, a little more engaged.

Of course, there were hundreds of people there, about five of us from the UK, and everyone else from all walks of life, all parts of the globe. She didn't want to say much more, she could sense the trap, smell the cheese.

Any men?

Ah! Here we go! thought Rei, it was never long before the venom was exposed, the real reason for the bite.

*There were a couple of guys there, in fact there were three of them, from America…*shared Rei happy that her answer could not provoke anything more *…two were gay and one guy married with kids* she felt it necessary to add as the silence loomed heavier around her descending like a thick fog in the dwindling light.

And outside of the course? Did you meet anyone? Any guys?

*F**** thought Rei!

She knew she was the worst liar *ever.* She hadn't done anything wrong on paper; she'd just spoken to a couple of guys. Yes, they'd exchanged numbers but nothing more than that. Time seemed to speed up, her second of hesitation felt like an hour in the spotlight, centre stage, the audience (him) hanging.

What are my options? she momentarily thought.

She knew he would see right through any lie and she knew he could tell if she deviated from the truth. More so she hated lying, despised it, had told herself on many occasions never to lie again, she wouldn't be able to live with herself.

I met a couple of guys she blurted out.

The chest puffed a little more. The clouds figuratively moved from expansive, borderless freedom outside in to the actual bedroom, caged and dark, in doing so their substance changed from lightness of form to burgeoning, fit to burst, oppressive and burdensome.

One when I was walking early morning and another in the restaurant before I got the plane home her voice and her words getting the better of her. She was trying desperately to downplay the situation, to let him know there was nothing to be concerned about, not that he had any right to be, but as every second passed the squall rose, higher and higher, deeper and deeper.

So did you get their numbers? he squirmed, seething like pus beneath the skin of a boil about to erupt.

*S***! This is it.* thought Rei.

Yes, but not like that, I helped them both out a bit and they wanted a bit of support potentially in the future; one of their sister's had committed suicide recently and the other guy is coming to England in a few days so wanted some suggestions of where to go, what to do - I wanted to ask you about that actually... she said trying to deflect away from her and bring him into the conversation. She could feel her temperature rising, feeling hot beneath the collar, she knew he had her cornered and that the red button had already been pressed. How long until detonation she wasn't sure, but it was coming.

Cool, if it was nothing like that, then let me see your phone he charged towards her lunging for her phone.

Now this was too much. *Enough!* thought Rei. She had said no to the wedding, said no to this oppressive controlling regime. She didn't need to live with it anymore. It was none of his business.

No, she said, retracting her hand, pulling her phone closer to her.

There is nothing on here that you need to see, nothing incriminating (which there wasn't) *I haven't done anything untoward, there is nothing to worry about or for you to be concerned by.*

She turned and got into bed clutching her phone and tucking it in beside her, both as a way to protect it and as a means to protect her. She knew he wasn't happy, but she also knew she hadn't lied to him as such. She hadn't *done* anything. She had got a kick out of the guy at the bar paying her some interest. Look where that had landed her. *Was it worth it?* she wondered as she nodded off to sleep, on edge but exhausted now.

Silly Girl.

It was 4.30am when he awoke, when he woke her up, a heavy thudding prod in her ribs.

Wake up! Let me see your phone. If you've got nothing to hide then let me see your phone…Now.

He already had her phone in his hands his whole body shaking violently with rage trying his hardest to conceal it. Caught off guard but now wide awake, Rei thought she may try the tired approach *Can we talk about this when I'm awake properly, please?*

No, I need to see it now, right now, before I go to work.

He wasn't leaving for work for another couple of hours at least, he just wanted proof and he wanted it this instant. Rei knew the simplest thing would be to hand it over to him on a golden platter, to watch the tide subside, but there was something inside that told her not to…not again! Not to give into the manipulative, controlling behaviour yet another time. What would be the point of walking away if you were left still living in the exact same way? It made no sense.

Babe, she urged (where did that come from, she asked herself? Habit she presumed) *Let it go, you know there's nothing there. I'm not going to give it to you, go back to sleep and we can talk about it all later.*

He was pacing the room, a caged bear, hungry, ready to rip to shreds anything thrown his way.

*If you don't open the f***ing phone right now I am going to put my sledgehammer to it…I mean, now. Right now!*

Go for it said Rei completely unshaken in her standpoint. *That would be a bit of a waste of money though, you won't have got what you want from it.*

She knew that was true, but she also knew he didn't give a flying f*** whether she had a phone or not, the more damage he could do the better, the more he could make her life difficult the more he felt he was winning, in control again. He stormed out of the room slamming the doors behind him for extra added effect. She heard the garage door open, his van bleep as he unlocked it, deactivating the alarm and then the back doors open. She knew his van inside out, she knew where he was reaching and she didn't like it.

Suddenly fearful she ran into the bedroom next door, her youngest son fast asleep serene and angelic as he was in his bamboo four poster bed white sheets blowing gently in the crisp, late summer breeze, closing the door behind her as silently as she could. She sunk into the wall behind the door, trying to disguise her breathing from the morning light, it was rapid and she thought it was loud, the silence around her deafening, even her heart beat seemed noisy, on full volume.

Time passed, she wasn't sure if it was quickly or slowly, she had no phone with which to check. She imagined walking out later, much later, once the coast was clear, to glass smithereens on the driveway, a sim card stolen and whisked away for detective inspection. She contemplated the possibility of three hours here, like this, and although cold and tired, it was definitely the place to stay, protected by a door with no lock and a sleeping angel. There was no way he would come in here like that.

As she was replaying what had just happened, slightly surprised by her own ability to stand up to that behaviour, the door slammed open. Not loud enough to wake Bodhi she was relieved to see but enough that her pounding heart jumped straight out of her mouth.

*Last chance. Open your f***ing phone* he said, in a slightly more hushed tone this time but exploding with fury nonetheless. Rei said nothing but held her finger to her lips as if to remind him they were in one of the kid's bedrooms and it was still officially night time, sleep time.

Shh! He's asleep.

That was it. Jack whisked her up by the neck and held her high enough slammed to the wall that her feet could barely touch the ground. The pressure unbearable around her throat. She tried to talk, tried to breathe, but nothing.

She considered her brother hanging from a rope, her (now) and his (then) eyes wide open, the whites never seen so clearly before. She tried to hit him, to stop him, but nothing.

This was the end she thought. She'd taken it too far. Once and for all.

*Get the f*** off!*
Get out!
Get out of my room. Now!

Rei had never heard Bodhi speak like that before, he was charging at Jack, defending his space, saving his mum from a potential death she should never have faced and one that she could never ever thank him for enough.

1981

Rei is carrying the bucket of feed down the garden, the goats Jemima and Gertrude waiting, looking longingly at their food being delivered by hand, the young girl, welly boots on, hand-me-down baggy jeans (two sizes too big) and a hand-knitted argyll jumper in Christmas colours, bobbing up and down joyously cantering towards them, as happy to see them, as they their food. Rei loved the goats, she loved having someone close, a living, breathing thing of the earth in her garden, in their shed. Every day there was purpose outside of herself, of looking after something and she loved it. Caring for things was an innate sensitivity, an acute awareness that Rei thrived with. As a family they also had a peep of chickens, a flock, a brood that lived in a man-made cage at the end of the garden. There were ten of them and each morning and night Rei and her dad would walk together hand in hand down to the pen to feed them, clearing up after them. It was perhaps the thing she looked forward to most in her days. She loved to be outside, to be in nature, out in the elements.

Aren't you cold? her mum would ask as Rei rushed in and out of the kitchen in her t-shirt holding the latest worm she'd found to show her. Her mum always squeamish at such things did not deter Rei, she wanted her mum to be included in the family fun. Later when they moved house, they would have a duck pond and two ducks, a he duck and a she duck, her mum liked them.

One early Saturday morning Rei and her dad were walking out of the back door ready to feed the *chooks* stopping off to feed Jemima and Gertrude on the way when their pace lessened…Rei looked up and across to her dad whose face had changed, who'd dropped hold of her hand, he was looking over towards the chicken coop.

What's wrong Dad? Where are the chickens? she begged.

I think the bugger has got in he exclaimed his pace quickening. They dropped the goat's feed and ran, Rei following in her father's footsteps, trying to keep up.

Go back inside and see your Mum he pointed slightly aggressively towards the house, shaking his head in disbelief. Rei not usually one to disobey orders was determined to see and know what was going on, *how could all the chickens have fled at once, together?* she wondered.

It's alright Dad, I want to see she exclaimed knowing full well he was trying to protect her in some way, defiant nonetheless.

Already in full flow her father did not rebuke her request and so Rei quickly caught up. She wished she hadn't. Thrown all over the floor were the chickens; it seemed all of them. There was no blood, no loose feathers, just deadness. So sad.

But why? Rei pleaded. It made no sense.

Sometimes foxes do that for fun he mumbled, clearly annoyed no longer trying to conceal it. *Bastards.*

Rei started to cry, she couldn't understand.

But don't they eat them? What's the point of just killing them? She couldn't let it go, silent tears falling from her face shrinking her woollen jumper.

I think they kill whatever prey they can whenever it is available, hoping they can come back and steal them away to eat later he replied.

So, he'll come back later? We will see him? questioned Rei.

She wasn't sure she wanted to see the fox in charge of such a heinous crime, but somehow, she could feel it was appeasing her dad, the thought of revenge, of retribution. They counted up the chickens; there were nine of them. They counted again to be sure, their bodies still warm, it had been a recent death which seemed to exacerbate the emotion; the closeness to saving them, yet the incapacity to do so. The neoteric act felt like an incentive to act, and act fast, like a detective hot on the case, hot on the heels of *the* criminal on the run.

Let's go, we might be able to find him, scare him away, deter him from ever coming back. The scoundrel! said Rei's dad.

And together they went across the fields behind their house, through the bushes and into the unknown.

It didn't matter that they would not find the fox, their chicken, or any signs of either along the way, what mattered was that they were together, on an adventure. This mournful eventuality would remain etched in Rei's memory for life, one of a handful.

A blend of sadness at the unnecessary death and a sense of belonging, of being needed, of being important to her dad.

1991

Rei was pulling back the wheels on the skateboard, edging them back a little further, hoping the tiny manoeuvres, these teeny movements would prepare her for the downwards slope ahead. She wasn't entirely sure why she continued to do this each time; the thrill was a little too close to the edge for her. She cared for her body, always had, and the thought of falling off the skateboard (albeit sat down on it) as it careered down the slope always gave her the shivers. But the two fingers up to the establishment by wearing down the heels on her school shoes having used them as skateboard brakes was worth it. It also meant that within a couple of downhill runs the shoes would be flattened, worn in as opposed to the torturous pain of wearing them in naturally over time. They were like clogs on her feet, they were nun's shoes, for children of God, poo brown, ugly, displeasing to the eye and on the body.

She edged rearwards holding her breath in anticipation. It was a steep slope followed by an immediate 90 degree turn right into the steps, or left into the front door which had a bit of a runaway escape lane before the wall commenced. If the heels didn't work then it would be straight slap bam into the glass door of the housemistresses office. Rei liked Sister Duncan, this outcome was not an option.

Off she set holding on to the rails for dear life her heart pounding. She took a turn to the left first, stopped and immediately bent over to examine her shoes.

Was it successful? Had it been worth the anxiety?

Yes!

The heels of her new shoes worn down excessively so on the left-hand corner of each, calling for a re-run to the right. Like their owner they needed to be symmetrical, inline, together, as one. Rei liked that. Since she was a little girl if ever she had bashed herself on her right elbow, she would immediately intentionally bash her left one to the exact same extent to balance it out. If she needed to rub her right eye, she would rub them both. She noticed no-one else did this and so tried to disguise her obvious strangeness, bizarrely apparent that she was up to something, tripping over her right foot to stabilise and equilibrate the left.

She ran back up the hill, skateboard under her arm pleased with herself and her achievements thus far. She never considered where the skateboard came from, who's it was, where it was kept? It remained a mystery and considering the girls had no access to anything else throughout term time it was a complete anomaly that it even existed, but she was pleased it was so and was adamant she would make good use of it whilst she had access to it. Confidence boosted, this time she sat down and took off immediately, aware that the dilly dallying at the top of the slope was worse than the reality of any other part of the ride.

Success! The right-hand corners of her shoes were sheered to insignificance too now. A couple more times straight up and down and she would be done, she took a deep breath in, it was nearly over.

As she walked back up, she saw the girls flocking back in from the right. The school coach had dropped them off halfway round the back end of the school, an unusual occurrence as the meeting and drop-off point was always at the front of the school. It *looked* good that way. That was her first question.

How come you got dropped off here? she asked interested but also a little perturbed for the answer as to why the unusual break of protocol.

They said we deserved it for being so good. Such a gooooood group! they all cheered in unison it seemed, high in spirit, smiles across their faces, their bodies bouncing up and down as one. Rei couldn't quite put her finger on it but it was as if they'd all turned into robots marching the same march to the same beat, there was something about them that felt different than when they'd left a few days ago, but she guessed that was just her, she was the anomaly, the *off* one. It had been said. They all knew it.

Rei remembered her First Holy Communion well (well maybe only a little), she had been in year six at primary school and it was the first time she actually got a new dress just like everyone else. She didn't actually really remember anything else about that day, other than having her photo taken in her new long handmade white dress with matching white satin ribbon around her. But she had remembered that much.

When at secondary school in Year IV they were told that as an extra-curricular activity and in line with the religious teachings, their year would be preparing to take their Confirmation next year. It wasn't posed as a question. It was what was expected of them. Somewhere deep within Rei was a sense that this was not true, not for her anyway. She spoke to the nuns about it, and said that she thought she'd quite like to sit this one out, to watch what was going on before she committed to anything. She knew this was a lie, there was not a skerrick of her that wanted anything to do with it, she was testing the boundaries, feigning interest when there was none. She was told in no uncertain terms that this was not an option, it was compulsory not voluntary and to get on board quick or else she'd fall behind and would find herself in trouble.

There was no need for contemplation on this one.

No said Rei sitting on the side of the room a-part from the rest, an invisible line drawn between them. The nuns not used to disobedience clearly caught off guard carried on, (pretending) as if nothing had happened, hoping that something would change, that Rei would realise the error of her ways and join the group once more. Unsure what would happen next, Rei sat knowing there was no other option for her, there was no questioning of herself, or preparing herself for the trouble she knew she would be in. For the first time ever, her own choice didn't disturb her, not one iota. She soon found out what was next as she was frogmarched to the Headmistress's Office and told quite clearly that

No-one, Not One person since the founding of the school in the early 17th Century had had the audacity to claim that they would not be confirmed, and did she realise what she was doing?

She would no longer be party to any weekend activities, no longer be able to go on the associated retreat, no longer have access to all the other students in her year for the next two years every time they were preparing for their Confirmation? Is this what she wanted?

Unperturbed Rei left the office, a deep knowing within her body that there was no other way.

~

It was now a good twelve months into the Confirmation process and her year group had all been away on a three-day retreat, she had gotten used to the leprosy effect that came on strong particularly at the start of the process every time they left busy with all things Confirmation; it didn't really touch her, but she could see it affected them. Some of her friends admitted they were jealous of her, wishing they didn't have to go either, but they knew their parents wanted it this way, they didn't feel like it was a choice they had. Sometimes Rei felt pretty glad that her parents didn't seem to care about her in that way. She was left to her own devices, dropped off at school at the beginning of term, collected at the end and mildly considered sometimes during part of the school holidays. Her other friends would speak to their parents most nights receiving phone calls in or calling home with their pre-paid phone card; they would receive letters or parcels full of tuck; and they would go home at the weekends and during the holidays to spend time together as a family. It was a different world to the one Rei had experienced thus far. Today the girls congregated around Rei as they piled out of the coach sitting down together on the front of house lawn. As they started to recount tales of what they had been up to over their days away Rei felt surprisingly glad she hadn't been involved. The girls started talking about Martina who had been *speaking tongues.*

It was ammaaahhhaaaziiing!!

Rei asked what *tongues* was and when they responded giving an imitated example, she wished she hadn't. It sounded like gobbledygook to her and the way the girls were contorting their bodies disturbed her, eyes vacant and possessed. In fact, there was something quite scary and sinister about it she thought to herself.

Cool she said, not sure if she'd gotten away with it, aware she didn't need to exclude herself any more than she already was, keeping her views to herself.

It felt lonely (but good at the same time) she thought, no longer looking for God in all the wrong places. She knew he wasn't here at school, or in the churches she'd been to as a child. It seemed to Rei that this thing called religion sucked.

She didn't believe in it, and she was closing the file on God now too.

2002

He may as well have been speaking Russian. She understood not the words that came out from his mouth, yet her whole body surrendered deep to a place she knew but hadn't felt for a very long time, not this life anyway that was for sure.

The people around her in the dark basement of the London church nodding in understanding, like they knew what he was talking about. The words flying over Rei's head like a jumbo in the night sky, not visible but known.

She was home.

Not just with her heart this time,
but with her w h o l e body,

her soul.

After the acid tab there were no more experiments with pleasure from outside of herself. She had entertained them, tried them on for size, three times now, but they gave her nothing in return. She'd got a short buzz from the ecstasy she'd tried a couple of times but nothing else, and the acid trip had been horrific dealing with Ethan and his psychotic reaction to it, three days later he was still reeling from it both pathetic and dangerous in his allergic responses, a threateningly dangerous concoction. Her heart remained untouched, she loved no less, felt no less around her, but felt oh so much more in her body now wrecked from the collision, the train crash. *What a self-inflicted punishment!* She wondered why she'd even bothered trying, she hadn't really wanted to, she knew drugs wouldn't deliver the goods, and what's worse she'd paid good money and now time (as her body groaned to catch up) for the pleasure.

In an attempt to not feel everything she was feeling, the reality that although happy on the outside she was still deeply unsettled within, and not knowing how to deal with it, how to change it all, to get rid of the tension she felt unremittingly so, she had lowered herself to depths otherwise not anywhere near her radar. As a young woman at university, she had done similar, knowing it wasn't necessary yet somehow drawn to participate to make sure that what she thought she could feel was true, actually was.

She had only had one relationship with James which had lasted five and a half years, so other than her first teeth banging snog in the depths of Le Palais, multiple kisses with an Italian Stallion and a smooch with a sexy Frenchman, by the age of twenty-two she was comparatively pure and untouched. The people around her not so much.

In a world free of internet, mobile phones and laptops it was only really those around you that shaped your views and perceptions on life. Sure, she had a strong inner compass but with everyone and everything else around her suggesting that she had it wrong and they were leading the way, and with no role models or people guiding her way, it seemed almost inevitable that she needed to try their ways of doing things on for size. She knew of people with a new bed mate every day and night of the week, she'd met people that had already slept with hundreds of people, who thought nothing of bed hopping whenever, wherever. She had housemates that cheated on their partners multiple times with less than a drunken excuse. That was the norm. Rei was the exception, not the rule. She wondered if she was missing out, missing a trick or two.

One evening with an unyielding fervour she set out with her friend determined to have *a one-night stand*. They rocked up at the bar early, already a new experience for Rei who would only usually be found out on a Wednesday night having watched the latest episode release of ER on Channel 4. Meeting her already plastered flatmates, who drunk away their student loans, she would drink water and hit the club's dance floor. That was how she rolled, simple and effortless.

With little to no appetite for alcohol or doing anything to her body which left her feeling out of control or open to the elements and paying her own way through university, two student loans down (a third on its way) and three jobs on the go, drinking water and frequenting free entry events was the norm. She was an *early to bed, early to rise* kind of gal and it suited her this way.

Tonight was going to be different though, she'd dressed up like everyone else usually did, and was visiting a bar with the sole purpose of buying a drink and at some point that evening finding a man…but only for the night.

They piled into the already crammed bar packed to the rafters of businessmen it seemed. They'd come so early that the uni students were probably still half asleep in bed and these guys had all just piled out of work desperate to forget their day. It seemed like too much of a waste to turn around and go home and what was more Rei was determined to experiment with a clandestine meeting, a booty call, a hookup, meaningless, promiscuous sex (maybe) just the once.

They edged towards the bar, pushing their way through the crowd. As their bodies squeezed through and past the stampede Rei caught sight of a suited man smiling sweetly at her, his eyes twinkling. He stood out like a diamond in the rough, the smell of beer permeating the air and already sticky beneath their feet. Rei smiled back and found her place at the bar.

Jostling back to her friend two lagers in hand they scanned the room and the outside space looking for the one, the victim for tonight's endeavours. They were losing momentum, there was no one around who fitted the bill; attractive, rugged, (not weird), and giving off the *don't give a shit but want to get laid* vibe that was frequently on full display in such establishments. Not prepared to give up just yet they ordered another beer; this was proving harder and more expensive than Rei had expected or anticipated. *How did people do this regularly on repeat?* she contemplated as she surveyed the scene once more desperate to finish what she'd begun and get home, back to the safety and comfort of her flat.

They ended up in their usual hangout on a Friday night rather than the *Free Wednesdays* Rei was used to. It didn't feel the same queuing and paying for entrance to dance on the soiled, grimy, tacky, glue-like discotheque, but they did it nonetheless. Rei had long given up on her quest for the evening, two hours in and the seeming effort, like a hawk locating prey, surpassed any need or desire for anything that had been there before. She was hoping for some good tunes through the speakers, some non-murky (but knew it would be) water in a plastic cup and some banging beats to dance to. She found her way to the bar and as she sidled up, she found herself next to old twinkle eyes and his mates.

Hello he said, wide eyed and surprisingly sober. *How are you?*

His smile disarming and settling all at one.

They got talking and didn't stop.

Rei never made it to the dance floor, but she and he made it home to her flat for the one-night stand that never was.

1986

Rei shunts across the kitchen floor, pretending it doesn't hurt, trying hard not to scream any louder anymore, the pain debilitating.

What happened exactly? her mum asks, concerned more so than perhaps before, Rei's arm hanging from its socket, limp and already turning green. Rei had always bruised easily just like Natasha Beddingfield sang…*so be gentle.*

I was running home and then two boys started chasing after me so I jumped the rail and tripped and fell on my arm.

She didn't dare tell the truth. She had been skipping home from the shops *happy as Larry* in her own little world, humming, singing out loud and dancing, truly content within herself. She had been jumping the rails but not because of anyone else, just because she could. She normally was adept at pacing herself, of knowing distances and heights, she could do it with her eyes closed, but today not so it appeared.

She re-ran the tape recording in her mind, one minute fine the next minute not, one second up the next down. She remembered looking behind her as soon as she could from the grassy floor, firstly to see what had happened who had pushed her, but as soon as she realised there was no one else there she turned to check no-one had seen her fall…All by herself.

How embarrassing. She felt stupid. Silly.

Silly girl.

She was sure someone, something had pushed her but there was no evidence, no proof, just the pudding. A ten-year-old girl excited to be at the end of the summer term ready to go on the school trip with her best friends tomorrow. Like *reallyyyeee* excited.

Her ability to act strong was waning, she knew she'd done something bad, irreparable and she knew tomorrow's school trip was looking highly unlikely. She'd been waiting for this all term. Her best friend Kiera Black and her were going to sit together on the coach, both there, and back!

The tears welling up in her eyes, Rei holding back the dam, the pressure building.

I'm fine she said convincing no-one, not even herself.

Can I just lay down for a bit? she asked half way to the sofa, trying to hide the shock clearly exuding from her body,

I'll be fine, I just need to sit down for a minute.

She went to sit as she usually would, banging her arm which was hanging a good few inches lower than normal, mad at herself for not being more careful. The pain now excruciating, the screams returning, her mum fetching a cold flannel for her head.

Crrr (or was that grrr), *let's get you to hospital, that doesn't look right!*

She knew it was an inconvenience for her mum to drive her that's why Rei was doing the shopping from the parade of shops on the main road around the corner in the first place. She didn't like the fact that her mum was being put out because of her, because of what she'd done. Rei knew she was tired; she always was, she worked long hours in a job in town and she made sure the girls knew about it, and they did. She suffered really bad migraines, was frail of spirit and weak of heart (Rei thought but didn't like to really admit to herself or anyone else).

~

Her mum never came to the school gates, Rei had always walked herself to and from school, and as her sister grew older, she would walk her too, dropping her off at the childminder on the way home. It was cheaper that way. Rei had asked her mum once a long time ago why she never came up to school remembering she said

She felt out of place, like everyone was talking about her. That she had nothing in common with any of them.

Rei could feel the pain and torment within her mum, she could feel how embarrassed she was barely having enough money to scrape by, let alone keep up with The Joneses, not that there were any Joneses in their sleepy Berkshire town anyway. Her mum's notebook and pencil out each evening, working out the expenses in her mind, on the paper, ferociously scrubbing out and rewriting the penny changes here and there, lists upon lists of numbers, of calculations that probably cost more to do than they saved.

Now because of Rei's *accident* they would be using unnecessary fuel, causing unnecessary wear and tear on the car. Rei knew these things (she had to). It was because of her. Because she had been happy. *What was she thinking skipping along, singing out loud? Look at what she'd done!*

The doctor in the hospital asked the same question pointing to her arm, he didn't have to touch it to know. *So, how did you do this little girl?*

I slipped and fell when I was walking home, she replied already knowing not to mention that she'd been out getting the shopping by herself, omitting the railings part too. They sounded dangerous. Nor did she mention the boys that didn't really exist, it may be misconstrued that they lived in a rough area. Rei knew exactly what everyone was thinking and what they wanted to believe, she had already learnt to dodge the bullets, *taking one for the team* at every juncture. Anything she could do to help her mum from the misery she felt day in day out. She was also acutely aware that anything might be used against her mum, incriminating evidence for a later (any) date. She was used to war, used to games, tactical, analytical and devastating, two sides, two opponents, teams of varying numbers, one against the other. Rei wasn't sure how exactly she knew these things but she did having observed life play out for others around her, watching and learning as they went about their ways. She was acutely aware of them. She read everything, was the grown up in life, of the situation, taking it all on as hers. She the parent, her mum the child. She wasn't sure she'd had a childhood, she thought she'd been born and then been fast-forwarded to the future-her once she hit five years old.

You've dislocated your shoulder and fractured your elbow, shattering the bones into tiny pieces said the doctor with a furrowed brow. *What hand do you use to write?* he asked.

My right she replied.

She considered telling him that she had originally used her left when she was little until she was made to change it at her first primary school. Not this one that she was at now, the one before in the village they used to live in many miles and counties away. She had been told it was wrong and it needed to be changed. And so, she did, and this is how it was that she wrote with her right hand now, not her left, a punishment for something that had needed correction. *Bad Girl. Naughty Girl.* But on reflection she thought this might add fuel to any potential fire and so kept quiet.

Hmm. Well, you're going to find this difficult for quite some time I'm afraid. Your arm is going to be in a sling for six weeks whilst your bones try and heal themselves. Because of the fracture we cannot operate or do anything to help. You're going to have to rest up for a few days, and no more walking home, okay? his eyebrows raised as he spoke with that knowing look.

The tears already in full flow *But I can still go on my school trip tomorrow, right?*

No lass, I'm afraid you're going to have to sit this one out. You're going to be in a lot of pain whilst you get used to this and you can't have anyone nearby that may accidentally bang you. It can delay and disrupt the healing process and we'd have to start all over again. Chin up, there'll always be next year!

Rei knew this wasn't true, this was the last year, the last school trip and the last week of term. Not only would she be missing the trip but the end of year, of school, forever. The dam burst open, her heart aching, knowing she would never see her friends again. Ever.

She didn't remember the journey home, or the six weeks that followed. She knew that what was before the broken arm was *then*, and what was after, *now.*

A whole new (unwanted, unprepared) boarding school world.

2024

The water plummeting downwards for 260 feet, 13,000 cubic meters of water per second. The noise present but not deafening; the spray stunning, glistening with rainbow arcs caught in the sun's rays, reflecting back to the crowds the magnificence and magic of it all. 275 individual waterfalls colliding into one, hurling themselves over the cliffs edge *Devil's Throat.* Rei & Gabriel spellbound by its magnificence.

The flora and fauna of the rainforest that they had been enjoying on their walk up through the National Park paling into insignificance next to the sheer volume of water around them. The natural wonder a reminder of the amplitude of their love, of how they were loved and of the love around them.

It was the perfect confirmation of their union. A moment in time that could never be erased.

Seeing and feeling the waves and torrents of the cascades, one could not even begin to entertain the brokenness of the waterfall. All paths led to this one point. No matter the meandering, no matter the distance travelled, they all arrived together, at once and from that point forward they served as one.

No droplet escaped the fall, they all survived, unified and stronger together on the other side.

One.

2013

The silence that followed his death gave way to the echoes of people and their thoughts, of thoughts from the underworld, dark, menacing, blaming, manipulative and suppressing.

Struggling to swallow the actuality of events Rei asked to see his body. Her dad suggested otherwise, it would not be a pretty sight. Rei momentarily considered the burning, straining rope marks around his neck, *would his eyes have popped out under the strain, the force, the pressure?* She wasn't sure, but she also knew she could not go on without seeing him, it still didn't seem real. She *had* to see him, in whatever state, to be able to close the door on this, for herself.

The undertakers were on the way to the church where Olli's service was being held. Rei knew she had to wake up earlier to make the journey down, giving extra space in case she lost it emotionally and needed time to collect herself and regroup. She was doing a reading during the service and she knew she had a responsibility to hold it together for everyone; her sisters, her dad, her kids and the hundreds of people that would be there.

~

They wheeled his body in, frozen in time and frozen to the touch Rei soon realised as she put her hand out to hold his face as she so often would speaking so dearly and tenderly to someone so close.

She had only seen one dead body before, the oboe teacher's at school. Being a prefect Rei had to sit at the front of the chapel on the individual stalls that flanked the aisle immediately in front of the decadent altar, in view of all. The body was bought in, open casket, and placed immediately next to Rei. She had felt weird, she wanted to peer inside, to take a proper look, but couldn't, all eyes on her, she knew the conventions, the etiquette it was screaming at her, rimming her from all sides. She angled her body as casually as she could, glancing over her hymn book pretending she was reading the type cast on the page and sang to the organ's chorale, the words imprinted subconsciously within having sung them so many times before.

She hadn't felt much from her glances around the school chapel that day, other than there was a lot of sadness, not just from the people within the building itself which had opened its doors to the public for the ceremony, but from the deceased herself. Rei could feel the different genres of grief both fiction and non-fiction; biographical, historical, fantasy, academic, self-help, even romantic. She had never stopped to entertain and ascertain the various types of sadness but it seemed that a long and drawn-out service was just the place to do so;

unhappiness,
sorrow,
dejection,
misery,
depression,
regret,

desolation,
despondency,
despair,
grief,
woe,
gloom,
melancholy,
heartache,
wretchedness,

…all different flavours of the same ice cream, a dessert rich in destitution leaving the recipient of these emotions battered by their turmoil.

She was bought back to life and reality as the congregation stood for the final hymn, Rei contemplating the scene around her wondering

Was this what it, life, was all about?

~

As she stood beside her chilled and frigid frame of a brother, she couldn't have felt clearer. She'd had a relationship with him for twenty-three years now, she knew who he was, she knew the essence of him. This, that was beside her, in front of her, was not him. There was nothing of *him* left. Yes, the veneer appeared the same (just about) but *he* was gone. Long gone.

It confirmed what she knew to be true, that his soul had already left. All that remained was the carcass of him. She could say goodbye now. She hadn't wanted him to go anywhere but he had.

He would be back.
He'd been tricked into thinking this was the easy way out.

What a crime. It would get worse before it got any better.

Rei walked back to her car with the kids, no tears, merely shaken by the simplicity of the truth of it all. She somehow felt more complete now. Any gaps left within herself would be revealed, a rich feeding ground for grief to grow.

Rei would hold his hand feeling the depth of the universes, the potency of their connection. She needn't imagine the necessity for stars to collide, nor the beating of a drum roll to signify the approval of their amalgamation from anyone outside of herself. They were already in the presence of the blessing each and every day. It was what they moved, what they lived, from day dot. Every time they met they would stand opposite one another holding hands looking deep into each other's eyes. Time around them frozen. Still. Nothing was as important as being truly seen, heard, met and at One, all without a single word being spoken. After that anything could be dealt with. Clarke Kent & Louis Lane each taking turns at leading and being in the background, whatever was needed from them.

Rei had spent all of her life doing things alone, or not in true, equal connection and partnership with another, doubt plaguing any opportunities of healing these patterns and moving forward from them in the past. Up until now. The past was in the past; she could let that way of being go now. As Simba in The Lion King had so wisely been shown ...*you can either run from it, or learn from it.* Yes, he'd been hit over the head with a wooden stick and it had hurt, but any emphasis or dwelling further on it was unproductive. *There was work to be done!* The same went for Rei, she had already learnt the principles of this lesson but realised that genuinely putting them into practise may have been a different matter. There could be no slither or percentage of protection or hardness being drawn in. She knew if she did it could be the end of the everything she had been gifted. Anyway, she realised she didn't even need to think like that anymore, it was completely unnecessary. Rei didn't need to be in protection, she had someone by her side who backed her all the way, who didn't impose, and who deeply honoured, cherished and adored her every way. She no longer needed to hold the whole world on her shoulders; she didn't need to go shopping when the shops were closing for the yellow sticker end of day deals; she didn't need to pace herself to be able to deal with everything that came her way, fighting off the herds single-handedly. She had already traversed these paths, lived this life, was out through the other side, only this time she had a husband, a divine one at that.

Rei was understanding more and more the power of all that she could sense, which to her was as simple as breathing.

She could feel his sensitivity too, like a deer in a field alert to any movements not in true harmony, and she loved that; he offered her a different reflection, took her deeper in unexpected ways. Together they were surrendering in ways neither had ever done before. True it was a healing for them both beneath the surface, but so much more was on offer for them.

There is and was always more.

Just as Rei had once looked at Ethan and his home life wondering how he could ever not have questioned what was going on, she realised there were entire chapters of her life that she herself had either hidden deep under lock and key, or that she knew little to nothing about. She knew her history was vague but had never asked more, never enquired. She was beginning to realise the reality of the situation for most; that they either actively did not want to or chose not to see. Or that they were so blindsided into submission by the forces around them, that the truth neither could, nor would, be revealed to them. She knew when she could ask something freely, and she definitely knew when she could not.

It was becoming clearer that it was the latter that was the most frequent offering. Instead of speaking up she had retracted becoming mute if anything. No wonder her recurring nightmare as a child screaming out loud with no sound. She actually had so much to say, she was reading everything around her, yet she knew no-one really was asking to hear about it. In a world where everyone points the finger at another without looking at what's going on within their own four walls, she saw the demand being circulated. People paying high prices to take the spotlight off of themselves. It was much easier to tut under one's breath, shake a head and raise an eyebrow at Billy down the road shagging his next-door neighbour than to look at the lovelessness within their own relationships. It was more comfortable questioning and bitching about the decision making of the guys in charge of the company than looking at all the lackadaisical ways in which they, the employees worked. It was rife everywhere, it was like everyone had blinkers on, moving like zombies in a film. Bodhi was formidable in his ability to see through it all, to know the truth and to not hold back. He would not entertain any of it and Rei admired that in him. She could see she had bought him and all the kids up in a safe space in that respect, allowing them to feel and express what was there; she hadn't stifled that, she had actively encouraged it. There was much she appreciated about her parenting but she still carried a guilt around all the things she hadn't done well, all the things she could have done better, much better. *What a bunch of silly choices that harmed so many people all around her, so unnecessarily.*

Silly woman.

Why hadn't she reached deep within and pulled it all out, pulling up the rot that weighed her down like an anchor to the deepest seas? Why hadn't she exposed it all at the time, truly gone there into the out-of-bounds, *do not enter, guard dogs present* world? If she had bought it all to the surface right from the start she could have spared themselves of all this post-cause play out, that she now bore responsibility for. A dead weight around her neck. She hadn't tried to hurt anyone, but she realised she had. She knew that now and she pledged never to do that again.

2002

Rei had spent years searching for the answer to her (non-religious) prayers, looking for home, (*the*) true home. She had rummaged through and to the end of cookie packets, scoured the globe, checked the labels on different goods of varying prices, surveyed nature, analysed (hers and others) bodies, steeplechasing life and its wares.

She no longer needed to explore; she was no longer lost.

Much that you seek has now been found. Search no more. Dive deep within to access all the glory now bestowed upon you in my Kingdom.

She was already full!
For real?
Already a diamond…?

In the rough maybe, but that was it.

There was nothing to do, much to undo. A bit of extraction here, some separation there, a few rounds of cleaning and sorting brushing off the false accumulated layers and imposter dust that was in the way of her shining bright, exploding in the universe.

It seemed like too good a deal to be true. Little did she realise how incarcerated she had actually become.

1994

Rei and James set off for Thailand, their first adventure past Europe, past Turkey. Their bank balances full from six months of working where and when they could, he predominantly in the law firm and her in the country pub. She'd met people she would never have otherwise moved in the same circles with, and she had learnt a lot about the people that frequented such establishments and the *why* behind it. Landing in Bangkok was another level of eyes wide opened. Some places and the people that had visited them felt lonely, the pub had been one of them the church too, now it was in every back corner and every street alley. She saw girls behind glass screens holding number cards, and wondered *Why?*

She asked and she was told.

She saw girls shoot ping pong balls from their vaginas, and wondered *Why?*

She did not dare to ask; it came into the *best left to the imagination* category.

They were mauled through the street markets their blonde hair causing a stir amongst the locals. The smells infusing wafts of grilled meats with aromas of garbage and sewers, the heat and the humidity adding to the acrid decaying food and pungent exhaust fumes causing sensory explosions. She was tired and overwhelmed, her senses had never been so heightened on every level, it was all new to her, to them.

They went back to their room and slept a deep sleep, their first experience of jet lag and strange foreign cultures, of obvious prostitution and of lonely men on the prowl.

Tâo-rài? How much? they would ask.
Short time, long time? they could hear echoing the streets.

The sleep was hot and sweaty and full of dreams, of smells and noises, of tastes and of sights, the seen and the unknown yet to explored. It was day one of the 150 nights away ahead of them; maybe she would get a girl guide badge after all she mused, slightly shell shocked by the prospect of the seven new countries ahead of them.

1984

There are places that smell like sleaze, this was one of them; the vending machine, the unmaintained chipped painted railings, the wet braids falling down the girls' backs drenching their off the shoulder t-shirt ever so, and the ogling men. The Man.

She walked the path up to the front entrance of the leisure centre, the hallway busy with families, some to swim, some to play badminton and table tennis, others to join birthday parties. It was the weekend and Rei was here for the latter. She was excited as this was the first party she'd been allowed to go to. Her friend Jessica Mannion's sister was ten today and Jessica had been allowed to bring a friend to keep her company, she had chosen Rei. As she wasn't strictly going as a birthday guest there was no present to buy, the family were paying for her entry fee and so with the *free* pass Rei was able to go. She couldn't have been more happy.

The smell hit her on her walk in, it permeated the air. She was only eight years old and didn't know what sleaziness was but she could detect it. Her body felt awkward, she wanted to contract somewhat, and internally she definitely shifted a key or two. But not to let anything stand in the way of her first real life birthday party she bounded in nonetheless, excited to see everyone dressed up, by an ice rink too! She'd never seen one of them before.

It was an ice-skating party and she was going to get to have a go. She found the Mannion family and the assembly of excited girls almost immediately, a chill enveloping her body. Yes, there was a sense of cold from the rink the other side of the plastic shield but it was more than that, she had the shivers inside, something was afoot.

Going to collect their skating boots from the reception block the girls parted company from the parents, some going for the obligatory pee before starting out on the next venture.
Rei could see shadows, perhaps less than she could feel them.

Eyes too.

On them,

the girls.

She moved closer still to Jessica Mannion, almost in her pocket now, the excitement of the party quickly turning to an alertness, an insecurity. She hadn't been briefed on the emergency exits by any air stewardesses; the escape routes were not clear. What was, was the mass of people congregating everywhere, the temperature rising, the capacity for bacterial growth growing exponentially. Like fire needing oxygen, heat and fuel it seemed all the elements were pointing towards an inevitable combustion. Pretty young girls in party stupor, dirty old men in sleazy meandering hazes, and a complete oblivion to energetic reading and discernment by all and everyone else to what was really going on around them. Together they were a match made in paedophile heaven.

Rei spotted a man, whose moves were out of sync with the dance wanting to play in her body; his rhythm moving to a different beat, moving fast as the maestro conducts slow, slowing as the starting pistol fires. He stood out like a not so friendly BFG *(Big Friendly Giant)* in amongst the crowd.

Rei's body decided all by herself that she would no longer be trying to ice-skate, it felt threatening and ice-cold, dangerous and un-safe. She told the parents she was scared of getting her fingers run over and sliced off by the other skaters if she fell which inevitably she would when they asked *Why the sudden change in heart?* It was true, but she didn't dare say she was scared of *one* man over there that she didn't even know, that wasn't even looking at her in particular.

She stood shivering on the inside the temperature plummeting, the noise of the crowd rising. She tried to watch the girls on the ice rink having fun but could not settle. The fair-weather cumulus forming over and around them, the Saturday happy-go-lucky vibe rising like a current, a thermal under the hyperbolic paraboloid, the cloudy atmosphere transparent in its blocking of the light, the sun, the warmth, the day, as it welcomed instead the following act…depths and darkness of sleaze.

As if a half time whistle had been blown, the girls came crashing in from the rink and off onto the bleachers. *It was a shame bleachers didn't bleach* thought Rei who had already grown accustomed to the powers of this agent. She knew it was a robust, potent, strapping kind of chemical compound that could kill almost anything, especially bacteria and contamination, she wondered if it could work to dispel and prevent the spread of human diseases such as perversity and waywardness? She doubted not.

She would call them *the stands* then, just like everyone else. She stood in *the stands* observing the girls happy and charged from their dancing and falling and merriment on the ice wishing she could have at least tried to join in. She was looking pathetic now, everyone knew it, she knew she would never be invited to another party again. Even when it was free, hinderance free, she somehow managed to mess it up for everyone.

Silly, Poor, little girl.

The girls pulled off their boots desperate for the loo, leaving them behind under the parent's surveillance, with Rei whose feet were firmly concreted to the spot. Silence around her, the parents now given up on trying to coax her into joining them, any of them. There were only forty minutes left to go of the party now anyway. Everyone could heave a huge invisible sigh of relief.

The time for them to return seemed to drag, Rei needed the loo herself but could not move, she guessed she would sit it out 'til the end. The parents intimating the girls must have got caught up at the vending machines or in the queue for *the ladies*. Rei never understood the queue for *the ladies* nor the smell or the dirtiness that seemed ever present no matter which *ladies* you were in. She always wanted to get in and out as fast as was humanly possible. Today the wait seemed to linger, longer than expected. Even if every single one of the girls had done a poo one after the other and then washed and dried their hands too, it seemed an implausible length of time, she wasn't convinced that's what was happening. She stayed mute waiting like a silent soldier on guard watching over the boots and the benches.

We won't have time for the cake at this rate! she heard Jessica Mannion's mum say to her dad. *Go let them know Jake.*

Off Jake went a little rushed, quicker than his usually leisurely pace, towards *the ladies.* He came back with a handful of the girls but not Jessica Mannion's sister.

Where is she? asked her mum.

I don't know, I couldn't see her and I can hardly go in myself.

Wait there! she paced, half running towards *the ladies.* Ten minutes passed. Rei knew because Jake had told her, under his breath. *What is she doing? It's been ten minutes already!*

Uncomfortable with a group of ten-year-old girls wanting to get back on the ice rink, wanting to know where the birthday girl was and also now waiting for a slice of the promised cake, he was pacing like a caged animal himself. It was as if the tide changed all at once, and suddenly in one wash everyone was on board. *Where is Olivia? Where has her mum gone?*

Where there had been high spirits now there were none. No-one had said anything, no-one had done anything, but it had all changed. Rei felt like the fulcrum of the seesaw watching everyone around her go up and then down, up and then down, connected to them yet neither side of the balancing act. She always felt steady and mono-tonal in life, more comfortable staying away from the dramas the Shakespearian tragedies and comedies. She was happy to run from those. The onomatopoeia *see saw* somehow symbolic, *she saw, she saw*. The reduplication of the word interchangeable, necessary *he saw, he saw.*

It was one the policemen would be asking them all in the cold of the ice rink's spectator stands hours later.

Rei understood why they were called *stands* now. She was on stand, a witness testifying under oath. It made sense.

Bleachers definitely weren't the right name.

Stands most definitely were.

2013

If only Rei had known this would be their final day together perhaps, she would have done something differently, spent less time with the wedding procession, more time with him. She watched him play with Bodhi carrying him on his shoulders, running with the kids through the grass across the freshly mowed and manicured lawn, guests dressed immaculately and splendidly for the August wedding, an amazing uncle to great kids. She had to watch most people, keep an eye on them, or guide or encourage the kids to be with them, but never with him. It just was.

It was *their* dad's wedding his third; the first producing Rei and her sister, the second him and his sister, and now the third gaining a brother and a sister. The family was growing, all well together, blended but split by distance and age, that was all.

They left slightly early, Aaron feeling ill and needing a bed, saying goodbye as every other time, huge hugs and lots of love.

~

A month later on his birthday Rei, the queen of remembering people's birthdays, forgot until late in the day. She felt awful. To make matters worse the family had all been meeting up nearby for the day and Rei *couldn't make it,* too tied up in the ugliness of her relationship with Jack. She was withdrawing from her friends, from her family, she had no poker face, was too embarrassed to be seen this way, living like this. She guessed people could see through her as easily as she could read them and so retracted. A woman who loved people was becoming isolated on a self-made, (wo)man made island with high walls and no windows.

She sent a message full of the love she had for him, knowing inside she was failing. It was a sickening feeling to be living a lie, unable to do the things she really wanted to do, felt to do. She didn't even call, she knew he'd know and ask her how she was, she didn't want to lie or pretend, not to him, and so she made it so that she didn't have to.

It was all about her and protecting everyone from the mess she had made and was making. It ate at her that she was manipulating her life around a cover up that she wasn't wholly enjoying; in parts she was, in parts it seemed great, like *The Little Girl Who Had A Little Curl ~ when it was good it was very very good and when it was bad it was horrid.*

The times it was good she counted in time. Every month there was a minute or two more *good* than the last. *Progress* (she kidded herself). She'd spent so much time and effort, invested so much in this relationship she couldn't give up on it. She had something to prove to herself to all the others, the naysayers. She didn't want to be wrong; she didn't want to fail at *another* relationship; she knew what a true relationship was. She knew she could do it. She thought she was giving him space to grow, to evolve. In reality she was saying *Go ahead treat me like sh**. I have no boundaries, no real self-love. I can talk the talk, but not walk the walk.*

She wasn't ready to let go of the things she was getting from this merry go round. The carousel of fibreglass animals on metal poles for kids ridden by adults, metaphorically clear in its offering - a repetitive cycle going round and round, up and down, achieving nothing, going nowhere. Motion and distraction, a whirligig for sure. She'd heard of the expression *throwing good money after bad* but didn't want to accept it this time, not now. She was in energetic debt, big time overdrawn, credit cards maxed out. What made it worse, was that she couldn't work harder to put money back in this energetic bank. If she could have, she would have done so, she was great at applying herself, of paying the way. But it wasn't possible this time, it wasn't how it worked. She felt it in her body, her body getting heavier each day. She wondered *How the scales would weigh at the pearly gates of heaven in front of God*? She knew there would be no judgment she'd learnt that much, *how could there be?* She wasn't stupid, just stuck in a momentum right now that she could not, would not, break. It seemed too much. She had coached enough people to understand how bound they became, knowing sometimes you had to hit rock bottom to do something, anything about whatever it was you were chained up in.

Every day something happened between them it felt like the pits, every time another lead magnet attaching itself to her body, invisible but known and weighty. She could try and lie to everyone else, to herself, but she knew with every cell of her body, she was trapped in a glass box with the keys in the lock, door wide open.

~

A month to the day after his birthday her dad called, *his* life had ended, her brother had ended his life and with-it Rei's miscomings came to the fore. They would release themselves over time, seemingly gently as if to give space but they were in-fact droplets more like water torture in their persistent drip drip-ness onto the exact required spot of most pain. The urgent needs and attention given to customers, children, schools, partners bludgeoning any moments of grief that attempted to rear themselves within Rei.

Two days later a sudden outpouring of tears as she was fetching something from the car.

What's wrong? Jack asked out loud in front of all the contractors working on site on the house. Rei had been trying to remain hidden, silent, embarrassed even that her brother had committed suicide. Grappling with feelings of anger, rejection, and abandonment that were trying to penetrate her, to make it her fault. *If only she'd called him, if only she'd turned up to his birthday, she would have seen, would have known, she could have done something, Anything.*

My brother has just died she snapped back agitated he could be so callous, she didn't like to be seen this way, didn't want to draw any attention to herself.

How was I to know, it could have been anything! he responded back defending his position in front of his peers.

She didn't understand that he might possibly think there was something else. *Was this not bad enough?* Rei ran inside. *Really?*

She felt like she was having to explain her grief to her partner less than 48 hours after the event. She withdrew some more. She had to put on a brave face for her, for the world. She learnt quickly that no one wants to talk to a suicide survivor. It makes them uncomfortable, they don't know what to say. Her world became smaller overnight, her prison walls thicker. She couldn't understand what was being triggered in Jack, it was *her* brother that had died, and he had only ever met him once before.

Why was he so aggressive about it, so uncaring, so ruthless and reckless in his movements towards her, and obviously so? Was he hurt seeing her so upset over another? Was he feeling less that he was unable to console her?

She couldn't work it out, but it was clear that this was a new minefield she was walking, she would side step the bombs as best she could.

~

It was the morning of Olli's funeral and she had arranged to see his body at the funeral directors on her way to the service before they too set off in the hearse. The decision had caused distress and disturbance amongst the family but she was sure she needed to do this, to be able to move on. Forward. They were still living in their makeshift annexe;

wearing a face mask to the toilet, dodging holes in the floors and sharing a bath with the tools. She had managed to rescue her black dress from a box in storage, had prepped the kids and their clothes the night before knowing full well it was an early start to a potentially emotional day, that she simply had no idea how it would pan out.

She woke to the alarm on her iPhone by her bedside just this once, the phone was normally far from the bed and their room at nighttime, a routine she established years back which supported her no end. Today it was loud, blatant, screeching the dawn of the day no one really wanted, but absolutely needed, to tackle head on. She rolled over and kissed him gently letting him know it was time to get up. Usually, the first to stir and an equally light sleeper, today Jack did not respond as usual. Rei didn't want to poke the bear, wake him up in any which way that may not be optimal. The last few days had been tough, there had been no support, no acceptance, no conversations, no hugs, it seemed Jack wanted to forget and ignore her brother's death more than anyone else. She tried again planting a gentle kiss on his cheek and then his head, stroking him tenderly as only she knew how. She was fragile, raw, yet wholesome too, but she knew she could not afford for the day to go any other way than smoothly, there was no room for additional drama or emotion. She knew he'd felt her, she knew his every move, yet right now there was nothing, he pretended he was back at pre-school playing sleeping lions, a game he'd clearly won before.

Desperate not to prod, not to impose, she got up and reasoned by the time she'd gotten herself and the kids up and ready he would be up too. They lived within 10 meters of each other, all in - beds, toilet, bath, kitchen, diner, clothes, office. You could be quiet but not silent. A mouse would be noisy enough let alone the four of them on this morning. Still nothing. Jack clearly now going for the World Record of sleeping lions, not just the county championship title.

She made sure their movements escalated in volume, but not too much, it was a fine line. She wanted the glass to vibrate, to be stirred, but not to shatter. They had to amplify the sound through resonance and intensity without causing it to break. She called up a few times but again nothing. She knew he had heard, was being awkward, but she also knew if she did not make it obvious that she'd tried to wake him all hell would break loose. Rei wasn't sure what to do, but she knew she had to get going. In a last attempt she sent Bodhi up to wake him, who came straight back down.

Nope, he's still sleeping.

And so, she went back up one final time kissed him, told him they were going and to sleep well and have a good day, leaving a note for good measure, to cover her back. It was clear he had made his choice; she was doing whatever she could to alleviate the aftermath.

They bundled into the car and she drove off half expecting a semi-naked madman running down the street after her, waving ferociously. She looked in the rear mirror to the empty street and the barren pavement. She tried to hold in the tear that was welling up within but it softly and delicately warmed her cheek and embraced her with the tender love she so needed right now. She pressed play on the CD player and they began to sing their way to the funeral directors.

~

Walking back across the tarmac to the parked car Rei catches her breath and thanks the kids for looking after her, for coming with her. They had sat so preciously in the funeral parlour waiting for her to see her frozen brother's body. She wasn't crying but she was shell shocked. She held their hands and hugged them tight, thankful for the blessing of them even more so than a minute ago.

Beneath the trees and the dappled sunlight of this new day Rei feels the enormity of the cycle of birth and death, of death and birth. It reveals itself with the sun's warmth, with the bird's song, with the kid's laughter. They knew what was going on but she had protected them from the misery and projection that was so obviously around them. The stigma, the shame, the isolation, the occupational hazard of self-slaughter. They laugh and play just as freely as before stunning her into settlement. She opens the car door ready for them to hop in.

Without warning the stereo kicks in, the phone hooked up to it ringing at full volume, breaking the silence in the otherwise quiet parking lot. Her stomach churns, a knife in her belly, a sudden, sharp burst of reality. The funeral director suddenly at her side too. Rei feels faint but knows she won't, she feels cornered but knows she isn't. They were just things she had to deal with one at a time, but which one first? To offend the funeral director by answering the call or to incite the partner by talking to the funeral director, the bomb detonating on impact? She asked the kids if they could take the call whilst she spoke with the funeral director. She closed the door gently, quietly shielding the two parties from one another, just as she had done as a child on the phone between her two bickering parents.

The funeral director had come to wish her well and shared that he appreciated it had not been easy for her coming to see her brother especially today, particularly with the furore it had caused within the family. She thanked him and apologised for the loud speaker. They nodded and said their goodbyes. Rei slinked into the car, the kids unusually silent letting them know Jack was on the line waiting for her. The kid buffer hadn't worked; the knife twisted a full 180 degree turn in her gut as she went to speak.

Hi.

She didn't remember much of what was said, it was the same as always now.

How dare she? Who did she think she was? Didn't she know?
No one would ever love her like he did…

It went on and they all unanimously and silently agreed (they had to) as quickly as possible between rants that it was her fault, and *all* her fault.

I'm sorry. I have to go she said *we need to go now to make sure we arrive at the church before the body and the rest of the funeral party do.*

She knew he was raging, knew he was mad, but she had no fuel in the tank, no energy to fight any fires, especially the ones she'd so called started all by herself. She was shaking, the energy violent and tempestuous down the line, hands coming through the speaker trying to attack her, to shake her down, put her in her place. She wasn't sure she could get much lower than a hole buried in the ground for a coffin, but perhaps that's where it was trying to send her, joining her brother six feet under that day, at least in spirit. She turned the car engine on and drove as smoothly and quickly out of the car park as she could. Embarrassed again, not wanting anyone to see her this way, to hear her conversations that she knew herself were wrong, but she could see no way out of. By the time they arrived at the church she and the kids had calmed herself down, resuscitated her back to life.

The hall was packed, her father determined not to make this a pity party, to remind the young congregation present that in no way must they idolise or think this (suicide) was normal. It was a reckless and stupid thing to do that had grave consequences. It was a harsh message eloquently delivered. Rei was proud of him; it could not have been easy. She knew how much he loved him, his only son, and his favourite child. There was nothing to celebrate here, it was a life wasted.

Rei stood with her siblings as they cried by her side and she read the passage holding them together, crumbled and shattered herself, barely keeping it together on the inside herself.

~

They left for the pub where everyone was meeting after the service for the wake, she had gotten away with avoiding everyone except her father up until this point and had made sure she steered the conversation any way away from Jack's absence. Now it was blatantly obvious he was missing. She made up some story about him not feeling too well hoping that may be a valid enough excuse that would also excuse him from further familial damnation, but it appeared everyone (but her) had received a text message from Jack apologising for his tardiness but reassuring them all that he would be there any moment now. Now she not only looked stupid but pathetic too.

*Crafty a**hole* thought Rei, *cheeky f***er. Sly fox!* She hadn't used swear words in a very long time but as they fell from her brain to the tiled floor below noisy enough for her to hear she felt a hand against her back and a kiss upon her head. She wanted to vomit. The lion had woken and was here to play happy families, the king of his pride. Rei wanted to scream, wanted to shout, wanted to kick and push and show him up for the toe rag he was being, but of course he knew she would do no such thing, especially not now, not today. Her brother's burial day, a sacred day. Shat all over from above, up high, by her partner the person she chose to spend her life with. It couldn't get much lower than that she reckoned. But just as she'd said to someone the day before her brother's hanging that she didn't think things could get any worse than they currently were she now knew they could. She wasn't going to fall for that old chestnut again, she was sure it could get worse, but she could now also add that it too would eventually get better. She pinched herself, holding back the tears, relieved and ashamed (*again*) to be using her brother's death as an excuse for the teardrops when really it was a whole heap of things (including his passing) she just wasn't sure of the order of them.

The psychological autopsy had begun, not on her brother but on herself, extreme and self-punishing, condemning herself for failing to intervene effectively or on time. She was trying to develop a narrative that made sense. She wasn't sure exactly what she was referring to, her brother or her relationship with Jack. The subjects were interchangeable it seemed. She was the constant. Anything she had taken for granted about herself, her relationships and the world she lived in had disappeared.

It was a day she would never forget. For all the wrong reasons.

2004

Rei stands there stunned.

It is the first (and last) time she will stand there and take sh*t from her mother. A loud, stinging slap across her face. Red finger marks imprinted, raging, burning, as if the force with which had hit her had been transferred to the surface it had come into contact with. Her mum shaking, spit still spilling from her mouth after her angry outburst at Rei for leaving him. For leaving Ethan.

How could she? Did she have any idea what she was playing at? Did she know how hard it would be?

Rei thought she had a pretty good idea. She had lived through it for her whole entire life. She had never felt unity around her since birth, and from five years old until now at the age of twenty-eight she still lived with the reality of *how hard* it was. Every interaction with her mum shrieked of it, every silence howled, every sentence loaded with encumbrance, every nuance arduous and onerous. Both her and her sister *knew*. She wasn't sure her mum had any idea of how it actually was for her daughters. She had always been quite self-obsessed, unable to see beyond her own four walls or even to the other two people living with her within them. They had lived the horror, had been on the receiving end of this journey day in day out. They had received the constant slaps on the legs like a toy clapper caught with the on switch *ON* banging resolutely between two buffers, had had their heads smashed together, their skulls cracking in sound from the thwack, had been pinched and scolded, had their arms twisted and mauled in Chinese burns and every now and then when they were ill, they would have their heads stroked. It wasn't all bad Rei (had to) remind herself, there were starving children in Africa after all.

One of the reasons boarding school had been palatable and often enjoyable was that it offered respite from the home environment. One of the reasons her sister had chosen to live with her dad was to get away from the depression at home that fogged every corner of life. They *knew* all right. They knew it wasn't right and Rei understood it wasn't personal, she could see the torturous strain her mum was under but it made it no easier to bear and she took it on as her own. She knew her mum was trying to protect her, protect her from the suffering she had endured and been through herself, protect her from all that would come. But Rei didn't understand, she was not her mum, she was a young (now single) woman with two young kids, but past that she could not see any similarities. Rei prided herself on having learnt how *not* to be, from both her parents, and felt she was doing a pretty good job at it.

They had been living in a two bedroomed house in Oxford for a couple of months now. She had moved out with Aaron and Bella knowing full well what she was taking on. She had found a place they could afford and had done it up gorgeously for them, their new home, their new life ahead. They were happy, and she was happy too. Yes, it wasn't always easy but there was a lightness that had returned and a joy she hadn't felt in a long time. She felt free again for the first time and it felt like spring time, blossoming buds and baby lambs prancing. She was not being naive, in fact on the contrary she was being very real about it all. The pros outweighed the cons; the hardships paled into insignificance against the clarity she felt in her body.

She had struggled herself with the guilt of leaving him, she had vowed and promised she would never put her kids through what she had been through as a child and here she was making the same choices, separating from the father of her two children. She had to let this go she told herself, she knew the truth of it, she was different and she would do all she could to make sure it didn't pan out in the same way her parent's separation had.

~

Standing there stunned, she could feel that alongside her mum's protective streak came a narrative; a heavy, substantial, consequential force, telling her to back down and to go back to him. That standing for the truth was too hard; leave it alone, put it back where it came from. It was not okay that she had chosen another way for herself and her kids. She was wrong. It was wrong. She must go back. That was the only way. She knew this wasn't true. It was not her weight to bear, not her burden to carry, yet somehow, she felt like this was something in the fine print of a contract she hadn't really read through properly when she signed. She knew she would have to consider her (their) return, otherwise the anchor that had just been thrown over and around her neck would take her down, deep down to the bottom of the sea never to be seen again. It seemed she had already signed up for it, this inevitable return. She could see no other way out from this tension she was feeling. It was as if King Kong was in the room towering above her, powerful and territorial reacting to her moves away from the non-loving arrangement she had been in. In fact, he was positively defending the compressed way of living she had chosen to move away from. The evident destructiveness of this giant ape like energy from distant shores was made manifest in what he was moving, what he had already moved and what he was threatening to further move, unmistakably and indisputably menacing. Protective of the environment he called *home* and that he felt safe with, dictating that this was the only way. *It's my way or the highway.*

Rei had observed energies before but none as clear as this, it made no logical sense otherwise. It wasn't just her mum she was seeing and witnessing. Her mum loved her deep down. What parent would actively encourage their child back into the arms of lovelessness, of unhappiness? She saw how un-dealt with issues can be used to manipulate and control others even if that was not the intention.

Rei went to bed glad that her mother would be leaving in the morning and that she would no longer be having to deal with the force of her fears and projections again.

1988

One night I dreamed I was walking along the beach with the Lord. Scenes from my life flashed across the sky the whole school read out loud.

Rei's heart murmured, a stirring back to life. Finally, a song, a hymn, a poem, anything that resonated with her somewhat as opposed to everything else in chapel and school assemblies that did not. Perhaps it was the reference to the beach, her mind whisking her away to wind swept walks on the Suffolk coast, the dogs running between her legs, hide and seek in the dunes, the sun beating down on her skin.

In each, I noticed footprints in the sand.
Sometimes there were two sets of footprints; other times there was only one.

Rei saw the dog's prints and those of the oyster catchers and the sanderlings running along the water's edge, their distinctive tracks left for all to see in the tide's ebb and flow across the now wet sand. She could see her own footprints but that was it. The wind whisking up loose sand around her ankles, blowing her hair, salty air upon her lips. There was no one around, no one to be seen for miles and miles, as far as the eye could see.

During the low periods of my life I could see only one set of footprints,

so I said, "You promised me, Lord, that you would walk with me always.
Why, when I have needed you most, have you not been there for me?"

Rei wondered if that meant she was always in a low period of her life?
Was she only always alone?
Was she really that bad?

The Lord replied, "The times when you have seen only one set of footprints, my child, is when I carried you."

Rei felt relieved. Perhaps she wasn't that bad? Or maybe she was? So much so that *The Lord* had to carry her the whole time. Gosh that must be exhausting she thought, she knew how heavy it was carrying her books to and from class each day in her arms, she couldn't imagine carrying her non-stop. Through sand too! That felt like walking through a muddy quagmire sometimes, she knew, she'd done it.

Thanks Lord she said inside. She appreciated that he'd done that for her.

This was as far as her relationship with God went now. *The Sand In The Footprints* as she liked to call it. She'd shunned what she'd been told about him, he didn't really seem to turn up in all the right places at all the right times like he should have done according to the scriptures, and she knew she wasn't *that* bad despite everyone telling and trying to make her believe she was.

She knew that something was in the air that she breathed, the ground that she walked upon, that had been majestically provided for her, and for everyone, by some grander power way beyond her or what her tiny brain could fathom. That much, she was sure. She didn't have a name for it and she didn't need to.

The Lord in the story tale could put her down now, and her him she reckoned, she had this on her own, that way she knew where she was going. It seemed simpler that way. She wasn't sure about the slight victim and better than thou vibes she was getting from the poem, it seemed similar to the judgemental love thread pumped out on stereo around her in the bible, from the priests; she just wasn't buying it.

Love was for everyone, not just the people that loved him back, The Lord, God.

Silly.

2001

Back when Rei was a child her nanny and grandad had been the most precious people in her life. They were the ones who looked after both her and her sister; they made them dinners; allowed them to jump on their bed like it was a trampoline when waking in the mornings; let them snuggle up for biscuits and tea (minus the tea for the kids who went straight to the biscuit tin for the pink wafers, custard creams and chocolate bourbons) whilst grandad read the daily paper just delivered through the front door, the dogs barking to herald its arrival; took them for a walk across the park to the allotment to pick the freshly grown and tended to fruit and veg; travelled with them across the country in the back of their beat up car to Suffolk each year; made Mrs Tiggy-Winkles with them each summer; took them to church, then the phone box and then finally the fish and chip van every Friday night; let them count up the coins from the church collection tin the pennies in one pile the two pennies in another; the list went on.

As Rei grew older and her life moved away, she saw them less and less, but she would always ring home to them. Grandad would without fail answer the phone *5739*, like a code from war times, stuck and out of place but comforting nonetheless. War had taken its toll on him but he didn't really let that be seen, outwardly only in his silence perhaps. He was a man of few words and although her nanny was the one that really got involved her grandad was an ever-present presence in the background. Mowing the lawn, washing the dishes, walking to the shops for a pint of milk, creating miniature golf courses for them in the tufty Suffolk grass, creating a rope swing from old fishermen's braid, filling up the paddling pool… He would do it all taciturnly, with a little chuckle here and there now and then. He called his wife *Duckie* and he held her hand, it was said with such loving endearment it melted Rei every time.

Now, standing in front of his coffin, in the church that they'd taken them to as children Rei felt different. The chapel had felt monstrously oversized back then; the pews and their cushioned kneelers seemed to go on for rows and rows without end but today before the altar everything felt smaller, shrunken in size, compressed and constricted.

She was eight months pregnant with her first child and nanny had said not to come, she didn't want her or the baby upset, she would be alright without them. But that was not an option for Rei, so here she was. She sat beside her father who was crying, uncontrollably as the service wrapped up and the people filed out. It was the first time in her life that Rei had ever seen him cry. She put her arm out across his back and held him his sobs getting stronger and more visible as she did so.

Are you okay? Is there anything I can do?

She wasn't sure her dad heard her amongst the sobs, weeping, head in hands, elbows on knees, shaking it side to side. They sat in silence and Rei waited, hand on the back of his heart.

He never once told me he loved me. Not once. Ever he said.

Rei remained quiet learning a lot in that moment, about her dad, about war, about not sharing your emotions. It explained so much, about,

well about absolutely,

Everything.

She already told her unborn child every day, multiple times a day how much she loved him. She would never let it go unsaid how much she loved someone; she was sure of that.

I love you she turned and said to her father, rubbing his back gently.

I love you too he replied, for the second time. Ever.

2024

Bella made a wedding cake for them (GF, DF, sugar free) covered in white icing with a pistachio buttercream between the moist lemon and nut sponge layers, finely decorated with green leaves collected from the tree outside and one white ranunculi stem to mirror the small, but spectacular bridal bouquet.

Everything about the wedding, the day, had been simple but exquisite. No detail spared, nothing held back on, yet all coming together with such delicacy, grace, ease and simplicity and costing near nothing at all. Rei had found her dress online not having any space to go shopping for one between trips, consults and presenting. It was an elegant, glamorous dress in its purest form; super sexy, slinky and delicate all at once. Rei knew keeping it simple didn't mean having to play it safe, and this was

f a r

from safe.

It fitted her like a glove; a part sheer, 90s inspired asymmetric slip dress cut on the bias which allowed the fabric to mould and show off her gorgeously fine womanly body.

When she showed it to Bodhi for the first time, it having just arrived through the post he commented *I think it could do with a little more fabric!!*

She called Bella over face-time who squealed *Yes mama, yes! That is soooo you!*

Rei knew deep down this was the one, she didn't need to ask outside of herself. It was indeed that simple; the first dress ordered, the first one tried on. *Bingo!* She knew it was risqué in layman's terms; she knew the ceremony was on a December afternoon in England, the weather forecast already indicating rain and sub ten degree Celsius temperatures, it all seemed to not make any real sense in her head, but her body gave her a resounding *Yes!!!* to it all. The drapery effect of the silky fabric showing off the all of her body left nothing to the imagination, yet somehow the elegance, regal-ness, purity and divinity in womanly form oozing from her transformed the dress into something beyond the term exquisite - a goddess beauty in the flesh.

They had all taken the Number 7 bus home from the Italian restaurant down the other end of Baker Street. Like kids returning home from a school trip in full spirit, laughing in full joy, they piled on the bus taking up the whole back bottom deck. They had been the bus's first pick up stop for the evening and the driver was pleased to see such a group of merry passengers alight his vehicle, as much as they were him. It had been a windy day, surprisingly mild yet hugely unsettled as Storm Dalglish caused disruption across the country. Trees had fallen, hundreds of thousands of homes had been without power, there had been flooding and most travel had been disrupted if not delayed or cancelled.

When they woke that morning, they faced the inevitable fact that perhaps many, if not most of their guests would not be able to make it. Two were flying in from abroad and other than the three children staying with them that night and one within cycling distance, everyone else was travelling a long way to be there with them. They looked at each other in the absolute knowing that everything would be exactly as it needed to be. They had each other and they had God, everything and everyone else were multiple scrumptious cherries on the top. One of the guests, a witness, sent a message; a screen shot of the airport departures board. Every single flight that day had been cancelled, every single one except hers. A sea of red with one green light. They knew they were being looked after.

The concierge from their flat building had arranged to drive them each down to the registry office for the ceremony knowing full well the weather implications for a December wedding, wanting to be of service to them sparing them the twenty-minute walk in blustery conditions. He first arrived to collect Gabriel, the best man and the four boys. He turned up suited and booted in a freshly cleaned Mercedes resplendent for the event, like a personal chauffeur with an executive limousine. *Pretty Woman* had nothing on these guys, they meant business. Just as a young Vivian had pretended she was a princess trapped in a tower rescued by a knight on a white horse climbing up the tower, the young Rei had always felt like she was a princess, but she no longer needed rescuing. Here was her King, her aide, her confidante, her equal, off to the ceremony, one ride ahead of her.

She opened the bedroom door where she was getting ready before he left and they spoke together, between the ajar-ness. *You, Me & God* they said, echoing the words engraved on the inside of his ring. They hugged each other through the door, their body as one. They had planned to be by each other's sides the whole lead up to the event but Bodhi had shared that he thought it was important to have the *Big Reveal* and one of their friends had agreed. There was nothing that irked either of them about it, about any of it, but step by step along the way they were being held and ever so gently shown all the small ways in which they were not being in the magnificence of what their union represented, of what it meant, of what it was. Both of them were quite happy to shy from the limelight, to underplay it all, but they were being asked not to, ever so lovingly so, and so they responded.

Ten minutes later Rei, Bella and her maid of honour went downstairs as arranged, for their lift. What awaited them was a golden Porsche cleaned and decked out for a Queen on such an occasion. Tears in her eyes, joy radiating through her smile Rei was in complete humbleness of what'd been delivered and offered so effortlessly to them without any need for thanks or recognition. The whole world seemed to stop spinning and there was space and zero time like never before.

They pulled up at the side entrance to the registry office and both drivers stood as if caps on and to attention, there for them in absolute fullness. Rei hugged them both and took a selfie with them, holding her bouquet and dress up with one hand and hugging them with the other. It was a beautiful start to it all.

~

As they sat at home that evening, a cup of fresh rose and mint tea in hand, they basked and bathed in the glory of the day, the wonder of it all. How simple, how effortless and how absolutely perfect all of it, every single aspect of it was.

Without any trying, without rush, or push, or drive, or pictures, or expectations they had been given everything on a plate. A golden platter. How blessed they were.

2020

It was only knowing *Him* that got her through it all.

That was all that she knew. The rest had been a blur, a torturous bedimming.

Rei sits on her bed in her beautiful flat given to her from a blessing on high. Covid 19 had just hit and the world had gone into lockdown. Her father had told her seven weeks prior in no uncertain terms to get on a train today, get to Oxford, pick up the kids and make a home for themselves, they were all going to get locked in and up. He had been right about this, and Rei was thankful for him overstepping the mark on this occasion. She still managed to take offence to his well-intended, but mostly ill executed plans, but was becoming less reactionary to the *do as I say (not as I do)* style of parenting that she sporadically received no matter her age. He knew she had no money and could still barely move seven months after all the operations. She had been camping out in a friend's working study in east London for a few weeks now having left Italy for good after an ultimatum of sorts. She was making moves forward but was still far from any semblance of normality in movement or energy levels. Her father had astutely (and very generously) booked and paid upfront for three weeks in an Airbnb for them and said she could take it from there.

No one had any idea how, when or what this covid thing was, only that it was a looming, menacing cloud at this point in time that seemed to be morphing very quickly into a cyclone, the eyeball currently above them ready to shift and whisk them all up and away at any point. They needed to lock themselves in and baton down the hatches. They stayed in the Airbnb for the three booked weeks and then some, as the lockdown swelled in size and voracity.

For people unable to leave their properties, hanging from their windows at 8pm on a Thursday evening banging their pots and pans had become the highlight of their weeks, the whole city out in unison, a sign of the times. The intended one-off event thanking the frontline staff at the end of March ended up being the social climax of everyone's week for months, the marking of another cycle, another week where nothing much had changed. Rei appreciated the noise each week from their underground rental the otherwise silence now the new norm. It was clear lockdown had no signs of coming to an end and so they had to find accommodation fast. Being unable to look at anything in person and after her too-good-to-be-true experience only a couple of months prior Rei wanted to tread carefully.

She had learnt from the last scam that the internet and even the estate agent's websites could not be trusted as clear or true verification. Scammers had accessed an agent's accounts overnight put up a heap of real properties (that were not available) for rental and taken deposits, legitimate looking ones. Rei had felt this was *too-good-to-be-true* at the time but given her circumstances she was happy to have a lucky break. Instead, it was another kick in the teeth, another reminder to honour what she felt at all times; the money she had put down for the deposit was now gone. Down the drain. The policemen came round to interview her, taking all the details, the emails, the WhatsApp trails, the bank details. She had been careful and wise enough to follow protocol and not be an obvious scammers muse, however she had now re-learnt (*again*) she could not dishonour even the slightest inkling she felt anymore. The policemen said it was great she had come forward with all this evidence as they had been trying to catch this high-end ring for some time, unfortunately the amount of paperwork and being put on hold normally deterred most people, who would cut their losses and run. Rei however had no job at the moment and was incensed at yet another heinous and nefarious crime so was determined to see this through. Her patience eventually paid off and her deposit was returned. Just in time to put it down for the next place, their home in Oxford for the next year, at least. She had a good feeling about this one.

With no belongings just her one suitcase full of clothes she'd been living out of since last year, she signed for the property asking them to remove some of the furniture prior to their arrival. There were no usual pleasantries just a set of keys in an envelope in a box ready for collection. No meeting of the agents or the landlords, everything silent, everywhere. They wheeled their cases the mile long walk wondering what may await them, but they needn't have worried, it was more than gorgeous. A place they could call their own in which to recover, the first in a year. There were two real beds and two bathrooms, one with a bath, they had never been so grateful. They unpacked their things and smiled and hugged, Rei and Bella reunited and *home*.

2015

Rei didn't have to keep a mental note of the things Raquel had done to her at school, they were imprinted in her body. She didn't think they had created scars or un-jumpable fences for her, more so that they'd acted as junctures along the way, moments that made her stop and take the right-hand fork instead of the left. Like a plane holding before landing, a seemingly unnecessary movement stalling the inevitable smooth pathway in, the distant memories of Raquel and all those years entailed often cast a shadow for her before the clear light of day was seen for what it was.

The old school friends had arranged to meet in a pub in London on a January afternoon, nearly the whole of their year flying in from all parts of the world to reunite some twenty years after their final farewells to each other at the age of 18. Rei had kept in touch with a few of the girls over the years, some more than others, been to a couple of their weddings over the years kids in tow, but had never seen everyone, not all together like this. She was happy to be seeing them all in the flesh after so long, to see beyond their Facebook updates and profile picture changes, their Instagram stories and their family portraits, she couldn't wait to hear about what they were up to, where they had been in life, where they were going.

With the odd text here and there prior to the event not much thought or consideration had been given to how the day might unfold. It was only when she arrived in London that she really considered how the meeting with Raquel may be.

Would she be there? If so, would she still be the same? she wondered. Regardless of whether she was or wasn't Rei agreed within herself that she would hold nothing against or towards her, the past was the past.

She arrived at the pub to a group of women already deep in conversation, high in spirits, recognising them all. It was as if no-one had actually changed, perhaps a little larger around the waistline, a few more wrinkles, a changing hairline and a new fashion sense, but all their names came flooding back, the houses they had belonged to at school; it was like they were in a Harry Potter film and had just gone through the wall at King's Cross Station onto Platform 9 3/4 everyone back and ready for the school term ahead.

It was mildly relieving knowing everyone and finding common ground immediately when potentially it was thought there may have been none. She turned around and saw Raquel stood behind her, still small in stature but less portly than when at school. Rei said *Hi,* and Raquel talked back as if they had been best friends which somewhat shook and disturbed Rei. She had subconsciously prepared herself for most eventualities, but not for this one, it hadn't even occurred to her that this could be an option. Knowing herself all too well she guessed her face would be giving her thought processes away, but even if it had Raquel carried on completely unperturbed. Rei had to catch herself internally questioning *Had she imagined her whole childhood? Had she made the whole thing up?* Right now, it would appear so.

She could see people around her staring at the two of them. *Were they staring for the same reason Rei's own face looked perplexed?* she wondered. She couldn't quite work out how to be with it, with this behaviour anymore, and before she realised, she had asked the question *You know you were a complete bitch to me at high school right?* not loaded, but inquisitively.

The women around her stopped to hear the response as if this was what they had been waiting for, the moment of truth. The women transported back to the girls they once were, unable to stand up to the bully themselves and so part of the gang, the clique that through their inaction became just as much wielders and a part of the bullying as Raquel herself.

Rei personally aware that she now no longer shied so much away from awkward situations, from confrontation, she wasn't riled or angry or bitter, just curious and with that her part in it all seemingly diminished too.

I'm sorry. I really was a cow, wasn't I? Raquel replied.

I'd say you being a cow was a pretty generous understatement if I'm honest Rei replied, amazed she was responding as such. *When I said you were a complete bitch, I meant it. You were horrid. Maybe not anymore, but there were repercussions.*

Rei had said her piece now; she knew that was all that she needed to say. She had expressed the truth, the reality, she hadn't held back against or before her arch-nemesis, she could relax now.

Was I really THAT bad? Raquel asked slightly concerned.

Yep! You sure were replied Rei with zero glee but with a sturdy mindfulness that it needed to be said exactly how it was. *But don't worry I haven't been scarred for life! I'm more than fine. Genuinely. You know what I even had a couple of fish in a fish tank again a few years back for the kids.*

Rei now smiled, out through the other side of the trauma, reliving the scene that took place in her cubicle in the autumn term of Year 3 some twenty-five years ago. *Except this time there was no hole-punch in sight!* Sometimes Rei wished she could wink just for effect, but it was probably just as well that she couldn't. Raquel's face turned from a polite smile to pure aghast-ness at the flashback bestowed upon her.

*Oh my God! I'm so sorry, I REALLY was s u c h a bitch to you. It's just you were so perfect. So tall and blonde and skinny - you still are! And you were good at everything and everyone liked you including all the teachers and everything you touched seemed to turn to gold, you could do sports and dance and maths and English and French and Latin, even physics, who's good at physics for f*** sake!*

God I was so jealous of you. There were no commas in her speech, it all came out at once like a runaway train coming down the tracks, she blew, she blew.

Wow, that's so crazy, that's not what it felt like to me Rei commented back, realising she had taken it all very personally. True it had been directed very pointedly at her but as soon as the words tumbled out of her mouth, she realised quite how evil the whole comparison thing really was, pitting each other against everyone else. There was no joy to be had, no backing of one another, just a stampede to not be trailing at the back.

Try being in the bottom set of everything all of the time! chirped up Frankie who'd made her way across the room beside them both now. *I can't believe we got away with half the sh*t we did* she said.

Your poor fish half-dead with holes in them; drinking out of a baby's milk bottle…What were we thinking…climbing over the cubicle partitions at night and playing cards 'til past midnight with a pillow propping up our duvet pretending that was us… Were they stupid or were we just geniuses? she mused out loud.

Everyone gathering round now reminiscing about the god-awful times and the terribly awful things that they'd done or that had happened to them, but everyone still with a part-smile on their face. There were no deep hurts or regrets, but a closed and silent realisation that they all had a lot in common with one another and that these times whether they had been friends or not highlighted a very significant part of their lives that had shaped their adulthood. Wild flowers grown in the same meadow, a beauty in the diversity present amongst them. Like puppies separated at birth going out to their new prospective homes, there was a natural parting of the waves but they would always be inextricably linked, a part of the same ocean with the same ocean bed. Boarding school hadn't really been that easy for any of them and they had all dealt with it in their own ways. They didn't need to talk anymore about it. They were here because of it and that was something to celebrate.

My parents were always arguing and there was a lot of alcoholism involved, it got nasty at times and so I took it out on you Raquel continued clearly needing to express some more. *If it makes you feel any better, I've been through years of counselling and am still in it, two hours a week.*

Rei realised more the evil that can be done if people aren't open and transparent with others around them, being used against each other to everyone's detriment. The truth was in fact that it could have bought them together, stronger if they had shared it with one another. It was all so unnecessary.

Gosh you always played happy families very well in that case then Rei responded. *You don't have to tell me how difficult that all can be. I'm sorry you had to deal with all that. It sucks. I hope you are alright?*

Yes, I will be, I'm getting there replied Raquel.

They gave each other a hug before the whole year bundled in on top and the group photo was taken. *Hoorah!* They all cheered. *To us!*

1985

As they pullback before going into class that morning they notice there is an unusual hubbub about the place. A bunch of nine-year-olds circulating the building whispering and giggling, the stuff that Rei has always hated but thankfully never really been part of. Their teacher Miss Wilson walks past and says *Hurry up girls! You may want to get inside quick; it's a beautiful day…* the message received was loud enough to give Rei the shivers. She knew something was up but she wasn't sure what yet. She hated surprises and the atmosphere around them seemed to be building. She turned to Kiera who looked just as perplexed and bewildered as Rei felt so they took each other's hands and walked the five steps up to their classroom together just as each and every other day.

They were in Year 5 now and every day the class rule was they had to come in and sit at their desks ready for the lesson to begin, everyone knew it, even Miss Wilson, so why was everyone stood around their desk? Why hadn't Miss Wilson reminded them of this like she did every other day on her way to collect the register from the headmistress's office? Rei was feeling a little apprehensive now. The throng around her desk burgeoning before her eyes.

After hanging their coats on their personally drawn and illustrated named pegs, their PE kits swinging with abandonment beneath the winter wares, they made their way across the room to their desk. The sea of classmates parted and they walked through like Moses and the Red Sea;

this sea swelling and eager to return to its previously amassed state. Standing loud and proud on the mini sized wooden school desk complete with inkwell and wooden lid flap were two cards, one normal sized one and one Super-Sized one…and one red rose tied in a red ribbon. For a milli-milli-nano-second Rei smiled at the beauty of it before really quickly realising it was *all* on *Her* desk. She scanned the classroom from side to side, back and forth. *Nope, there was nothing on anyone else's.* Fear took over her body, embarrassment like she'd never known before. She hated being the centre of attention and right now all cameras, lights, action and eyes were on her. Her heart beat loud in her mouth the whole class able to take her non-resting pulse rate for how loud it was thrashing and thumping through her body.

Ooooohhhhh!! started the class.

Who's it from?

Rei has got a Valentine they sang somehow in harmony like a rehearsed choir, although it sounded more like a ruckus in Rei's ears. There was no room to breathe, let alone swing a cat.

Someone loves her!

No, two people love her!!
Who's your valentine Rei?

Open it, let's see….

The waves were crashing in on her now, she was feeling a little nauseous and her whole body was tingling, she wished she could just disappear. She could focus on nothing other than getting rid of the source of the attention. Now. The fight-or-flight response already kicked in, Rei wanted to be alone with no evidence that any of this had ever happened, ever even existed. She ran out and down into the girls' toilets and into the middle of the three cubicles, opened both cards, scanned the messages through tear streamed eyes and promptly ripped the cards and their two envelopes into shreds, throwing them down the toilet with such wolfishness she shocked herself, stumbling to the floor against the cubicle wall. She'd flushed the handle but the cards with nine-year-old handwritten love letters and pictures of red roses circled the pan, determined not to be rejected just yet down the mini sized toilet basin. She flushed again, this time more card seemed to come to the surface, the red roses circling mirrored her red cheeks, her red eyes. She sat there frozen, unable to move, unable to get past the whirling dervishes in the commode. The porcelain goddess stood still and proud not gulping this time, or the next, or the next still. Rei could hear the not so muffled sound of Miss Wilson calling the class to attention.

Settle down now, settle down. If you can all take out your books and start reading where you left off…

This would be the first time Rei wasn't in her desk for the start of class and it was the first time Miss Wilson hadn't shut the door before beginning class. It wasn't looking good.

Rei couldn't move. She didn't know what to do. She could *never* be seen again. *Ever.*

Whilst time stood still she was able to digest the longhand notes scribed in the Berol handwriting pens she had seen a few minutes prior in her clamour. They had been from Nathan Shaw and from Cameron. She could tell Cameron's handwriting from a mile off the letters all joined together, long and thin, a bit spidery, a typical boys' writing but all within the invisible lines they'd been taught how to write on to get their hand-writing licence last year. Nathan on the other hand had beautifully arched, curvy letters that were separate from each other and spacious, she actually *r e a l l y* liked his writing, but right now she despised it, every part of it. He had written her a long poem he'd obviously carefully crafted which she couldn't remember and wasn't sure she had even read in full, but she could feel it. It was sweet and loving, flowery, kind and gentle. It made her want to throw up right now. Pass out even. She wasn't sure what she was feeling, but the earth was not swallowing her up like she wanted it to.

How could he? How could they?

Nathan had been one of the group of four best friends since Rei started at primary school along with her best friend Kiera and his best friend Max Wilson. Together they had seen each other's bits under the table in Year 2, played together in break times (although now Red Rover was getting a bit more popular sometimes, they weren't always on the same team anymore) and would always sit together at lunch.

Cameron on the other hand was the class reject, oversized around the waist and going through puberty already, he was an outlier amongst the thirty-six children. Rei knew he was sweet and was always kind to him unlike the others in her year who said nasty things about the way he smelled *B-O Baddie* and the like, turning up and holding their noses for dramatic effect whenever he brushed past. She also liked Cameron because he would take her milk bottle from her every break time. She hated the stuff it made her want to puke every single day. They were made to drink it in the depths of winter and the height of summer and everything in between. Curdled, rancid, warm, frozen, it mattered not. Thankfully Cameron had an appetite for at least two bottles a day so they would carefully swap bottles (his empty one for her full one) in the hall near the window, their backs turned momentarily to the crowd and the teachers, whilst they performed their magic switch. Rei would always line up the thin blue straw perfectly centrally piercing the middle of the silver bottle top through the crusted layer of cream that rimmed the milk beneath. She found the smell of the milk way worse than Cameron's body odours and couldn't understand how anyone could drink it, so was grateful she had an ally in Cameron, and he one in her.

She could see that it made sense that either or both had a soft spot for her and she knew they hadn't meant to humiliate her, in fact it really was actually rather sweet and she was flattered deep down, but above all this, *way* above it all she knew she had no tools in her pocket to deal with what she was actually feeling at the surface level…and to make matters worse she still had not been gobbled up and engulfed into an abyss.

Rei hadn't really known what Valentines Day was until this point in time. Absolutely no idea, but she knew that she hated it already. *What was a Valentine anyway?* Rei had zero concept of love or romance in her life. She didn't see it around her; she was used to broken people with broken lives. Shattered, in pieces on the floor for all to see, although she also knew it could be swept under a rug too. She'd already vowed never to get married; it seemed like a stupid thing to do; a piece of paper that meant nothing, it ended badly, and even then, it was bitter and painful, noisy and angry, hurtful and spiteful, all the things she hated.

She thought that perhaps that was one of the reasons why she was friends with Kiera, Max and Nathan, because they were a little bit (not too much) broken too. Kiera was the only other person in the class whose parents weren't together and Max was *orphaned*. That had seemed as big and scary a word as being a *bastard* to Rei when she first heard about it last year in Year 4. She hadn't believed him when he told her, she thought he was making it up, because his parents clearly loved him. Loads.

Wasn't that how it worked? she pondered. She had *real* parents and she wasn't sure they loved her very much, so how could these people that absolutely adored Max not be his *real* parents? She had ended up upsetting Max when she didn't believe him, so much so that he got his mum to come over and talk to Rei, to tell her *the truth,* at school pick up before she turned off on her walk left down the alleyway.

Rei never forgot how badly it had hurt him that she hadn't believed him; things were never quite the same after as Rei had been *soooo* adamant that he was lying to her, to them. His parents cared and doted on him - it could not be true! It took her a while to get her head around the fact that it was, that people could be loved like that even when they weren't *theirs*. She wondered how bad she must have been to not be loved by her own.

She really must be very bad.

~

So, what were Nathan and Cameron thinking sending her a Valentine's card? she pondered. Firstly, she wasn't even loveable like that, she knew she was nice but it was impossible for someone else to actually *love* her, even if it was pretend Valentine's Day love.

Every time her mind travelled back to the cards, the ribboned rose, it was like all her senses got turned up…the volume of the loo pan flushing, of the classroom murmurs; the disinfectant smell in the girls toilet fresh from the morning cleaners; the feel of the cold floor under her, the colder wall behind her; the whirlpool of spinning card pieces like lotto balls in a bingo cage, the bars of the invisible jail cell she had imprisoned herself within thick and heavy;

the taste of confusion, shame, awkwardness, humiliation, ignominy, abashment...all together a chicken Chow mein of intermingled emotions, the perfect combination of ingredients for a lavish meal of desperate measures. It took Miss Wilson to come into the toilets some while later to coax Rei out and back into the helm of the student amphitheatre a few steps away. She had to (pretend) *promise* that no-one would say anything, that it wouldn't be mentioned at all,

ALL day.

Rei returned to her classroom with her head hung low and buried her head as deeply into her book and her desk as was physically possible. She had a hunchback bigger than the old people she sometimes saw in the street who looked like an upside-down U shape. She felt like the man who came to school with his van full of animals at the end of each year. It was the annual highlight, less so because of the owls, or the snake, or whatever he would pull out of the shrouded black boxes he bought in with him, but more so because they couldn't keep their eyes off of him. He had a way with all of the animals undoubtedly so, it was mesmerising, but all they (everyone else in the school) could see was his non-existent thumb, a stump of a digit. Everyone tried to *not* look at it, but they could *only but* see it. No-one dared say anything as they knew it would be rude to, so everybody said nothing. The students were silenced, entranced by the animals and his hands, each probably believing they were interlinked, adding mystery and a fear factor that this could happen to them too if they stepped out of line, the animals loose and capable. It was the only assembly for the whole year, each and every year without fail, that everyone sat exactly where they should have sat without fidgeting on their bottoms for the longest time ever. Not one teacher ever had to interfere or interject with a *Shh! Keep still. Stop fidgeting! No, you can't get some water, you can wait,* like every other day.

Rei felt like him now, like something of her had been taken. That everyone would look at her, talking on the inside but saying nothing. She'd asked Miss Wilson for it to be that way but she didn't want everyone to be looking at her differently. More than anything she just wanted to be the same as everyone else.

To fit in.

That's all she'd ever wanted.

And now it was too late. She didn't.

2024

Walking through Hyde Park hand in hand with Gabriel she felt amazing. He stopped her and pulled her aside whispering in her ear how sexy she was.

Did she know how sexy she was? Could she feel it?

He asked her to never hold back on being sexy, everyone needed to see it so that they too could be reminded to be seen, to be sexy. She could feel very clearly that he wasn't sexually objectifying her, that there was no *him* in the statement. Unlike the small but still obvious buzz her dad would get out of having her by his side, on his arm, people thinking he'd scored himself a tall, young, leggy blonde; or like other men before who became possessive of this beauty not wanting it to be shared or seen, keeping it to and wanting it for only themselves. Gabriel was different, he didn't need recognition from anyone else and above all he loved Rei and wanted her to be everything that she was, no holding back. It was not for him, it was for her, for all.

Rei realised that she did indeed feel sexy. It was oozing from her every pore. It wasn't that she was wearing anything that displayed her flesh as such, she had a pair of black leggings on that her dear friend had custom designed, a pair of boots and a cashmere jumper that soon came off with the heat of the walk to reveal a simple, plain tank top beneath. She didn't need to show flesh to be sexy, but neither did she need specific clothes either. It wasn't about her body shape or her weight, it was about what she was emanating from within, how she felt about herself and the way she was moving, not just right now in this moment but in general, in life, all-ways. It wasn't something that she could hold back, and nor could she put it on, she and it just was.

She let herself settle with this as they continued through the sun lit, people laden park. It wasn't until they crossed the house lined streets towards Waterloo Station that she was able to put it into words.

Thank you she said.

I realise this is the first time I can actually really be me. It's as if being with you gives me permission to just be me, like you are my body guard. I actually needed you, needed this.

Gabriel looked at her his eyes silently asking for more information, more understanding.

I don't feel like I've changed at all, in fact I know I haven't but the pressure is off me now. I'm allowed to be sexy and there's not a thing anyone can say about it. Before it would be claimed I was being sexy to try to hook a guy. I knew I wasn't but it was still there. Now I have a ring on my finger and they can't use that one on me anymore. Before it would be said that I was talking too openly, being too forward, trying to flirt with someone. I wasn't but it was there. Having you beside me people can see that I'm not doing those things, I'm with you. It's only you and me. I don't know if I'm able to describe it, articulate it very clearly. It's ever so subtle and I'm exaggerating for effect, but that's the essence of it. That energy that circulated before has nowhere to go anymore, and being here with you in our relationship has taken the lid off the pressure cooker, so thank you.

I don't think I've really done anything, but thank you for recognising that Gabriel replied in his ever so humbled way.

Rei snuggled into him and the knowing that their union was moving mountains as they continued their walk back to the station, closer together than even the moment before.

1999

It was New Years Eve, they had had a week on the island already and had a few days left before their return back to Japan, to the school term. As they ate out in the local restaurants on the beach by candlelight, they would look over to other couples sat silently across from one another, nothing to say, and wonder if this was the inevitable route for them all. They disagreed believing they would be different, that wasn't the way they would turn out, as they delved head first deep into conversation.

The week had gone by quite swimmingly. Ethan had managed to turn Rei's hair a vibrant shade of ginger by convincing her to let him put *Sun In* in her hair. The lemony hydrogen peroxide spray that *would naturally highlight your hair in 30 minutes under direct sun* gave no indication of results under an isolated burst of clouded sky and heavens deluge! It was not a good look and in truth neither were amused, but Rei shrugged it off knowing it was only hair, hers thankfully grew at an alarming rate. Ethan said she should get to a hairdresser as soon as they got back to Japan, which she did. They bleached it all over to give it any chance of an outcome other than the colour green it was threatening to be. Rei wasn't sure if that was really how hair colouring worked this being her first foray into such avenues or whether this was the Japanese being polite and not having worked on *gaijin's* (aliens) hair before. Ethan seemed pleased with the final product, it had all been worth it. Rei wasn't convinced, she now felt like a コールガール a *kōrugāru* (call girl) all she needed now was a mini skirt and some large platform shoes and the look would be complete; bright, sexy and cute.

She would learn later on he had quite the obsession with hair, both his and hers, at various times and wondered if it was a *man* thing. Her father had always demanded that her mother keep their daughter's hair long, way past their bottoms, long enough for them to sit on. It caused her mum and the girls great distress as the weekly bath and hair wash on a Sunday afternoon came ever closer each week, hours spent tugging and pulling, scraping and holding, tears between sections parted and parts put back together as the whole became whole again. *What was this preoccupation, fixation, infatuation with tresses and locks?* she wondered. Hair was the first thing most men noticed supposedly. It was said that a woman's length and quality of hair served as a marker of genetic strength, of health, of youthfulness and of their reproductive potential. Rei had good hair so it was easy for her to not worry about it, although today in its titian, burnt state, it may have been a different story.

~

With a tad of the *ginge-minge* about her and the start of the new year only a few hours ahead Rei played on the sand like a child, content within herself and the beauty of the island they were on. She hopped between beach and sea, ocean and land, enjoying the simplicity of island life and the stunning majesty of the nature around her. Ethan sat tanning on the side lines, bottle of local beer in hand, and watched on enjoying himself in the global inaugural new year's eve build up. Rei was looking forward to dancing tonight, there was a beach party along the shore which they'd bought tickets for a few days ago, it was the only thing that she'd requested that they do this trip, everything else she was easy with, but she wanted to dance and this was her opportunity.

As she made dolphins in the sand a group of locals came and sat with her completely immersed in what she was doing. They spoke together, laughed and moved as one despite the language barrier. In truth there was none, they understood each other perfectly. Ethan shuffled his feet through the sand, grains sieving through his toes amused and bewildered by the constant magnetism around and towards Rei.

I only have to turn my back for a minute and you are always surrounded by people he said.

Rei could detect not only a compliment but also an underlying whiff of insecurity. She let it pass. She watched on as he sipped and gulped his way through more of the local draft brew. As day turned to night, they went back to their room to change for the evening out. They shared dinner and began their walk along the beach to the party beneath the night stars, shining brightly in the clear, dark skies. They stopped to sit on the shore in the sand and take it all in, the beauty of the cosmos. Ethan lay down on his back and looked up to the stars Rei beside him, he said he was feeling a little tired now and needed a nap. Rei glanced at the people now walking past her, past them, on their way to the party, the numbers increasing as the party drew closer.

Okay, but we'll need to get going soon Rei said aware that she felt like Cinderella with a ticking time bomb, her dancing shoes were primed for action and she only had one shot.

Yeah, yeah, I just need a minute Ethan replied, promptly falling into a deep and heavy sleep. One where no-one can wake you and one cannot wake oneself. He lay there motionless for the rest of the night until sunrise on a happy New Years Day where he woke and stumbled home to Rei in bed in their room. Icy and cold. Dancing shoes hung up to dry.

It had been early retirement for the shoes and punishment of sorts for Rei. She hadn't felt safe going up to the party by herself, the crowds passing, rowdier and more drunk as the minutes progressed. She took herself home after numerous attempts to shake and wake Ethan from his slumber, realising this was no way to be treated and no way to treat someone.

She felt sad and alone but there was no way this was going to affect the rest of her holiday. She would take herself to bed and begin fresh the next day. *Hmm, happy New Year* she thought to herself.

1981

The walls are full of moving shadows as the tree outside sways in the wind, the moonlight reflecting through the leaves upon the Artex ceiling. The swirls stippled by the moonlit glow amplifying the patterns and giving grandeur to the semi dark silhouettes of the leaves outside, appearing like potential monsters on the inside. Rei looks closely at the shapes and tries to form pictures from them, a dog maybe, a cloud, anything happy, but instead she feels a menacing darkness overshadowing her. She tries to regulate her breath to tell herself it's ok and that there is a pane of glass between her and the threat outside and around her, it cannot get in, and so she pulls the cover above her head and talks herself to sleep as every night before.

She wakes in the morning and with both parents pre-occupied she slips into the bathroom and reaches for the kiddie nail scissors. She loves the colour of the plastic-coated metal handles where you put your fingers through, a soft mermaid blue. To her they are as big as a pair of scissors downstairs that the grown-ups use. She'd never been allowed to use them before and they fell clumsily around her thumb and forefinger. She creeps lightly into her parent's bedroom and stands on tiptoes before the mirrored panel on the front of their wooden wardrobe door. She grabs a bunch of her hair and with a few (perhaps with hindsight, clumsy) stabs cuts the front part as quickly as possible so as to not get caught. She picks up the long precious locks (evidence) from the wooden floor beneath her feet and missing the creaky floorboard on her way out replaces the scissors, content that her mission has been accomplished. She had wanted a fringe like all the other girls for a long time now, she also wanted her ears pierced too but was told that *if, when you are eight years old you still want them done, then you can, for your birthday.* Somehow though there was no leeway or explanation regarding the fringe. It had seemed like an awfully long time in Rei's world waiting, wanting a fringe with no conversation about it. Murmurs of expense and time fell idly to a young girl with a desire and a pair of shears in her hand. She thought she was doing everyone a favour.

As she appeared downstairs, the shrieks thundered through the house. Her hand was grabbed and she was dragged, pushed and thrust up the stairs to whence she came from.

Show me what you have done!?! came the voice.

Rei relived the moments prior.

Everyone at school has a fringe! What's the problem? she wondered internally, knowing not to say that much out loud.

They said I should get one too. I haven't hurt anyone she offered up as means of an answer. Her defiance and complete naivety to the situation aggravating the scene further. She was lifted up and held point blank, short distance range facing the looking glass. Rei herself could see she definitely was not *the fairest of them all*, she didn't need to ask the magic mirror that much. She had a few tufts of hair left pointing out at 90-degree angles in no particular order, no symmetry, no continuous direction. She wasn't sure she could liken herself to anything much, but it was *Ugly*.

Between parents blaming each other for the mishap and grabs and attempts to tame the tufted, clumped hair with clips and grips and water and gel it was evident there was nothing further to do than to march into school and be presented to the headmistress before the day began.

Rei shrank into her skin listening to the rants and raves the accusations and the upset. She hadn't blamed anyone and she knew she wouldn't dare mention anyone *ever* again. This was her doing and hers alone. She felt bad that the headmistress was having to listen to this and she willed the conversation over. Her parents none the happier returned to their working days and Rei to hers, learning that hair always grew back and not to do something so silly ever again.

Silly.

Silly girl.

1976

Rei was born in a hospital in a town with the same name as her surname and so her passport would show the name twice in two different places, or was that locations? She always felt it was kind of special - grown, born and named in and after the one place.

Who else in the world could say that? she wondered.

Later on in life she would smile to herself filling in forms as people stopped her to say, *no dear not your surname, where you were born!* Every time a fresh dialogue would begin, an opening into an unknown world of communication between strangers.

Her birth town was not a particularly special place, comprised of five villages *On the Up* transitioning from the manufacturing industry to a service led sector; it was pretty grimy in fact.

They live in a small flat above a shop on the high street, the walls adorned with large brown and orange flowered wallpaper and a high pram in the hallway. Her great grandmother's hands shake as she holds her cup of tea, the milky potion toppling over the china's edge and into the saucer beneath each and every time she comes to visit and walk Rei. She has a hanky tucked up her dress sleeve which she uses all the time, for everything, but it always smells of roses.

The sweet smell of roses.

This is what Rei remembers.

2002

Rei knocks at the door, Aaron at her side and Bella in her arms. She is not entirely sure what she is letting herself in for but her friend Kassie assures her she'll love it.

All of the rugby club have been and had it done now too. It's great for clearing, you'll feel amazing afterwards. Promise.

A slender woman with long blonde hair and striking blue eyes opens the portal and as they cross the threshold she asks Aaron,

How many angels can you see?

Three he replies nonchalantly.

Rei had never spoken of angels before, never even contemplated them so was taken aback by his matter of factness, completely unfazed by the question. They walk into the adjoining room where the colonic would take place and settle in at the desk, wooden toys in hand.

She had been on a mission to clear herself of everything that did not belong in her body for some time now and having written to her father she felt she had dealt with the emotional remnants. She ate well, not having consumed gluten or dairy since her days in Japan feeling so much brighter and lighter for it. She had only had one glass of wine since her alcohol poisoned night in the Land of the Rising Sun many years ago but not a drop more alcohol.

Having had Aaron, she realised the importance of being fully present and alive, ready for him, she knew she would never drink again. He was too precious to her. She could not afford to be anything other than 100% ready for action.

Whilst he grew in her belly, she could not get enough carbs, pasta and potatoes which she never ate any time before or after. With Bella it was tuna that called and a family size pack of Maltesers each day, not a choice as such more a necessity, that came with a smile as she recalled her solitary Malteser, piano playing childhood.

She had forgotten quite how clearly her body spoke to her demanding its needs. Immediately after the birth of them both she had sprung back to her pre-birth shape and her pre-pregnancy eating habits so this calling for clearing now was much deeper than she could explain. She was fit and she was healthy, but something within told her there was more.

Today was the first (and last) experimentation into such realms, she trusted her friend and believed that *the removal of unnecessary toxins and waste* could only but help her cause and so she jumped up on to the treatment table and the session began. Once finished she jumped off, glad she'd done it but knowing she didn't need to come again.

There was something enchanting about the woman that Rei admired, she was clearly much older but had such a youthful vitality about her. Rei hoped she may look and feel this way when she was her age, it was quite remarkable. As they packed away their toys which had kept the kids entertained for the last forty-five minutes she turned to Rei and said

I know a guy that you would absolutely love. He's from way over in South America, his name is Noah.

Interesting thought Rei and gave it as much thought as bumping into a friend in the street saying *let's meet for coffee.* It never happened, but it was lovely to feel the offer was there.

They packed up and left waving goodbye, three happy faces to one other.

2020

Rei wrenches her heart and her mind from their vibrations calling them to attention. She had back up and had conducted everything accordingly. *It was safe, she was safe,* she told herself.

She had had no dealings with Jack for a while now too frail to deal with anything but her health; that had been the main priority, getting back to at least semi-fitness. It had been well over a year since they'd left, backpacks in tow for the night, never to return. So much had changed since, yet here they were attempting to claw back their home, retrieve some money from it; anything so they could move on and move forward in life. Rei had emailed him well in advance and let him know they would be going in with an estate agent at 10am that morning to get a valuation on the property.

The last dealings they had had with each other he had sworn

I will never leave, never move out, it is mine now and there is nothing you can do about it.

She didn't expect a response this time and neither did she get one. She spoke to the police and informed them of her intentions, there was a file logged and they knew of the situation well, it had gotten quite big over the past few years.

Her two feet carrying her to the front door, feeling the pavement beneath her she breathed in the crisp winter air and looked sideways for assurance from her friend Nina, who half smiled, and then glanced across to Aaron to check he was ok. He seemed so, unperturbed as he so often was. The estate agent was yet to arrive so they hovered like fireflies in the front garden on the path, close yet far enough away to not be seen to be encroaching even though it was *her* home. He ran up the pathway catching up with them, apologising for being a few minutes late, aware of the tense and precarious situation. He had dealt with Rei across many previous years through her own house sales and those of her clients so they had a great working relationship. Rei had felt close enough to share the bare bones of the situation, she didn't feel it was fair to let anyone into open territory without warning. He said he thought he already had a potential buyer for her if Jack was open to it. She let him lead the way, the professional, unsure of what may await them. He knocked at the front door and then stood back waiting for a response. Nothing. He knocked again, and then again. After the third time they nodded between themselves that it was safe to go in, they could all bear witness to one another's moves.

As they turned left into the first room Rei could hear water, a shower on in the next bedroom. Her heart leapt to her mouth, she wanted to chase the promise of fresh air and safety outside, but knew this was something she had to address. Here and now.

Hello? she called out. *Hello? Is there anyone there?*

As they shuffled forward towards the bedroom, she saw love cards whispering sweet nothings and displays of grand affection with flowers and presents strewn across the windowsills and furniture around them. She saw Rose wanting to peek inside and told her not to.

The rainfall from the shower came to a close and Rei called out once more.

Hello? Is there anyone there?

Who's that? came a woman's voice. It definitely wasn't Jack's daughter.

It's Rei. Jack's ex. She replied. *We are here with the estate agent as notified a few weeks ago. We only need a few minutes. A quick walk around and then we will be gone. Sorry to disturb you.*

Rei turned to see Aaron, Rose and the estate agent's horrified faces before her. Their concern for her and what she was having to deal with. The steam from the shower room permeating the hallway now, as the girlfriend part opened the door wrapped in a towel, faces red from worry, concern, rage and fear.

Dispassionately Rei led them away and through the house to survey the changes. They were not to her taste and she would not have done it that way, but it was all irrelevant now. They heard the girlfriend call Jack from within the bathroom walls behind the hall door ajar. Him on speakerphone angry, irritated, shouting at her to *Get them out! Call the police!*

But it's her home, she's done nothing wrong. She told you they were coming…

They left not needing to hear the rest, their job was done. Shaking within, Rei felt relieved they had managed to get this far. She felt for the girlfriend, she knew it all too well. She could hear it in her voice, eggshells cracked and trampled. They were no longer beneath Rei's feet and they would be there for all the others until they were not. It was no longer her cross to bear and just as she had taken responsibility for staying in the relationship there was no sympathy to be had, empathy yes and understanding for sure, but nothing more.

She walks back to the car quickstepping past the roses that she'd once planted, and on into the future, away from the ugliness of the past knowing and feeling there were tendrils still so present now no matter how hard she wished they were gone.

2006

It's the final term of her Dance Movement Therapy Certification and they are preparing for their finale performance in the theatre, the marking of their graduation and the culmination of the year's work with local communities. Rei is huge, her whole body swollen, engulfed by the baby. Unlike the previous two pregnancies there is no hiding this one. By three months she looked fit to burst. Now over six months pregnant she looked like she was full term with twins (or more).

When they had begun putting the routine together a few months ago a backwards roll didn't seem too unusual at the time, now the team members were worried she would be getting into all sorts of mischief by performing the move. Rei assured them she would only do it if it was there to do, she certainly wasn't going to put her or the baby at any risk, she loved being a mum, they were her everything, she couldn't wait for the arrival of number three.

It had been another pregnancy that just happened, not planned, irresponsibly occurred through *innocent* ignorance. With such a big gap between the baby and the top two now, Rei was convinced they would need to have a fourth to balance the scales. The other two were co-joined, they even called themselves *The Cuddle Twins,* embroiled and unified moving together as one in everything. But a couple of months in and Rei swore this was the last, her body reminding her of all the things she'd forgotten about pregnancy from day one.

Her feet had grown from a size 5.5 to an 8 overnight; like a heron's webbed feet designed to spread weight over the largest possible area, or a goose's adapted to bring greater force swimming and propelling its body like a paddle through the water, Rei felt like a dinosaur with a foot span of a woolly mammoth, her feet struggling to keep up with the rate of growth and stability needed above.

Rei loved the aspects of movement and dance by themselves and wholly enjoyed watching people be able to express themselves in a way they could not elsewhere in life. It was like watching someone walk through a door from one realm to the next, completely transformed, like the contestants on *Stars In Their Eyes* walking through the curtain *Tonight Matthew, I'm going to be…Myself!*

Sometimes she could see the pain and the anguish clients kept locked within being released, other times the pure freedom and joy of having the space to be themselves catapulted the clients to a new level. Either way so much was revealed without words and the clients always left a little lighter and clearer each time, their relationship with themselves and with Rei stronger, deeper and more transparent. It was a beautiful time and she knew she was going to miss these few hours each week and the people she worked with but there was no regret, there was another stunning being on its way soon to be delivered to her care.

She could feel the auditorium hold their breath, all eyes on her (and her belly) throughout the performance. She hadn't meant to be the distraction, but it was inevitably so, like the underdog in the championships who finds everyone's favour she stood out like the proverbial sore thumb, everyone slightly uncomfortable but intrigued and spellbound at what they were witnessing nonetheless.

The backwards roll went down a treat, the whole crowd gasping and then up on their feet cheering, the students rushing in and flanking Rei on all sides. She had never been one for attention, but the love she felt from her clients in this moment nearly swiped her from her feet many of whom never spoke, had developmental disabilities and never shared their emotions. The power and strength of their relationship so clear for all. The crowd went wilder still.

The blackened hall once cold and empty now alive and vibrant with love and appreciation.

Rei slinked up the side walkway to Ethan, Aaron & Bella and gave them a huge hug. They could go home now. It was done.

1992

Rei sits for what feels like forever but was perhaps a few nano-seconds unsure of what to say, feeling the intensity of everyone's eyes on her. James had just professed his love for her across a room full of people. A group of teenagers in one of their parent's homes on a Saturday afternoon, in full light of a summer's day. There was no hiding. The bottle had come out and it had been spun. The game had seemed pleasant enough up until this point in time although definitely arousing anxiousness and anxiety with each twist of the glass bottle as it gyrated, rotated, whirled and revolved around its starting point on the carpet between them all.

As the red Château Lafite-Rothschild threatened to spill from its cork as it rotated on its invisible wheel, it stopped, pivoting towards James.

Truth or dare? the group cheered happy for a new victim.

Truth, he replied.

Who in this room do you fancy?

A pause.

The silence echoing around the room with its floral wallpaper, gingham fabrics and classic furniture; the coordinated accent chairs, the comforting pastel sofa and the wooden sideboard adorned with family photos and fresh flowers. It was Laura Ashley *Cottagecore* to the max. Rei felt queasy in its presence, she thought it was all too *matchy-matchy* despite knowing its monetary worth.

Rei! came the response, the eyes leered towards and upon her; now she felt sick.

Spin, spin, spin! Arose the chorus, and as he did Rei knew what was coming. A bottle top her way.

Truth or dare? cackled the crowd.

Truth, she replied wishing she didn't have to, knowing full well that a dare would have meant trouble for sure.

Do you fancy James?

Rei's heart sank. She looked over to James, sweet, innocent and clearly holding on for her very next word, she felt the pressure of the group, they were pretty much the only friends left not coupled up at this point and it seemed so obvious. Rei wasn't attracted to James, she didn't even really know him, but more than anything she didn't want to hurt, embarrass or humiliate him, that felt inhumane.

Yes, she said, not telling the truth, but opting for what seemed like the safest and most comfortable option.

Yey!! cheered everyone from all sides as they sprung up celebrating before returning…

Spin, spin, spin!

Rei could feel what was coming once more and despite her silent pleas and her industrious spin convincing herself otherwise, the phial of alcohol weaved and pirouetted its way straight back round to James.

Truth or dare? jeered the pack now feeling more like a mob.

Rei could see James realise the intensity of the situation, at the same time realising he was actually very similar to her, both wishing they were not a part of this preferring the quiet and the shadows to the loud limelight. She could see him struggling to work out which was the worse option, saying truth or saying dare. Neither seemed pretty.

Dare he whispered hoping the quiet murmur would let him off entirely.

The ineluctable, and somewhat necessary for the comrades, proposition was proffered.

Snog Rei! Yey! Wha-hey!

It was as if coming into bat for the first time a batsman had struck a ball high into the air clearing the boundary line, hitting a six, to take them through to the final of a Test match. The spectators were up on their feet storming the pitch, the bottle of red shooting across the room (still corked at the very least).

Thankfully the unrest gave a bit of scope for anonymity as James slowly got up from his cross-legged position and made his way across to Rei. He knelt down gently, and moved in for the kiss. They didn't snog, but they kissed lips and from that moment forth they were an item. Rei didn't ever have the heart to tell him the truth, it seemed as if it would have been even worse to reveal it then as each day passed by. Days became months became years, and the two were as solid and close as brother and sister.

As all their friends fell apart and their relationships crashed and burned Rei and James stayed close and went the distance.

2002

As she pushes the buggy into the lounge, she glances into the mirror, catching sight of the purity of her form in a white summer's dress. She had been on a breakfast fast of freshly pressed apple juice with apple cider vinegar and garlic this past week since having the colonic and felt great for it. Her eyes seemed brighter and her mood too.

As she unpacked the wares beneath the pram seat a white leaflet fell from the shopping bag, seemingly from nowhere in particular, like a white feather falling from the sky on a summer's walk with no bird in sight making you stop and wonder at the marvel of it all. She picked it up and took a look, it was a flyer for a session with Noah, the guy the hydro-therapist had told her about. Rei sat down on the floor flabbergasted. She didn't believe in magic, but this was a clear sign as any she had ever been given.

Within a week she'd been given three signals and communications about this guy Noah. One verbally suggesting they could be friends, the second in a health food shop in Woodstock later that same day, and now this back at home many days later.

She read the leaflet once more knowing she must go. She would speak with Ethan on his return that evening.

And so, she did.

2024

Rei stands as the car salesman approaches her, she's already made it clear she is not looking for a new car and is happy with hers, a sporty version, black, sleek and compact. She is only here as the car needed servicing and given it was so cold outside, she opted to sit in with a cup of peppermint tea and wait for the works to be done instead of taking her usual walk around the block.

His smile is effervescent, bubbling over and Rei cannot help but join in his joy. She speaks with him and he offers to show her what cars they have available as her three-year contract is up. She reiterates that she is not in the market for a new car but shares she is happy to look and learn if he doesn't mind sharing his time. He asks what she pays each month and she tells him and then he walks her to a brand-new Mini Cooper on the showroom floor inviting her to sit in and make herself comfortable. He's a kiwi with a strong accent and they get talking about New Zealand and where he is from, they talk about the latest news over there and it transpires the school Rei had stayed in for five weeks when she was nineteen was where his cousins were educated.

Such a small world they mused.

The car stereo on, the sound resonating through her body, the twelve speakers configured around the car for greater quality proving their worth. The sunroof pared back to reveal the starlit showroom above. The dashboard and display clearly much newer, simpler, brighter and up-to-date than her current six-year-old model. She admits it's a great car.

She had never thought of a Mini before her last purchase, she'd had VWs for life, a whole troupe of them after her Japanese Mazda MX5 and her first Fiat Cinquecento. The Mini worked well. It was fast, sporty, efficient and easy to park in the city being so relatively small. She loved it, surprisingly so.

She recalled how it had come about, walking into the Oxford showroom after covid. They had bought their flat purposefully for the fact that it was central and they didn't need a car, cutting down expenses from the outset; yet after training to be a celebrant she was being used far and wide and needed transport to get to the next of kin's houses and to wedding venues across the country. The bank balance was still frighteningly low but she'd looked online and saw there were some steals to be had. She waltzed up to the salesman at his desk and said she was looking for a black mini, that much she was sure of. The only criteria other than the colour were that it must be automatic and it Must (with a capital M) have heated seats. She had grown accustomed to the warmth on her back, on her kidneys, even in the height of summer and it definitely took the chill off a winter's day in England. He asked what her budget was. She replied that she didn't really know, she would just know the car when she saw it and would deal with it from there. He looked perplexed and pressed for a more specific answer, *the size of the deposit even?*

She told him that the car would determine the budget, she didn't have money in the bank but she would know and it would be fine. Rei could see he seemed a little unsure whether she was a time waster or not with such vague unknowns, but she also knew he knew she was legit. He was just struggling to settle with his heart and his mind's different version of events. *Ok* he said swinging round his screen, lets input black, automatic, with heated seats. 34 came up nationwide with a price range starting at the bottom and reaching to the very top. He was still scrambling for a normal way to be with this, but Rei assured him she'd know. He smiled timorously as if he may be in trouble. They scanned through the first few pages, Rei saying *No* to each.

He asked *Why?* trying to understand her reasoning, if any.

I can't explain she replied *they are just not the one.*

He flicked the screen again and there it was. *Yes, that's it* she said.

Why? he asked again hoping for more clarity this time.

I'm not sure, everything about it, also the number plate, it just feels right she replied cheerfully. He was happy she was happy but still he asked again, *but how do you know? You don't know the price of it yet.*

Well let's see what we can do Rei responded.

He got out his calculator and worked out a monthly price, with a nice round number for Rei spread over many years, and what was left was the deposit, which of course happened to be just within Rei's bank balance. Rei asked if he could round this down too, to a more palatable number which of course he did. *Bingo!* The transaction was done. The car would be delivered in two days time and that was as easy as it was. She knew it had been gifted from Heaven, it had served her well and she was happy with it. It was within her monthly budget and still worked like a dream, there was nothing more she needed or desired.

~

Hard out! he exclaims as she appreciates the sound system for what it is.

They've done a good job with the sunroof and the stitching she says, always a stickler for the details.

Yeah right, he says less formal and more at ease with her now, he knows there is no hard sale to be done here.

You know what give me a moment, let me see what we can do he says marching off to the glass framed office.

See about what? Rei thought to herself.

She continued to take a look at the cars on display and felt hugely content that she loved her car, and even if she had the money (which she didn't) she preferred hers to all the other flashier ones here on show around her.

He came back out a few minutes later papers in his hand.

What if we could give you this brand-new car for the same price that you are paying for yours now? he beamed.

Rei now perplexed herself asked *how is that even possible? My car is six years old and this is fundamentally a better car with all the gadgets and a sunroof too…*

It's the end of the season and we have got to hit our sales targets he said. *This is the last Mini Cooper left in the country; it was meant for another customer but they have just failed their credit check. It's meant to be being dispatched up north to a different salesroom tomorrow, but if we can sell it today, and I'd love to sell it to you, then we all win.*

Rei contemplated what she'd heard and immediately thought they were pulling her leg, the office assistant now joining them to hear her response.

I don't understand said Rei. *How is that even possible?*

The office assistant ran her through the figures and the situation they were in as a branch. Rei understood what she was saying and knew it was true but she was still shell shocked. Her mini's vehicle check had just come back needing £2000 worth of work something she had not been prepared for. She was trying to work out how she could pay for that right now her mind running the math.

Look if you sign today, you can drive home with this new top of the range Cooper and we will pay for the work to be done on your car he said. *How about that? Super simple. No money needed, just drive home in a different, brand spanking new car.*

Rei felt like she was in a reality TV show, the cameras hidden behind screens, everyone watching her laughing at her for being such a mug believing such a spin off. She couldn't quite take it in. She had come in for a two-hour vehicle check and was quite literally being given what seemed like a free upgraded car to drive home in right now whilst also not having to pay for the work on her old car.

Bonkers. Crazy she thought.

The two colleagues looked at each other unsure as to why Rei wasn't biting their hand off.

This is the best deal you'll ever get, it's the best that we've ever seen. It's virtually impossible that it will ever be possible again. You'd be mad not to take it!

Rei knew they weren't lying to her but she still wasn't convinced it wasn't a great big hoax. She asked if she could take a moment to call her fiancé, explaining she couldn't quite take it all in.

Of course, take all the time you need they said.

Rei called Gabriel and talked him through it. A great lover of cars and a mean machine with finances he was the perfect person to check in with.

Absolutely he said, go for it!

Holy smokes thought Rei as she got off the phone. *This is real! It's actually happening. Thank you God. Truly.*

She walked over to the office and let them know she would love to take up their deal, she was happy to sign for it all today but could she please go home and come back in the morning to do the hand over. She needed a bit of space to really let this all sink in, it seemed too surreal otherwise. The owner of a brand new upgraded on every level car, having saved money not having to repair the old car, and winning with future savings on this, and not an ounce of energy spent on the deal *at all*. It was literally as if the car fell out of heaven, onto and into her lap.

Within the space of a few months she'd been gifted the perfect flat, the perfect (soon-to-be) husband, and now the perfect car.

Rei knew there was no perfection, but by jove these were as near perfect as could ever be!

2019

Rei meets up with Dan. A friend who probably on another day in another situation she would firstly never have met and secondly not really had the chance to be so close with, but right now he's the only person in the country she actually feels safe with, who has her back, wants nothing from her, and perhaps most importantly who does not judge her.

They had met in a lounge room in Soho House one morning, Rei escaping from the torment going on back home to work in the quiet room there, him stumbling in hungover asking to take refuge on the sofa in front of the fire. They got talking and later exchanged numbers after he told her he felt like he'd had ten years of therapy in one hour, he felt like a new man.

How do you know how to ask all the right questions? he asked.

I'm not sure she replied *I just follow the flow.*

Would you be up for interviewing me? he asked. *I've just published a book and I've got another going to screen soon so I'm being asked to give interviews but I always tense up, yet with you it's easy.*

Sure, replied Rei, she needed more work at the moment and was happy to try anything.

You are an absolute diamond he said,

You are one of life's diamonds,
You are one of my diamonds.
I cannot thank you enough he shared.

~

It was a cold winters day and she could still barely move. The final operation had occurred over three months ago now yet her strength seemed to diminish rather than grow. He drove down from Cambridgeshire to collect her from their Airbnb and drive her to her old home. Three hours driving each way to help her pack up some boxes in an inhospitable house and then return. She was beyond grateful.

They had become close over the months rarely speaking but with a deep knowing of each other, he knew the story of what had gone on. He said he'd help wherever he could no questions asked, no strings attached. She was so appreciative to have him as an aide right now, it seemed no one else was capable of not being critical, imperious or disparaging, he was a breath of much needed fresh air.

He helped her into his car as the few steps alone seemed too much and they drove pulling up outside Jack's home, *her* house. She had emailed Jack in advance letting him know she would go in and pack up the remaining stuff. She hadn't been back for over six months now and wasn't sure what to expect.

All their stuff had been collated and thrown into the end bedroom piled high, some stacked, some fallen, some jettisoned. It did not feel nice. What was expensive furniture now looked like it belonged in a closing down charity shop, or better still the tip. She had not been prepared for this. Over flowing bags; pillows, cushions, rugs, lamps, rails, mirrors, pictures, paintings, stools, beds, baskets, books, DVDs, shoes, clothes all stored into the one room. It was overwhelming. Her whole life up until this point crammed into this small space. What had once felt luxurious now felt empty.

Dan pulled her down a stool and she sat unable to do anything else. *Where shall we start?* he said *Tell me what to do and I'm on it!*

Truth be told Rei wanted to set the whole lot on fire, being here bought up so many bad memories she just wanted to be done with it, but she knew that wasn't possible or realistic.

Ok she said *I'm really sorry I literally can't do anything and I don't want to sound bossy but if we can make three piles that would be great. One for the tip, one for charity and one for me to take.*

She knew they only had a couple of weeks left in the Airbnb they were now staying in, the money from her savings had completely drained now and she was incapable of working, she couldn't even move still. The council had come out yesterday and they had been declared *officially homeless.* They were now being placed on the register and as of two weeks today they were out on the street without a home and penniless.

Rei looked at the stuff and knew some of it was worth money but she neither had the energy or the wherewithal to deal with it right now. Besides if she sold it, it would not give her much past a basket full of groceries, it was not worth it. She took a pair of shoes and a suitcase (an upgrade from her overnight bag) with her, that's all that she could afford to take, she knew not what was ahead of them and she needed to make everything as simple for them all as possible.

Dan got to work and assured her if it got too much, he would take her home and come back another day to help her out. He could see how frail she was and knew even sitting there was a big ask.

But you've driven all that way she shared, embarrassed and anxious.

And I would do it all again tomorrow if that's what is needed, he replied.

She feigned a smile and pointed out some pieces for the charity shop. After forty-five minutes exerting as little energy as possible directing exactly what was needed where, she was fully spent. It didn't look like they'd made much progress but the car was full of stuff for the hospice, and there was just enough space for them both to squeeze in and to return Rei home to bed.

To oblivion.

2006

Rei the size of a house now calls her friends to tell them she won't be allowed on the flight to Sicily, she is bursting at the seams. It doesn't look like she is *carrying* a baby, more a grown man is playing hide and seek under her clothes. In her body to be precise.

She had been asked by the nursery staff if she knew who she was talking to having got into a deep and meaningful with one of the dads at pick up.

No, she replied, *should I?*

One of England's greatest musicians and songwriters! they chortled.

You seemed to get on well came the slightly loaded nuance.

Yes, we're meeting up with the kids tomorrow she replied not remotely disturbed. *He seems like a nice guy and Aaron and Ben play nicely together. It should be fun!*

She hadn't realised this would be the start of a very beautiful relationship for them all. Aaron was a deeply gentle boy with boundless creativity and didn't really enjoy the usual *boy* things. Rei had bought both him and Bella up appreciating both the masculine and the feminine, no colour was ruled out, and violence and force was a definite no-go. Consequently, not many of the young boys or girls around them were used to drawing or art, more guns and destruction, but not so with Ben. Together in each other they'd found their first true friend.

Rei had got to know most of the village by now teaching them all yoga and both the kids and adults alike loved her. The kids couldn't wait for her lessons each week and she loved seeing them transform before her eyes, the parents relieved at what they came to pick up each time, a healthy restored child, calm and responsive. It was a job she loved doing and something she could take Aaron and Bella along with her to. It worked well and they enjoyed the interaction with other kids of varying ages and the responsibility of work it gave them despite their young ages of four and three. Ben hadn't been yet but was keen to come.

They ended up spending most days together at the Oliver's house, the boys merrily content and Bella equally part of their tribe. Rei got on fabulously with both Mark and his wife Milena and by now they'd already spent three holidays together. Rei didn't share this fact with anyone else in the village it was unnecessary to, yet tongues wagged and the village rumour spread that Rei and the world-famous musician Mark were having an affair. Nothing could have been further from the truth and this was an early insight for Rei into the pernicious effects of village life, of adults with too much time on their hands and not enough purpose. She had never really fitted in anywhere; she was too young, had not enough money, had too many kids…there never seemed to be quite the right balance or the right reasons to. She was used to it now and took it at face value for what it was. She was super happy and enriched having the Olivers in her life and she didn't need anyone else. If their name was spoken around her, she would feel the universe stop, the air contract, as people toyed with the unspoken questions inside their heads. She learned to keep her head down and sidestep any possible jibes or probes. She thought if she couldn't hear it, it would go away. It never really did, but it was nicer not listening to it anyway.

~

Unable to take the flight abroad Rei grabbed the small handsaw from the potting shed and took to the garden outside. They'd just moved into a bungalow that could house the growing family, it came with a tiny orchard in the backyard and although she was not fit to fly there was nothing to stop her getting down on her hands and knees and sawing down twenty odd age-old conifers that were blocking out the neighbouring light.

Her mum who was visiting suggested it wasn't the greatest idea given Rei's size or how far gone in her pregnancy she was, but she also knew she was probably wasting her breath. Once Rei had something in mind, it was done, no stopping her.

It was later, as Ethan returned home from work, that Rei realised the magnitude of what she had taken on and achieved as the sunlight now streamed into their garden, the space so much grander and vaster. The space was nearly ready now for his arrival, as was she.

1998

Living with the boys was grand, she loved each and every one of them and knew them all so intimately. They'd shared bathrooms, dinners and washing machines for over a year now, she knew their every move and they hers. Each bill meticulously gone through, each telephone number called attributed to its user. A couple of the boys had mobile phones but it was still cheaper for them to use the landline, so everyone knew who spoke to whom, when and for how long. They were all wholesome and clean cut, not perfect but they looked out for one another which was great.

They tired of Rei's Tuesday evening vegetable pasta surprise and hoped for steak and chicken but knew she did not have the money for such luxuries like they did. Skiing and drinking were as much as their student loans touched, Rei's paid the bills and she bolstered her rent payments with her three around university time jobs. They would take the mickey out of her and sometimes it would scar but she knew they didn't mean any harm. Secretly, not secretly, she knew they all really cared for her and if she had given them a chance, she knew a couple of them would have taken it, but she was clear, they were not for her.

She had been on a date with a guy she had recently met who turned up to take her out in his Mercedes convertible, not your usual student vehicle. He was well educated, suited and booted, smelt of cologne, and took her to the fanciest of restaurants a short car ride away. He was the son of an electricity empire mogul and clearly not short of a buck or two. He was well spoken, had all the right features in the right place and all the manners to go with it. Yet Rei was completely turned off by it all, by him, and he'd done nothing wrong, it had all been *right*.

He asks her out again and Rei mumbles *Mm, I'm not sure, I'm sorry.*

Gobsmacked that someone had not been bowled over by his chivalry and toys, which clearly won all the other girls over and had them all fighting over him for, before Rei, he shared *…but you're the nicest girl I've ever met. You're not like the others. You don't ask for anything from or of me. I would love to see you again. Let me give you some space. You've got my number, call me.*

Rei jumped out of the car and said goodbye never to see him again.

She got back to her room and closed the door behind her, the boys wanting to know what had happened. She knew they would ask, *of course they would, who wouldn't?*

She sat on the edge of her bed, her hand-held typewriter within view and her next assignment ready ahead of time and pondered *Why she was so sickened by a nice guy? By nice guys in general? Why did she still feel the need for a bit of something else?*

She knew it made absolutely zero sense, but she also knew that was exactly where she would go next.

Like a moth to the flame.

1990

She feels given up. She's no longer waiting for anything. No prince, no rescue boat, no parent, no school teacher, no friend. She feels the persistent pressure on her eyelids forcing her to sleep. She feels safest here. Asleep.

She hears the daily routines go on around her; the 7am wake up calls, the stripping of beds, the placing of all the sheets and duvets and pillows on the study chairs now placed in the corridor for all to see, no one to escape this chore. The windows all opened wide to let the fresh minus zero temperatures in and all the nasty school girl germs out. Her body weighted to the bed, her bed.

She had been a school prefect every year and every term now since she had started, no one else had that record, yet here she was in the confines of her cubicle alone. Soul sick. Given up. Withdrawn.

Sister Duncan had told her that they would be taking no further action with Raquel, they couldn't. Her father was one of the largest donators to the school and they would not put that relationship in jeopardy. Rei understood loud and clear. It was about money and who you knew, not truth or love.

She wanted to get back to her body conditioning classes that she'd been teaching for the past couple of years now alongside aerobics and Step Reebok but her limbs would not carry her. She thought of The Sound of Music and of Maria waltzing through the abbey and climbing trees. Rei wished her sister was with her now and they could sit down and watch the film together for the eight-hundredth time at their nanny and granddad's house cross-legged in front of the TV, the video player whirling and churning its way around beside them, but her sister was living with her dad now far away, never having being sent to boarding school like Rei had. They hadn't seen each other for years it seemed. Rei knew the words off by heart and recounted her favourite parts.

How do you catch a cloud and pin it down?
How do you keep a wave upon the sand?
How do you hold a moonbeam in your hand?

She had always loved thinking about these predicaments as a child and they bought solace to her now too. She wondered if she was like Maria? *A problem to be solved?* It didn't really seem that way, no-one really seemed to care very much whether she stayed put or not. *Should I Stay or Should I Go* by the Clash now ringing in her ears

This indecision's buggin' me
If you don't want me, set me free
Exactly whom I'm supposed to be

She had no idea of who she was supposed to be. Her friends all knew what A-levels they wanted to take, what university they wanted to study in, what job they wanted, where they wanted to live and how many children they wanted to have. Rei couldn't see past the end of her nose let alone into her future self. The thing she did know was that sometimes you had to let go and open your hand instead of scrunching tightly to the thing you wanted most. If what was inside the palm of your hand in the first place was meant to be there, it would return or even just stay there, of its own accord.

She thought of a butterfly and let go of wanting to have any energy or to be able to participate in life again and promptly fell asleep.

2019

As she waits to go back in for surgery, she realises she has absolutely no idea where she is. She had been admitted into one hospital and then transferred to the next by chauffeur driven ambulance. She wanted to call the ho(s)tel and ask them to pack up her few things, so she could collect them when she was out the other side, as she couldn't afford to pay for a dank room laying idle for the night, but it was not possible. She looked around her for signs she might recognise but found none, a street alley, a brick wall, a graffitied lamp post, all usual London signs. She lay back on the bed and appreciated the light from the window behind her. She'd seen a few too many hospital beds by now and was pleased to see this one had a window attached, for the moment at least. She sees a vase of flowers and a thank you card for the nurses and smiles at the simple beauty of them. She can see them trying to grow stretching out towards the light wanting to unfurl, just as she is, and wonders if she will be here long enough to see their unfolding evolution?

She wakes and for a moment hesitates to place where she is. *Oh. In a hospital somewhere in London, that's right!* she reminds herself touching her belly to see if it's still there. Nothing had changed on the outside but now the baby and all its remnants had been fully removed thank goodness. She asked how long she could stay, hoping she could get a free non-paying night there, but they assured her she would be good to go home in a few hours once the doctor had checked her over. She wondered if she could get a taxi driver to be the responsible adult to take her *home* but was spared the process as she switched on her phone to find a message from João saying he would be there shortly. He'd managed to take a day off work and had caught a flight over. She was relieved that he was on his way, she could rest for a little while until he arrived.

They caught a taxi back to the ho(s)tel and João nearly died. He thought he'd walked into a murder scene. He tried to open the windows to alleviate the smell of dark, damp, yellow and now blood stained hotel rooms but they were locked and triple bolted.

I can't stay here he exclaimed *it's disgusting!*

Clearly not reading the situation or Rei's necessity to rest or her fragility after yet another surgery he proceeded to call numerous hotels on speakerphone trying to find a room for the night. He had to leave early in the morning to get back to work and Rei had to move on to her next client.

It's ok she said trying to assure him no green-eyed monster would eat him up alive, nor would the sheets or the carpet. *I just need to rest. I'm sorry* she said. *Thank you for coming over, I really appreciate it.*

He lay on the bed trying to hover above it as if he might catch something. He could well have done; his skin hadn't touched anything but the finest Egyptian cotton bedlinen and the finest cashmere jumpers in years. Rei knew that.

It wasn't ideal for sure, but right now it's what they had. He didn't get much sleep, that was obvious, Rei a little more so perhaps, she wasn't sure.

They said their goodbyes in the morning as he left for his flight home and Rei collected her car, paid her bill (another day's worth of work money down) and drove across country to her next client and accommodation for the next few nights. She prayed all the way there that she could see this one through.

She had, and there was, no back up plan.

2019

All her belongings had fitted into the smallest lock up storage unit there was available. She had met the removals man at the house and he had loaded her sorry state of affairs onto the back of his truck. He had seen her move many a time now.

This one is on me he said not needing to know anything but sensing it all.

Rei was dressed in a woolly hat and one of João's old jackets that he'd given to the boys five months prior. She hadn't heard from him since her third operation, he'd gone AWOL never to be heard from again. Rei knew it was all too much for him. It was fine when she was alive and kicking, but now she too was half dead it was another matter, the baby now obsolete and gone and with it the idea of their life together.

With an ocean between them and one half of the party unable to move it was an easy tactical manoeuvre. Fool's Mate played against Rei's weak opening moves, checkmate ensued, she had nowhere to go and no pieces left to play herself. Thankfully she had no energy left and no tears stored in the well to grieve. She was breathing and that was more than enough.

The van now packed up, she got back in her car and drove to the nearest town. She had arranged online to sell her car to webuyanycar.com. The beautiful new custom spec'ed VW Tiguan's Hire Purchase had been put in her name to aid with Jack's tax rebate, and subsequently post break up had been left to her to deal with. It was another part of the puzzle she'd had to pick up the pieces for. She had been complicit in these dodges and reaped the benefits of the holidays abroad. At first, she had questioned these actions and had said no to them all but then gradually over time she'd given way to the end of year purchases and the cash under the floorboards, not that she had access to it for it would be taken at any hint of turbulence between them, which there undoubtedly (and nearly always) was.

She had just about broken even after the monthly payouts to date and was relieved at the thought of the car having been sold, another string to the past cut, and buried. With her one suitcase of belongings in the boot she pulled in and signed away ownership of the car, handed over the keys and sat outside the perimeter fencing. Another step closer to having nothing.

She had flash backs to her car keys being stolen and the car removed so she couldn't go out; of her clothes being thrown out of the bedroom window onto the mud trodden wet footpath below; of him driving off on their holiday to the airport without her, leaving her stranded. So many memories from just one moment in time triggered by a car and a suitcase. She was glad she was no longer collecting these kind of memories anymore. She had no room for them in her body, and her body had no need for them.

She recalled driving empty handed to a friend's home after Jack had bolt locked their front door from the inside with some new *extra length, extra strength* builder's merchant screws, she can't remember whatever for, but he had damaged their newly constructed front entrance in the process and did not seem to care, as long as she was on the outside unable to get in, the rain lashing and howling at her feet, drenching her inside and out. The tears imperceptible from the monsoon flood occurring outside, him in their warm mansion on the inside. Her friends had not been in when she arrived but their son and his wife were. They opened the door appalled to see anyone in this state. Horrified they asked *What was up?* Rei too embarrassed and still not wanting to paint a bad picture of Jack said he had locked her out. She made it sound casual, an everyday occurrence, nothing too much to worry about. Both their eyes screwed up and their noses lifted, so they could look down them with perfect and immense disrespect. *Err, I don't think so. That doesn't sound like something Jack would do* and they closed the front door abruptly on her.

Rei got back into her car, drenched and stone cold. She was unsure why they had treated her that way, she hadn't lied about any of it, in fact she had omitted and hidden most of the facts. She shrank a little more inside believing for real it was all her fault, all because of her. Everyone could see it.
She was a failure.

She turned the heating on max and the car steamed up. She drove a few miles away and pulled over by some trees. There was nothing in the car, she always kept it clean and immaculately tidy except the few empty shopping bags neatly folded ready for the next weekly shop. Just this time she'd wished she'd let the kids keep their swimming kit in the boot, a towel would have come in real handy right now, to soak her up and act as a duvet. It was going to be a long, cold night.

This car. That car.

Thank God this one was going, going, gone!

In one day, she had said goodbye to her kids, her home, her belongings, her car, her life as she knew it and had always known it.

There was

n o t h i n g

left.

As the clouds form above her head, the chill whipped round her chest and reacted as it caught her warm breath, the green bus pulls up beside her and disappears. Another passenger onboard.

2024

Rei wakes and sets about her day as usual. As she hoovers the flat, she gets an impulse to call him, to say hi, but she ignores it. She removes the plug from the hall socket transferring it to the one in the lounge, the chord extended as far as it can reach and uses her foot to press the start button. As the machine kicks into action, it comes again.

Call him.

Like a voice from the depths of the ocean. She entertains the thought in her head and then buries it deep. She had nothing to say to him *What would be the point?* It would look weird like she wanted something when she didn't.

The guy that she had been talking to in South Africa a couple of months ago messaged her back thanking her for her honesty. He had been busy and dropped the ball on a few things including his relationship with her. Rei could feel the dishonouring although she couldn't really criticise him for it knowing all too well herself the demands of single-parent working life, she knew this budding relationship was a no-go area, and she had told him so. They had never met and hadn't known each other for long but they were close already. It didn't matter, she knew deep within, like that sleepy New Years Eve moment on the beach in the Philippines many moons ago that this was not the honouring she deserved. Everything she had been through had taught her that much at the very least. **To honour what she felt.**

She now knew her worth and was not prepared to settle for anything or anyone. She was beyond happy now and had everything she could ever possibly need. It was simple, manageable and gorgeous. For the first time ever, she could say with absolute certainty that she was happy to be alone and was not looking out for any potential match. She had accepted that she may well be single for the rest of her life, and it felt great! The thought of ringing Gabriel then for no apparent reason seemed silly and perhaps even provocative, something she was not prepared to entertain.

~

A few months prior after moving into her new flat she had invited Gabriel round to see her new home; they'd known each other for years now and she knew he would enjoy it. She made sure the invite was strictly between meal times and very clearly stating it was for a cup of tea and home viewing only; under no circumstances did she want him getting the *wrong idea*.

He came and they shared a nice hour or so together with Bodhi, it was refreshing someone talking to her son as the aware, wise gentleman that he was rather than judging him and reacting to his teenage choices. He offered to help him with his bike and so off the two of them went downstairs to the storage unit beneath whilst Rei warmed up the lamb and apricot tagine she had made for The Celebration happening in the building that afternoon. By the time the boys re-emerged it was time for Rei to leave. As they walked back down the stairs together Rei asked Gabriel if he wanted to see the communal areas, she had to go to drop the tagine off there before she could give him a hug goodbye anyway.

Of course, he said opening the door for her *I won't stay long though.*

The room was already full of sweets and cakes and people chatting over drinks so Rei placed the offering down much to the delight of the guests, a hearty warm savoury meal was the stand out piece. They took a seat by a couple of sofas, Rei talking to some newly moved in neighbours and Gabriel to some others. She knew she didn't have to worry about him; he was as great with people as she was.

The lady she was talking to some minutes into the conversation commented *Is your partner…?* Rei laughed, *oh no he's not my partner, just my friend who's over for the afternoon, he's just leaving in fact.* And with that they both excused themselves and said their goodbyes. As they got outside, they both smiled at the absurdity of the comment, but also deeply valued that it was clearly visible how much love they both moved with.

~

It was a couple of months until they spoke again and this time Rei was over for dinner at his place. Once the food was finished, they sat together on the sofa and Gabriel showed her a watch he was considering buying. Many years ago, he had commented on her own watch over a dinner table appreciating the finer details of it so knew she would be interested. They talked and laughed and then Rei noticed him deep in thought.

What are you thinking about? she asked.

Whether there was any purpose in us being in a relationship together? he replied matter of factly.

They both laughed and in chorus replied *Nah! We're good.*

They said their goodbyes and Rei left for home.

~

Yesterday had been a beautiful day and despite all the tears in the car after his question she hadn't felt drained or emotional. They had held hands all the way back from the party too, a hearty, full, settled silence between them. They said their goodbyes as he dropped her home, hugging as every other time, two friends appreciative of the time they'd spent together and of the day that they'd shared.

She cleared away the hoover and sat down to read, interrupted by a call on her phone. It was him.

Hello, she said *Fancy that! I nearly called you earlier. How are you? What do I owe the pleasure of your call?*

Hi, I'm well thank you he replied *Actually I'm not sure I am, I was just with my friends in their home and I couldn't get out fast enough which is unlike me, I just knew I had to call you. So here I am…What were you going to call me about?*

I'm not sure she said *I didn't really have anything to say, but thank you again for yesterday, I really appreciate you coming to get me and drive me up and down, I couldn't have gone without you.*

How's your arm today? he asked

Still the same she said, *I just managed to hoover left-handed so am pretty chuffed with myself and order feels like it's been restored.*

They continued talking for what seemed like a few minutes before Rei detected a silence down the phone, and perhaps even tears.

Are you ok? she questioned, the roles now reversed.

I have to love you she heard him mumble between the falling droplets almost visible they were so felt, *because by doing so you can love the world.*

As much as Gabriel had received an instruction, so too had Rei.

Like the thunderbolt from the sky the previous day this was a double strike; much needed and now embedded in stone so they could not miss it like all the times before.

I'll come and take you out tomorrow evening he articulated. *I'll be there at 6pm.*

They hung up none the wiser but perhaps a little more humbled.

2020

Rei looks around the room in awe of the fact that everything from their tiny storage boxed lock up fitted perfectly in their flat. The one linen cushion cover of the set of four that Jack had thrown into the end bedroom was the identical colour and tone of her lilac bedside dressers. It was no coincidence. It had always been her least favourite and she'd been uncertain about buying it at the time some years ago, and although it had *worked* in its previous homes, it never fitted as it did now. She smiled. She knew it was a spiteful move from Jack leaving this one especially without the large goose down inner, and she had questioned herself why she was holding on to it at the time that Dan packed up her stuff for her that winter's day, yet despite all of that, here it was, shining, resplendent. There had been a plan and a purpose for it all along. It was only now she could see it. She was glad she hadn't doubted herself that moment and had kept it despite how nonsensical it had seemed at the time.

Covid was still rife and they were locked up inside. In some ways she felt relieved and lucky as it took the pressure off her incessant need, want and desire to be fitter and more capable than she actually physically was. It had been nearly a year now since the operations and she knew she was so far from being able to work and be in life like she had been before. She still struggled to do anything other than walk to the shop at the end of the road at the culmination of each day to buy the reduced produce clearly marked with its end-of-day stickers. Although still physically demanding on her body she valued her daily walk, it gave her purpose and focus in an otherwise bleak existence.

Thankfully her work with the large global corporation had continued. They came back to her as the pandemic showed no signs of reprieve and asked her to write an online curriculum for them. Years prior she had posited it would be a great move for them and they had rejected the idea wanting to keep sessions and training in person. They relied heavily on Rei and her ideas and although the US government had denied her a work and residency visa into the country as their Global Director, she was happy to work alongside them for free from across the pond through a computer screen. It made her feel like she was still living, still capable. She hadn't quite lost everything; there was still a part of her that worked (sometimes). She hadn't told them what had happened, what had been going on. Their zoom calls were scheduled so she could always prep herself and her face (email taking the brunt of the work most times with the time differences) and so life and Rei appeared as normal, covid aside.

She wrote the course overnight and pitched the process to them assured it would be great. She had worked with so many clients online now over the years herself she knew the nuances, she knew what was needed. It was completely different teaching an immersive three-day training course in person to hundreds of global consultants to doing it online and she had the experience and expertise with which to do it. She was hungry to get her teeth into anything and was gutted there was not more work like this she could do.

Whilst doing this work though she realised she now had the emotional strength and mental capacity at least to start to deal with Jack and try and get her share of the home back. It was a dark time and although she appreciated everything she had, her flat beyond luxurious and her kids safely back with her sleeping on the lounge and bedroom floors, it was not easy. Both Bella and Bodhi were suffering mentally and physically. There was no one nearby she felt she could call on for support.

She had four friends dotted around the world whom she spoke to irregularly and who never treated her any less for all that she was going through. She knew how special that was. It was only really through all of this hardship that she truly got to feel the evil of judgment, of projections, of expectations, they were so heavy and so toxic she still could not be anywhere near any of them or the people through which those energies came. Her world had shrivelled and she had become quite solitary and isolated out of necessity rather than choice. It was taking its toll.

There were others she knew that would perhaps not judge her but she was so embarrassed by everything that had happened, that she had gotten herself into, that she could not bear to pick up the phone to them, to ask for help or even to just talk. *She had got herself in this mess so she had better jolly well get herself out of it!* The thought of pity, or sympathy seemed just as gross and malignant as the judgement, and so she told herself it was safer this way, she could just about deal with her own emotions and mental constructs without having to worry about or navigate the potential of everyone else's too.

It was the first time she understood how people could commit suicide, when there seems no break, no respite from the dark. She learnt that it's an eerie place in the depths when your mind has space to roam and wander through the shadows. She knew very clearly the only thing holding her here, different than the others who actioned such deathly steps, was her knowing of *Him*. He held her and she knew he was true. Everything she had seen, witnessed, felt from him ever over the past eighteen years was truth and was love. A beholding love she could never un-feel.

It didn't matter how bad it got; she knew that ***Heaven would never give anyone more than they could handle.*** By God it seemed like it was too much sometimes, thunderous tidal wave upon next, thrashing down on her in sets of twenty let alone threes, but she breathed (gently, not gasping) and she held on to the knowing that she was loved, deeply so, she just couldn't feel it right now.

Life experience had taught her that *this too will pass.*

~

She wondered why the only thing they were really *without* in their new flat was a kitchen knife of any sort. It seemed like a strange state of affairs. It had been months now and they had gotten by with their usual four-piece dining cutlery set and a forty-year-old small wooden handled butter knife passed under the (covid restricted) door from the neighbour below. With all the shops shut there was nowhere to buy a decent knife. One was all they needed, a set would have seemed ridiculous, they had gotten used to living minimally to the highest order having thought they were minimalists before. The local Waitrose had taken all dangerous items off the shop floor since covid began and it was forbidden to buy any kind of knife over the internet at this time. They learnt to work with what they had, buying things that they could rip or shred with their hands or between a dining and butter knife. They felt like cavemen and appreciated even more the simpler things in today's modern world.

She looked at her bank balance, titteringly low, talking pennies not pounds, and no sign of a zero in sight. Ethan despite knowing she had been in and out of hospital multiple times and the kids sharing with him they were worried their mum might be dying still continued to pay nothing nor help or contribute in anyway at all. He had evaded the legal system for over ten years not paying anything towards or for his kids, ever. Rei had paid for them all single handedly since they split getting no allowance or payout when she left. It was her way of appeasing the guilt she felt for leaving. She was learning the hard way that she didn't have to bear the brunt or take on the burden of everyone else's responsibilities, feelings and emotions. She had worked hard to get over the frustration and resentment she felt towards him for being this way, she could understand him not wanting to give *her* anything, but not his kids. *Why would anyone be like that?* It had caught her out for many years until eventually she came to terms with it and let it go; it was only affecting her and the kids more so otherwise.

In their new apartment they kept the heating off where possible and although they didn't have to change their habits, they were grateful they always turned lights off after leaving rooms and that they mostly cooked just once a day, it kept their costs down. Heaven had thus far looked after them to the penny, every single pound she earned spent to the dime. Nothing left and nothing below the overdraft limit every single month without fail. There was absolutely no doubt they were being looked after from above.

She didn't *need* a financial contribution from Ethan, although it sure would have helped out, alleviated the pressure and perhaps afforded some simple luxuries every now and then. It felt clearer without his money but she could feel somewhere within she perhaps distorted that clarity, getting off on being the strong independent woman that provided for them all, the so-called goodie in the situation. She gave herself kudos for the fact that she *had* managed to look after them, no one really needing or wanting for anything more than they had, whilst being there for them at the start and end of each day - that had always been important to her after her own childhood experiences. Yet she recognised that there was a fine balance between appreciation and self-gratification, having found yourself in a self-dug deep, black hole. It could be easy looking like the conqueror, the martyr digging ferociously and reaching the summit when actually behind the smoke screen you'd created the crater in the first place. She also knew she had the hugest propensity to take on everyone else's responsibility as her own and to blame herself for everything. She was still learning this. So, she tried not to give any of it much thought.

~

She knew she had to make moves with the Jack situation and she knew she couldn't do it alone, she would need professional help, which came at a cost way beyond her means. The buyer the estate agent had lined up last year had been eager to buy but Jack would not budge on it, he was not moving out or selling up, it was his now.

For so long she had never wanted to take legal measures, they'd always seemed scary, like she was dobbing someone in or getting them into trouble. Her whole life she had protected evil in one way or another by not calling it out for what it was. She didn't make it personal like most, but she had been caught with her pants down playing the same game on the other side of the fence. There was no right or wrong, both victim and perpetrator were complicit enablers. The bully and abuser believing they could act as they wished, and the scapegoat prey allowing it to continue, not calling it out or reporting them or the evil that was running them.

She recalled Eva, a parent, that she knew from the kid's first school in Oxford whom she'd gotten on well with and had helped out a few times along the way child minding her kids Polly and Estelle after school. She wondered if she was still in Law and could point her in the right direction? She googled her name and found she was working for a family law firm in the city. Acting immediately, she called expecting no response but was surprised to hear her voice as she picked up, and evermore surprised that she immediately recognised Rei. She asked Rei how she was and Rei gave her a brief description, a rough draft, without the details.

I'm sorry you're having to go through this, especially during this time, it's tough, even more so now said Eva compassionately.

Rei sits on the other end of the phone, vision smeared, holding her voice, willing back the tears. Any sign of empathy or kindness and she broke, like a punctured geyser latent beneath the skin's surface, erupting periodically and forcefully from the built-up pressure within.

Eva knew Rei well enough to take a bold leap of faith and offered to help her out. *I cannot charge you any less but you can pay as and when you are able. Once we get the house sold and this sorted out, and we will, no matter how long and arduous the process, you can pay me back anything outstanding…and then you can take me for a cup of tea* she chortled, knowing full well Rei didn't drink, but asking if this had made her consider *turning to the bottle*? Rei reassured her it hadn't funnily enough, and thanked her innumerably for her generosity and support. She was a scary lady from the outside when you didn't know her and Rei wasn't sure anyone stood a chance up against her, even Jack. She put down the phone trembling and relieved at what had happened and at what was yet still to unfold.

~

A few days later needing to be outside, moving, in the fresh air, her phone buzzes, her friend across the ocean, calling to say hi.

Rei shares the magic of God that she has been witnessing around her and the divine blessings that have been bestowed upon her. She stops in her tracks, smiling, realising she has said ***God*** out loud to someone for the first time ever this life, not protected, not guarded…*And,* in a complimentary way.

Holy Shit, she exclaimed *something h a s shifted!* No longer slave to the binds of religion as she'd known it, or to her own reaction to it, she wasn't navigating her words to fit around what made someone else comfortable, she was just expressing openly, freely, with no need from them, with a purity she recognised and knew so well.

~

As the proceedings unfolded the solicitor worked tirelessly with Rei pulling up and going through every email and every text collating the facts and building the case. It was suggested to Rei that she contact those who could share factual experiences of what had happened between her and Jack if indeed there were any. There were many. Past employees, accountants, neighbours, dentists, strangers in the street. Rei's stomach churned, she didn't want to involve

anyone else but it was true they needed the facts. She needed more evidence, every receipt, every bank balance.
She emailed the accountant first who'd looked after them for years. He had originally been Jack's accountant and they had a long friendship that went *way* back. She didn't want to have to tell the truth about what had happened, she didn't want to mar anyone's name but all their accounts, house documents, etc were neatly filed away in her old house exactly where she had left them and she had no access to them. Their bank accounts had been immediately closed by Jack having transferred the money to a personal account in his name, in doing so there was no access to anything from the past, no proof of anything, it was as if the bank accounts had never even existed. She had to provide exact figures about house sales, percentages owned, money earned, money spent. She was not prepared to be loose about even a penny, no rounding up or down, it needed to be pin point precise and accurate. Emailing Nick was her only hope as she had always sent him bank statements along with the end of month accounts.

As her finger approaches the *Send* tab on her email application, she hears Bella and Bodhi laughing, the sound of the kitchen in motion seeping through the crack beneath her bedroom door. She feels pecked open and raw knowing she must continue, it is the only way. For one crazy moment Rei imagines putting out a local broadcast getting it all off her chest,

*Yes, it's a s**t show! I made some really silly choices and now I'm paying the price for it. BIG time. Yes, he was abusive; physically,* *psychologically, emotionally. No, I know I never showed it. Yes, I covered it up. No, I'm not stupid. Yes, the signs were there. All seven of them, like deadly sins. For anyone out there here they are, listen so you don't have to learn the hard way, save yourself...*

constant criticism, and being put down;
threats, fear;
love-bombing followed by abuse;
gaslighting, denial, doubt;
walking on eggshells;
worthlessness, being unsure;
control, isolation, guilt;

...but it wasn't an option. And she knew she wouldn't. Something nagged at her that it was still all her fault, and because of that she couldn't possibly incriminate another, no matter what they'd done. This doubt and guilt and shame still lodged in Rei, yet to leave, left a void that creatures of the night could still inhabit and take refuge in, partying 'til the early hours, leaving Rei's body further battered and broken. The crack still showed to everyone else, but not to Rei who held it close and covets it, the one thing that she has known all her life. That it is her, that it is her fault, that she doesn't belong.

Silly girl.

~

Whenever she shared space with Jack, increasingly across the years, in person or out and about alone without him, her world became smaller, him becoming her centre of gravity, her book of knowledge no longer herself and all that she knew herself to be. It was as if he were a permanent magnet attracting all the iron filings that made up her body, pulling them all from their own north and south poles to his. It didn't matter what the pattern or formation as long as they aligned. She would watch it happening, feel the pull, knowing it was not true, as if her soul was hovering above her watching it from outside in, telling her, imploring her, to realign herself back to her true north, *The* true north.

Like a drug addict high on something, she kept returning for her next fix, monthly, daily, needing more of the same drug in a greater potency to get the same effect. A visceral damage that jeopardised the well-being of everyone around her not just herself. She wasn't blind to the impacts, on the contrary, but she'd invested so much time and effort into this relationship it seemed *a shame to waste it*. Throwing good money after bad she told herself it was changing, he was changing, for the better. But it wasn't, he wasn't. Each abusive occurrence like a recurring crater; dark, narrow streaks descending downhill reappearing, growing and fading with the season. For Rei at the time of each explosive strike, a nuclear explosion detonated and vaporised both the surface and within the depths of her body. The impact and its impingement complex, vast and intricate.

Unlike everyone else who raved about the newly *à la mode* ancient technique of *kintsugi,* Rei found the gold crafted cracks that pieced together and mended the broken ceramic fragments, disarmingly grotesque. She felt the story of her life was unique for sure but with so many flaws and mistakes the gilded lacquer couldn't possibly beautify or accentuate the original precious object that was her. Magnificence in imperfection yes, but this, *No*. She wanted the cracks gone, erased, more than concealed. If she could have it her way she would start again, but she couldn't, she had to learn from it and move on. All the motivational quotes she'd ever heard on the subject springing to mind; Albert Einsteins's *Failure is success in progress*; Henry Ford's *The only real mistake is the one from which we learn nothing*; rang in her mind. True, but not the whole truth.

~

Recalling all the past events in her mind to recount to Eva, way too many incidents than she cared to remember, her eyes prepare themselves ready to scan the room, in the search for something, anything to distract herself with. She reigns the desire back in, the picture 0.1 degree of an angle slightly off-line to the right can wait, as too can the plant pathetically whimpering for a drink. It reminds Rei that she needs watering too. She takes a sip from her glass and recollects a time with an incident over a water bottle.

They had been walking through town and Rei had taken a drink from the bottle she'd been carrying back from the market, she was thirsty and it was hot. Unhappy with the fact that she hadn't offered him any first Jack piped up, raising his voice to an aggressive derogatory shout almost immediately, swearing, puffing up his chest, his momentum escalating as everything done or not done that past week was thrown as fuel into the combusting fire.

A passer-by walked past and then turned straight back round towards them intervening *It is not ok to talk to anyone that way, let alone a woman.*

Jack already ablaze, crackling, acrid, searing and billowing, now also incensed, told him to *P*ss off! It's none of your business.*

Actually, it is, it is everyone's business said the young man looking him straight in the eyes and then back towards Rei with kind, caring eyes. *Are you ok?* he asked.

Yes, thank you. She said embarrassed she was being saved by a stranger his family waiting patiently behind him. She knew Jack all too well and if the family hadn't been there he would have sized him up, taken him on.

Let me put my number in your phone he continued. *If you ever find you need it, call me and I will be there.*

He held out his hand and Rei gave him her phone, his family smiling awkwardly at her, Rei shaking feeling the pressure build within Jack who then upped and left, storming off. *Bitch* he swore (not so) under his breath. *Typical f***ing bulls*t.*

Rei stood trembling, the family moving in closer. *Will you be alright?* they asked.

Yes, thank you she shared grateful they had interjected but knowing full well the repercussions would be even greater later on.

If you're sure they offered, *Call us, whenever*.

Thank you. Rei gently bowed at them ashamed, mortified, uncomfortable, sheepish and internally disturbed. She turned to walk in the opposite direction to both them and the way Jack had gone. She turned the corner and ran down to the supermarket carpark and hid, squatting behind the cars in the back corner. The shakes in her body now uncontrollable convulsions.

She messaged the guy with the kind smile and warm eyes (a ray of sun between the menacing clouds) immediately thanking him profusely and then promptly deleted his number saving it in notes in code, trying to make it look like something else, a bank account or something. *No, Jack would think she was up to no good, it couldn't be about money,* she wrote some colours next to the numbers so they looked like paint codes. *That might work.*

She contemplated her options and decided she felt safest here parked up between the littered bushes, fag ends and dirty car exhausts. She knew that later, whenever that maybe, for there most certainly would be a later, Jack would take her phone and go through it and she didn't want to get anyone else involved or into trouble so she went back to her notes and deleted the newly created paint numbers, afraid something awful may happen if she did not. She was back alone now, no safety net or blanket in sight but at least not involving anyone else in the firing line.

She reminisced that out of every single outburst witnessed by others there had only been one time, this *water bottle incident* in time, where someone stood up (*and in*) to try and break up the outplay. She wondered what had become of the world that we let these things pass right before our eyes, and then asked *What would she do in a similar situation if she saw it happening to someone else?* She was none the better, she always reasoned there were two sides to every story and she didn't know the back history, which was true, but also realised it was also a convenient excuse to not deal with what was there to address. She didn't want to hear this of herself, she wanted to be better than that but she didn't know the answer, how to fix this conundrum. She didn't know what was right or wrong. *Did that even exist? Was right the truth?* She knew it wasn't. She closes her eyes and prays for a time when all *this stuff* will be as simple to her as breathing. Her chest rising and falling as she lays on the bed half slumped, half alert. The space between.

Beyond the bedroom door, the sound of laughter returns to the fore.

~

Legal letters were sent out to Jack asking for immediate attention, laying out how this would proceed with the courts if he did not comply. They had crossed the unspoken border but not with hostile intent. Rei had always been very clear with the solicitor what was and what was not acceptable. She was not fighting to take him down or win it all, she would state the truth and ask for what was hers, nothing more.

The solicitor said *Rei you are remarkable, I have never, ever, seen anyone go through what you have been through and not only that but not be resentful, bitter, demonstrative, angry and spiteful. I could learn from you* she said. *You're still gentle, generous warm and smiley exactly as I have always known you to be!*

It didn't matter how low Jack stooped, how long and how far he dragged his heels, digging his steel capped boots in, it did not rattle Rei one little bit. It had been a long time since she felt this steady, there was no entry point. She remembers her friend saying long ago that Rei was *always strong and absolute when the s**t went down, less so in the good, plain sailing moments*. She wondered if that was still true. *How could it be if she found herself here, now, in this situation?* she pondered. It wasn't as if Rei had stayed mute during her relationship with Jack. She had always spoken up and out, calling everything out as they went along, but ultimately, she never said no and walked away.

Another friend questioned her *Why and how could an intelligent woman fall prey, and continue to actively choose to stay with a narcissist? I just don't understand…?*

Sympathy from introspectiveness; porous childhood boundaries; a desire to be loved taking precedence over the truth; and excusing the behaviour of the wolf in sheep's clothing; were some of the answers that sprung to mind immediately for Rei, knowing herself so very deeply and intimately now. Rei knew she did not have to blame herself on repeat, it was a viscous cycle that got her nowhere fast. Pictures of her and her friends dancing to Fire Inc's *Nowhere Fast* in the sixth form lounge, volume on max, came flooding in. Her body imaginarily bouncing to the beat in her head,

…Your body's got a feeling that it's starting to rust
You'd better rev it up and put it to use

And I don't know how I ever thought that I could make it all alone…

…Everybody's goin' nowhere slowly,
They're only fighting for the chance to be last…

Godspeed, Godspeed Godspeed, Speed us away

She smiled, back in the moment, realising that instead of focusing on what she didn't or couldn't do she needed to substantiate what she *did* know and what she *could* do. One step at a time.

One

foot

in

front

of

the

other.

It was the only way forward.

2021

As Rei watches Bella and Bodhi in the garden training Karla, the hoop perceptibly too high for her little legs to make it, she feels the sun's warmth on her arm as it peeps out from behind the cloud. It is the first time in a long time her body has felt the warmth and she likes it.

Newly settled into their new home, Karla slotted in immediately, theirs from the time they found her, the waiting time between viewing and collection was only to allow space for the flat purchase to complete. She was both a timely addition and a celebration of a home that was actually theirs, their first in two years. As she sits on the edge of Bodhi's old four poster bamboo bed now being used as their outdoor lounger, Rei watches the skies, meandering through the clouds. She had always loved clouds and what they represented to her, a grandness and vastness that put her tiny human-bodied self into perspective, a small dot in the vast, universal landscape. As the fluffy balls quicken pace speeding past, Rei, the kids and the dog are dappled with sunbursts below. Warm air runs across her skin. She smiles.

Rei carries a cushion and a blanket back inside, the diamonds in her watch catching the sunlight and reflecting thousands of tiny rainbows across the limestone wall. She glances back to see the three of them happy and content. She smiles again. It has been a long time since she has seen either of them outside, together, and smiling. As spring is in full bloom it appears the tide has turned.

It didn't take them long to unpack having so little, their relatively few possessions bolstered by a couple of items of furniture from the sale of their old house. There should have been a few more, but Jack had gone back in to their old property on the day of completion and stolen the remaining pieces which had been dutifully organised to be collected later that day. The buyers so fed up with his behaviour and completely exasperated by it all did not want to call the police for his *breaking and entering*. This was meant to be a new start for them, something to celebrate. Instead, they called out a locksmith and got all the locks changed there and then. Pronto. They called Rei apologetically explaining what had happened. They couldn't believe it. They had never come across anything like this before. Every turn underhanded.

If it wasn't for your steadiness through it all we would have run from this sale and this home many a time throughout the process. Is there anything we can do? We can contribute to buying some new furniture as a replacement. We're so sorry. We were so worried you'd think we were in on it with him and we gave him the keys or something…

Rei thanked them too for hanging on in there, now she was free and could begin to rebuild her life. She too was happy to cut her losses, yet again, to be rid of the beast. *Thank you, I really appreciate it, but no. I think I'd rather start afresh, free from any of this.*

First, she called up the removals man to cancel her booking, well aware he was probably already en-route, and then she called up her friends to let them know the furniture she'd promised them would no longer be coming their way. More than anything she felt bad she'd let them all down, it didn't really matter what he was doing to her, but what his actions through her wee doing to them. Even when she had thought it was all over, the money hitting her bank account that morning, it still hadn't been. She realised that evil never stops, it had no endgame.

Rei's solicitor called to say that Jack's solicitor would not hold his money for him, despite the fact that it would earn the company money, they wanted nothing more to do with him, no matter the cost. Not one of the solicitors working on either side of the case, with over one hundred years of experience between them, had ever seen anyone stoop so low and behave so atrociously. The level and sheer number of infractions, misdemeanours, wrongdoings, violations and infringements that had gone on throughout this case by one person alone had them exasperated. They were washing their hands (thoroughly) of it. They all wished Rei luck for the future and said she deserved it.

Rei was glad she only had a couple of pieces of furniture left from their time together, she didn't need any further memories or objects clogging up their new, clear space or their ability to move on.

She called the wedding dress shop who had been holding her dress for nearly three patient years now. They had been so generous in their offering to hold it for her after seeing what was going on. They didn't want the dress ruined as much as Rei didn't, even if there was no wedding to be had. Thankfully it was not a full, meringue style dress and so took up next to no space in their stockroom and they said they would sell it on for her if anyone wanted it.

Rei had the strength now to deal with all the little left-over strands and tendrils outstanding and untied, and this was one of them. She intended to get it back from the bridal parlour and put it up for sale herself. She doubted she would get much for it even though it was *brand new, with tags* and resigned herself to maybe a couple of hundred pounds in the bank on a good day. If not, she thought she could cut it in two and make a sexy little skirt and top number.

The shop assistant asked if they could call her back, which they did some days later, leaving her an answerphone message. *I'm really sorry, but we seem to have lost your dress. We moved premises a few months ago and we have clearly misplaced it. We would like to refund you the total amount immediately. Please accept our deepest apologies. I'm so sorry.*

Rei couldn't believe what she was hearing. She had been looked after, *Again*. Not only did she not have to deal with the past, her dress, its sale or its alterations, but she was being given back way more than she had accounted for or could have possibly ever imagined receiving. The money would come in handy allowing them to buy some essentials for their new home. *Thank you God* she said, looking at the pink neon sign she'd had made up that stood atop her mirrored bookcase and smiled within.

God's Got This.

~

Each day as she walked back and forth to the supermarket she would pass Rory in the street, they would smile having vaguely known each other for many years having lived in the same city, their paths often crossing. It was becoming too regular an occurrence for Rei to let it pass and when she got home that day she told Bella about it.

I'm going to go in and say hi to him tomorrow, there's clearly something there for us to explore together, maybe it's something to do with work she said. The next day came and Rei chickened out, she thought it may look weird, but the following day as they passed each other in the street again she chuckled as they said *Hi* to one another. Bodhi asking what that was all about. She told him. *Clearly, I do need to go in* she said. *Lesson learnt.*

That evening she went on her phone and onto the recently downloaded dating app that had been calling her name for some time now. She had been postponing it but right now it was beckoning her over. She opened it and swiped right a few times; Rory's picture came up before her next and she nearly laughed out loud. She didn't have to wait to go into the shop the next day she could message him here and now.

Hey! Love that you're here, saves me a journey in tomorrow! I was going to come in and say hi, we're clearly being constellated for something. Don't worry, I'm not hitting on you. Lots of love xx

She pressed send. She felt like she already knew Rory, his family had been a presence in her life when the kids were young growing up in Oxford. He messaged her straight back *Fab! Let's go for a walk sometime. Are you free this Friday lunchtime?*

Absolutely, shall we say 1pm by The Gardens?

Deal, see you there at the east gate. Look forward to it!

Rei puts the phone down not remotely surprised at the simplicity of it all. She was learning that when she got herself out of the way life could be really straightforward.

~

Up ahead, the pathway unfurls before them, it was a cold day and the ducks were taking refuge in the water's banks. The canal boats still, in contrast to the cyclists and joggers jostling for pole position. They walk and they talk, walking and talking some more, it was as if they had always known each other, been friends since the dawn of time. They say goodbye and say they should do this again after his weekend away, he'll be in touch.

~

As the seasons change from warm to cold and back again Rei appreciates the blessing that Rory is. Living proof that men could be more than decent. He would do everything that he could to support Rei whenever she needed it.

Sometimes it wasn't the help that she could have done with or wanted, but she saw that without fail he was there. Their relationship reminded her of James, her childhood boyfriend; like a brotherhood, they had each other's back and knew each other inside out, it was beautiful, but there was something niggling inside her, just ever so, that this was not it. That *there was more*. It wasn't about Rory as such, she thought that perhaps she was just ready for the next chapter in her life as the kids were growing older and moving out, perhaps something new was round the corner for her too.

She follows her feelings and they remain friends. Close friends. Nothing really changes, but she knows he will always be her brother.

2025

Fresh yellow water lilies, close in numbers, nestle amongst the enormous cabbage plants, growing in clusters, stretching out towards the pontoon. Their petals spiralling towards their centre, more opulent for doing their job carved out by God, transitioning into the concentric circular stamen at their centres. Its continuous gradient highlighting its ancient lineage.

Sitting just above the water, the pads reflect the sunlight, reminding them of last time they were here. Friends not lovers, neither husband nor wife. A party of people and a gate crasher. An outsider not really invited. Yet here they are now, their roots in the substrate of Heaven having found each other, thrown together; growing, emerging into the world as one but each a full delicate, established root of its own.

The swans and their cygnets glide majestically across the water's surface, buoying before them begging for food. They have become friends now. A far cry from Rei's childhood memories of swans attacking the family and their picnic, hissing menacingly at them chasing them back into their cars where they felt they belonged. She had never forgotten that gaggle of swans and had since characterised them alongside wasps and mosquitos, a species that she could do without.

Now today, the bevy before her reflected something far grander than the previous fear she'd associated with them;

intelligence, grace, elegance, beauty, a strength and adaptability, a creature with tremendous flying stamina. She could see her in them and them in her.

She marvelled at how far she'd come knowing this was just the start, only the beginning. She was clear and free of so much and yet her eyes were only just opening to everything else around her. She'd taken off the blindfold and removed the blinkers, now it was time to walk with her eyes wide open.

She reminded herself *there is always more.*

The swans nibbled at the pontoon reminding her to feed them, their royal reputation so understandable and perceptible to her, as they feasted from the bottom of their garden.

No longer the princess she always sensed she was as a child, she felt more than that. She turned round to see their bedroom and its balcony which overlooked them all on the bank of the River Thames. No longer a princess but a Queen with her Prince Consort.

The crowned King and Queen of Real England.

Evil is

because we do not speak up and out

and not because it is more powerful.

Addendum

Dear Reader,

Whilst writing this book, a couple of days after penning the passage that included the reference to Janet Jackson's song, I was walking the back streets near home.

I looked up to see a lady pass me. Nothing special or out of the ordinary, just two women passing by each other on the pavement, her with her head down and cap on, me grocery bag in arms. I walked on by, whilst my whole body screamed at me *That was Janet Jackson!*

Not having seen, heard or anything Janet Jackson for nearly 30 years I got out my phone and quickly Googled her, and yes, from her build it could well have been. Thinking I may well be mad and in some kind of book writing haziness I hesitated for a moment before turning round listening to my body.

She was gone. As if the whole thing had been an apparition.

Trusting it was not, I crossed the road and ended up right beside her as she sat in the driver's seat of her car. I took a moment and gently tapped at her window, asking if she was indeed Janet Jackson. Thankfully she graciously gave me the space to share that I had just written about her song; we discussed which one, and I thanked her, communicating *What were the chances?!*

I went home completely bedazzled by the magic of Heaven and had to pinch myself, not because it was her, but because of the seemingly nigh on impossible chances of that not only happening, but also at that very point in time when it was so poignant. Perhaps on another day I would not have *noticed* anything or it may well not even have transpired.

Over the next couple of days, I bumped into her twice more, the last culminating in a grand hug. Now, more than strangers.

The Magic of God.

Afterword

Were you ready to be whisked through time, jumping backwards and forwards into memories that capture the raw experiences of Rei's life? It was hard to put this book down, I was sometimes left wanting to know more, and then feeling rude for invading her life further than it was already invaded. Sometimes I wanted to answer back, sometimes laugh out loud, sometimes hope what I was reading was not what I was reading. That is the glory that lies in this book.

It confirmed for me how potent words are with a theme of belittling, control, and jealousy through so many different people and circumstances, that you could be fooled into thinking this was a Rei problem. On some level, it could have been. Why did so many people in such diverse settings behave that way towards Rei? How did Rei not see the similarities in the situations and the way people behaved towards her. You could say – that wouldn't make a good 'story', but our lives seem to be those stories, those repeating patterns and reading this book brings that cyclical pattern front and centre.

For me it took the challenge with abuse to a different level. I saw it as a horror movie, a theme of possession where the behaviour comes through people rather than from that person. This made it really hard for Rei to detach from personalising it to a person - a partner, a friend, a family member, a potential mother-in-law, and see that the energy of abuse can come through anyone. It is an energy that became so familiar that it became harder to question whether or not it was 'normal'. Inside she knew very well it wasn't 'normal' but so much on the outside of her told her it was that she doubted her own inner radar.

This is really common in relationships in general and what leads to the inordinate rise in family and domestic violence statistics. 1 in 4 women or 23% of women have experienced emotional abuse from a current or previous partner. This has led to greater awareness of coercive control. Coercive control is when someone, often a romantic partner uses isolation, monitoring, denying your freedoms, gaslighting, criticism, controlling money, domestic duties, controlling your body, turning children against you, jealousy, sex or threatening children or pets. 2024 saw the criminalisation of coercive control in Australia, nearly 10 years after it was a criminal offence in the UK in 2015.

This is where Rei's story is so compelling. Angelica offers snapshots, moments in time of people, behaviours, memories, feelings. It shows the similarities of the behaviour through different people and scenarios. It shows the consistency of the inconsistent behaviour which is so prevalent in abusive relationships where the fluctuation makes it harder to recognise the difference between love and care and control and abuse. There should be no trouble recognising that difference, but Rei didn't, and this is where Angelica introduces another theme, one that felt painfully familiar. The theme of our education to be 'nice' and 'good' which meant Rei wanted to keep the peace rather than nominate what was happening and question what was coming through others who she knew to be innately loving and caring people. The nominating and questioning would potentially have given permission to the part of herself that knew it was not loving and caring, to walk away or even move in a way that did not allow this controlling and abusive behaviour anywhere near her.

Even though Rei is a fictional character, the unfolding nature of the story is so entirely relatable that it illustrates the danger of settling for something 'better' than the last, of feeling 'this is the one' and then facing the disappointment that, once again, that same energy is following you around disguised as something else. Different people and situations yes, but in Rei's case still the elements of control, neediness, and being reduced to a possession rather than a glorious woman, friend, partner, wife, mother still remained.

For Rei to stand up and work out how to build again from scratch is a powerful message to anyone who feels they cannot be alone or cannot rebuild their life after leaving an abusive relationship. Statistics tell us that leaving is not the first thing we do when confronted with abuse. On average it takes 7 attempts to leave an abusive relationship and that is likely to be an under-report after potential multiple visits to the hospital or calls to the police, perhaps in the constant hope that the behaviour will change or that we will be 'strong' enough to leave, before recognising the pattern and understanding that at least one party has to change or nothing is going to change. Rei did, Rei may need to again.

What is very clear from the book is that settling for being in a relationship that tries to control, reduces both parties to a poisonous game of victim and perpetrator. Happy endings are not happy endings if the seed of what has poisoned relationships before has not been ousted. When there is a constant hope and search for a 'happy ending', that calls for a whole other level of honesty and integrity.

Despite the content covered in this book this is not a heavy emotional read, in fact I read it in 3 days, but it leaves you with an insight that will sit with you. That our much-championed education to be good and nice, to keep the peace, to overlook the subtleties of jealousy and control, serves absolutely no purpose. I have seen it through others, I have seen and felt it through myself. As a result of reading Angelica's book, I have been even more aware of the subtleties of that 'being good and nice education' that fosters a sense of numbing to coercive control. It has changed my movements, my communication and my relationships. It is the most glorious gift to actually recognise such education for the poison it is, and to be able to change the way we move and communicate so it has no entry to our lives.

Amazing and much needed writing Angelica Lamb.
Thank you.

**References to this Afterword, helplines and further information on the subject of domestic violence are given on the final page of this book.

Book Club Questions

What is the purpose and significance of the title Into the Arms?

How does the novel explore themes of protection? Is there a preservation of self and, or a shielding of others?

To what extent do you feel Rei would prefer to go with the flow of the crowd rather than standout, and do or say what she knows is true?

Rei finds it hard to speak up and out. Is this a product of her familial upbringing or is it more than that? How does society actively encourage us to stay quiet?

When the truth is concealed is this a positive or negative concept in the realms of this novel? How might it have looked in a parallel universe, if Rei hadn't done this?

Rei couldn't get away to Japan quick enough. Was she running away from something, or towards something she knew was true?

The theme of abuse occurs and reappears throughout Rei's timeline. Is this a one-off extreme case story or do we live with, accept and tolerate abuse within our homes, behind closed doors?

Rei feels a sense of embarrassment and self-ownership around many of the themes in the novel ~ sex, suicide, abuse, to name a few. Why could this be so?

Rei is clearly a very beautiful, articulate and loving woman and mother who looks for the best in others. In doing so is she truly discerning the truth of those that she meets?

By protecting individuals and not calling out the evil running their actions, how do Rei's own movements impact her children and those around her?

Do you feel Rei has learnt her lesson and truly moved on from accepting abusive behaviours from others, noting that abuse comes in various different, sometimes subtle, forms?

Bullying is rife in schools, society, work and homes. What advice would you give to Rei in how to deal with it?

Rei is clearly a very strong individual. Was Rei doing her and her children a disservice by trying to do things all by herself? Why did she find it so difficult asking for help?

Religion is a very subtle but key thread throughout the story. What impact do you think religion had on Rei's life?

What was the catalyst or turning point for Rei to look within herself for answers rather than relying on the outside?

Despite being through hell and back Rei does not hold a grudge against anyone. What is it about Rei that allows her to forgive and *let go* so readily?

There is a hint that Rei is in a much better place now, but what does a *better place* look like, in terms of her own relationships with others close to her?

Rei describes being delivered a brand-new car from heaven. Have you ever experienced being gifted something far grander than what is considered normal or beyond what you yourself have manifested or achieved?

What is your main take-away from reading Into the Arms? How would you encapsulate it in one sentence?

Acknowledgments

This book was written in five weeks amongst the hustle and bustle of everyday work and life. It poured forth and thus I feel I cannot take credit for it. I put my fingers on the keypad and they typed everything that was given as it was given. I got up and turned on the tap perhaps but the volume and the clarity with which it came through was so powerful I could only but observe it, in awe of what can happen if we get ourselves out of the way. This is the work of something far greater than the body of me Angelica Lamb.

I wrote whenever there was space, sometimes 15 minutes, sometimes half a day and anything and everything in-between. Each time *time was up,* the laptop closed and that was the end of the *chapter/year/event* being written about. I did not revisit it and neither did I have any idea of what would be coming next, I didn't give it a second (or even a first!) thought. Afresh and anew, I would sit and be given *something* and then away my fingers would run. The body is an amazing instrument that I have an ever-increasing appreciation for. Without its glorious, sexy, magnificent wonder it couldn't have happened. An unbelievably perfect Godly design. Thanks Mum and Dad for making me, and thanks Reformer for building its physical strength!

Only when the book was complete did I go back and read it, astounded by the beauty, synchronicity and sheer wonder of its precision. How each chapter moulded carefully and flowed seamlessly to the next and so forth and yet how *I* had been completely oblivious to the magic that had been unfolding. It is and was that simple. Go simplicity!

None of this would have been possible without the encouragement and support of so many along the way. *You should write a book* heard so many times across the years that e v e n t u a l l y it transpired. The seed had been planted. A woman with no writing skills but a wealth of *life experience* willing to be obedient to a call without any expectation, drive or ownership as to what that may look like. Yay to letting go of ideals and beliefs, restraints and compression from everything that tells you it has to be a certain way!

Thank you to Leonardo Da Vinci and his *Study of Hands,* the beautiful artwork that envelops and tenderly hugs this book.

Heartfelt thanks go to Hanako Footman for doing what Mrs Potts' character never did, providing the springboard for all that followed *the first sentence, something…anything* that unleashed the unravelling of this story, just as My Love pulled the plug on any temporal restrictions and gave me an unspoken wind beneath my wings. Wings that were given to me, to us all, since birth. Tarnished and muddied along the way and throughout the years perhaps, but never lost, always ready to fly, to soar, deep into and with the expansiveness of the universes.

We are never alone, and neither are we meant to do life alone. *Heaven has our back, front and sides*. For that I am eternally grateful. Thank you. I couldn't have and wouldn't have done it without you.

Domestic Violence

****Forward References**

https://www.cps.gov.uk/legal-guidance/controlling-or-coercive-behaviour-intimate-or-family-relationship

https://www.aihw.gov.au/family-domestic-and-sexual violence/types-of-violence/intimate-partner-violence

Helplines in USA ~

Life Line 988

Domestic Violence Hotline 1 800 799 SAFE (7233)

StrongHearts Native Helpline 1 844 7NATIVE (62 8483)

Runaway Safeline 1 800 RUNAWAY (786 2929)

Sexual Assault Hotline 1 800 656 HOPE (4673)

Victim Hotline 1 855 4 VICTIM (84 2864)

https://www.justice.gov/ovw/resources-for-survivors

Helplines in the UK ~

Victim Support 0808 16 89 111

National Domestic Abuse 0808 2000 247

Refuge 020 7395 7700

NCDV 0800 970 2070

The Men's Advice Line 0808 801 0327

Women's Aid helpline@womensaid.org.uk

https://www.nationaldahelpline.org.uk/i-am-planning-to-leave-my-abuser/

Helplines in Australia ~

1800RESPECT 1800 737 732

Lifeline 13 11 14

WWILD 07 3262 9877

Family Relationship Advice Line 1800 050 321

Relationships Australia 1300 364 277

Men's Referral Service 1300 766 491

https://www.australianfamilylawyers.com.au/information-centre/leaving-domestic-violence-relationship

Printed in Dunstable, United Kingdom

71673430R00241